THE UNDOING OF WALTER WOODSWORTH

PROLOGUE

A howling nor'easter had blown the night's snowfall into a blanket of purity covering the dust and dirt of the city and the gray house at 9 Forest Street. Inside, swollen with child, a small voice screamed and writhed with pain. “Agatha. Help me.”

The stem woman's felt slippers made hardly a sound as she hurried down the dark hallway and opened the heavy oak door. She walked to the bed. There in the muted light, she saw blood staining the pristine whiteness of the bed sheets and the girl's nightgown.

Without a word of comfort, the woman turned in a quiet panic, left the room, ran down the stairs and dialed the phone in the foyer. Listening intently to instructions the man was giving her, she replied, “I understand,” and hung up the phone. She paced like a soldier on guard duty until she heard a car moving down the driveway to the rear of the house. When she unlatched the back door and opened it, two burly men dressed in black asked, "Where?" Stiffening her back, she replied, "Up the stairs. Second room on the right."

Silently, the men wrapped the semi-conscious girl in the stained bedspread. One at her head, one at her feet, they carried her down the stairs and through the rear door like an old rug. Laying her on the back seat of the long black Cadillac, they took her without notice into the night. Before the car lights faded as it slowly made its way down the street, the falling snow obliterated the drops of red on the driveway that had seeped from her blood-soaked wrapping.

VICTORIA'S SONG

Who dare bring these pictures

To my slumbering mind.

Someone unknown has so divined.

They come just as night discovers

Early morning.

Fright replacing the joy of sunshine's

Dawning.

In another time and place, this

Story's author has no face.

Trapped in dreams for many a year.

Tired from sleeplessness, tired

Of fear.

Come on my journey and you will see

How I found what has set me free.

Chapter 1

MAY, 1971 - NEWARK, NEW JERSEY

Victoria's eyes sprung open wide as if someone had yanked the cord of a Venetian blind. She lay there staring straight ahead and tried to catch her breath. The darkness of her bedroom intensified her fright. Her heart was pumping wildly. Beads of sweat covered her trembling body dampening her silky blue nightshirt. It was 3:30 AM according to the digital clock on the nightstand. In the darkness, being as careful as she could not to wake her husband Mark who lay asleep next to her, she lifted the lilac patterned comforter and slid quietly out of their queen-sized bed. She walked as fast as she could to the living room to turn on a lamp hoping that its light would bring her back to reality and dissipate the terror that was gripping her mind and body.

In her haste and still in a sleepy stupor, she stubbed her big toe against an end table. Biting her lip in an attempt to stifle a scream, she did a painful little dance before falling onto the sofa. Holding her foot, she rocked back and forth until the pain subsided enough to allow her to turn on the lamp. The light made 1971 come flooding back. No longer caught in that ethereal world, she had escaped to the present from a different time and place. Victoria had never felt compelled to record any previous dream she had ever had; but this one was different. It had left her disoriented and so filled with terror that it was doing things to her body and mind that she could not understand.

Brushing her long red hair away from her tired brown eyes, Victoria's hands trembled as she retrieved a pen and paper from the end table drawer and began to write down all that had happened in her dream. Even with the light on, revisiting the details made goose bumps rise all over her five-foot-four inch plumpish frame.

When she finished her scribbling, logic seemed to replace panic. Going over what she had just written, she thought to herself:

There was nothing in the dream to provoke the absolute terror I felt when I woke up. Why did my body react to something my mind is telling me was not threatening? Maybe my subconscious mind knows something I don't. It makes no sense and I'm too tired to deal with it all now. I have to get some sleep or I'll be a zombie tomorrow.

Victoria put everything back in the drawer and reluctantly switched off the lamp. She made her way back to bed in the darkness and snuggled deep into the warmth of Mark's back. With her arm wrapped around his six foot two-inch tall body, she felt safe enough to close her eyes, Sleep eluded her the rest of the night; dozing and waking almost every hour until the alarm went off.

Chapter 2

Never a morning person, Victoria faced a daily battle of getting Mark, Diana, their nine-year-old daughter, and herself out of the house on time for work and school. Their little family of three lived in the second-floor apartment above Victoria's parents in a two-family home on Sylvan Avenue located in the Northern Italian section of Newark's North Ward. Rubbing her eyes to clear away the morning fog, Victoria walked into Diana's room,

"Good morning kiddo. Time to get dressed."

"OK mom. I brushed my teeth and washed up before dad this morning."

"Well, you're the early bird just like your dad."

Victoria then made her way to the bathroom. Mark was just coming out. He had showered and was on his way to their bedroom to dress for work.

"Hi sunshine. You look beat."

"Had a nightmare last night and had a hard time getting back to sleep."

“Is Diana up?"

"She's getting dressed."

While brushing her teeth, Victoria saw her reflection in the mirror and what looked back at her made her cringe.

Oh God, she thought. I look and feel like hell. It's going to be cereal all around this morning. If I cook anything in the shape I'm in, they'll arrest me for poisoning my family.

Pulling back the shower curtain, Victoria adjusted the water temperature to cooler than usual hoping it would perk her up. As the chilly water bounced off her very white skin, she leaned her head against the shower wall and groaned, I'm a night person. Why am I trapped in a morning person's world?

Her shower done, she wrapped her pink terry cloth robe around her and headed for the bedroom. She had set out her black pantsuit and red blouse the night before. Victoria found it difficult to make decisions in the morning. It took a while for her brain fog to lift. She knew if she left the task of selecting an outfit until morning, she would spend endless minutes staring into her closet when she had no time to spare.

Mark and Diana were dressed and seated at the kitchen table talking baseball. The New York Yankee's would be hard pressed to find two more devoted fans. Mark took her to opening day every year. It was their date and a vacation day for Victoria.

Victoria put out the bowls, milk, cereal and sugar. Mark already had the coffee going.

"We're having cereal, Diana. Guess Mom is not up to speed this bright and beautiful morning."

"Yes, and you will enjoy it," Victoria responded with a crooked little smile as she clicked her heels.

"I told you dad, until Mom's had her coffee, you shouldn't talk to her in the morning."

"Are you guys ganging up on me this morning?"

Victoria didn't wait for a response. She grabbed a cup of black coffee and headed to the bathroom to apply her makeup and fix her hair.

Mark finished his meager breakfast and kissed Diana,

"See you tonight sweetie. Have a good day at school."

"See you later dad," giving him a big hug.

Mark walked into the bathroom to give Victoria a kiss goodbye.

"Got to run. See you tonight."

"Love you."

Her tan handsome husband looked so good in his blue suit. Feeling like something the cat dragged in, she thought,

If we didn't have to eat, I wouldn't let him go to work with all those pretty secretaries.

Mark rushed down the stairs and out the front door. It was just a short walk to the end of the block where he caught the New York bus which took him into the Port Authority in Manhattan. From there, Mark walked to American Chemical Manufacturing Company's corporate offices on Park Avenue where he worked as Traffic Manager. It was his job to make sure his company's products made it to their destination within government guidelines and at the lowest cost.

Victoria finally had it all together and called to her daughter,

"Are you ready, Diana? Got your books and lunch money?"

Victoria always set out Diana's lunch money next to her books each night so she wouldn't forget.

"All set mom. I'm ready."

They walked down the stairs to the front hallway where Victoria's mother, Angela, was waiting. She always stood there to wish her two little girls a good day.

"You two be careful today. Do you have your lunch money, Diana."

"Yes, Nana. I love you."

"I love you too," Angela answered, smiling and grabbing Diana up with a big hug.

They both kissed Angela goodbye.

Victoria and Diana were the most important people in Angela's life besides her husband Victor. She always worried when they left the house. She knew the city had changed. It had become less safe. Lately, there had been a lot of muggings. She reasoned that was why Victoria and Mark had decided to move and had put a deposit on a house in Nutley.

Victoria and Diana waved goodbye as they drove away in Victoria's old station wagon. Angela had tears in her eyes as she closed the door. She would only have them a few more months before their move to Nutley.

Victoria quickly drove the few short blocks to St. Peter's school. She parked in front of the building and leaned over to give Diana a kiss,

"Have a good day sweetums. Do you have your homework?

" "Yeah mom. I have everything. See you after school."

"Love you, kiddo." "Love you too. Bye."

As she watched her little brunette munchkin enter the school, Victoria stared at Diana and thought,

She looks so much like Mark, tall and thin with olive skin. I'm glad she didn't inherit my whiteness. She'll never have to worry about sunburn like I did. No one would believe I had anything to do with bringing her into the world.

Chapter 3

Victoria drove down Franklin Avenue to the subway parking lot. It was just a few blocks in the opposite direction from the school. The subway cars to downtown Newark are not like those in New York. They are more like trolley cars and travel mostly above ground. The ride is usually pleasant and fast. Taking it was so much easier than driving downtown in morning traffic and paying a high parking fee. The lot across from the subway station was cheap; only $1.50 a day. Victoria parked her car and walked across the street where the subway car was waiting. She dropped the coins into the box and sat in the empty second row on the right.

Still groggy from sleeplessness, Victoria closed her eyes as the subway wheels made their monotonous clacking against the tracks, lulling her into a half-sleep. Last night had been ordinary, just like so many other nights for Victoria. She washed the supper dishes, checked Diana's homework and made sure she was bathed and ready for bed. She and Mark watched the news together and went to bed. When she closed her eyes that night, she had no idea it would be the beginning of the end of ordinary. Insidiously, the dream crept back into her mind.

It had taken place on a stone veranda which lay beneath a brown stone mansion's menacing facade. Bathed in shadow, Victoria and Mark were seated on steps that descended from the veranda to the great lawn. Victoria was holding a book belonging to their daughter Diana. She was expressing concern to Mark about what was written on its pages. The words made her frightened for her daughter's safety. Fearing for her daughter, Victoria looked towards the grassy sunlit knoll to her left; there she saw Diana playing happily in the sunshine. Suddenly a large boar's head appeared in the air near them. The beast looked at Victoria, became frightened and disappeared.

The subway screeched into Broad Street station jarring Victoria back to awareness. It was a short walk from the subway to Landis Advertising on Halsey Street in Newark, where Victoria worked as Secretary to the President. She took the job because it was not full time. Mr. Landis was getting on in age and only needed someone from nine to two-thirty. This allowed Victoria to pick up Diana from school at three-fifteen.

Most days she walked at a fast clip to get out onto Broad Street as soon as possible; but today was different. She was more afraid of the danger stalking her mind than what was around her. The station was not very well lit. It stank of urine and sometimes there were homeless men lurking in the corners.

Chapter 4

Victoria had made it safely to her office once again. Not wanting to appear tired, and in an effort to fend off questions of "What did you do last night?" she lit up her face and gave a bright smile and a hardy good morning to all her co-workers as she passed their desks on the way to her own cubbyhole outside of Mr. Landis' office. She had a lengthy dictation tape on her desk waiting for her to transcribe. Dropping her purse, she looked out the window and asked God to get her through the day. It wasn't just fatigue that plagued her this morning, she was scared. She intuitively knew the dream portended trouble.

Struggling through the morning with several cups of coffee, Victoria was relieved when Maria, her co-worker, announced, "It's one o'clock, want to have some lunch?" Olive skinned Maria was barely five feet tall and had a slight Portuguese accent that sounded like music when she talked. She lived in the tightly knit immigrant Portuguese neighborhood in the Iron Bound section of Newark. Victoria replied, "Let's go," happy to give her eyes a rest. The two grabbed their purses and headed for the elevator. They walked down Academy Street to Halsey and into Louie's Deli. The place was crowded as usual, but they found a small table in the comer. After they had ordered their sandwiches, Maria commented,

"Your eyes, they look tired Vikky. Is there something wrong?"

"Didn't sleep too well last night. I had this dream...more like a nightmare. It was on a veranda of a mansion. My husband and daughter were in it and a beast. I don't know why it's bothering me so much. Maybe it's because I ate a salami sandwich before going to bed last night," Victoria joked, trying to make light of the whole thing. "I'm being silly I know, but this dream really scared the hell out of me."

Maria, seeing Victoria's distress, offered, "Listen Victoria, I know someone. He's a medium, a friend of mine from Portugal. He can interpret dreams, make potions and remove hexes. Write down everything you can remember and give it to me before you leave work. I'll bring it to my friend and then he can tell you what it means. When you have a dream that really affects you, sometimes it's because one of your dead relatives is trying to warn you about something. "

What the hell, thought Victoria, Maybe, he can give me an explanation for the fear.

Chapter 5

Victoria was changing into her sweats when she heard the doorbell ring. She ran down the stairs to open the front door. It was her cousin Rita who unexpectantly decided to visit. Although Victoria was an only child, she had a large Italian family and relatives would just drop in at will.

"Hi Vikky, I was in the neighborhood and decided to stop. Haven't seen you in a while and wanted to catch up."

"Come on up...I'll make some coffee?"

"I could really use one. By the way, where is Diana?" "She went for ice cream with my parents."

Like Maria, Victoria's co-worker, Rita could see that something was amiss. There was a far-away look in Victoria eyes. She could never hide her problems; they were always written on her face unless she made a conscious effort to change her countenance.

It's ironic that Rita would choose today to visit, Victoria thought, as she put on a pot of coffee and set out some Stella D'Oro Anise cookies on a plate.

"There's something wrong Vikky. I can see it on your face. What's going on? Did you and Mark have a fight?"

"No, no. I had this crazy dream of a mansion last night and it's just bugging me."

Rita was always up for strange dreams, ghost stories and the like. She was married to a man who was deep into the mystical and had gotten Rita interested in those seldom talked about subjects.

"Vikky, my husband knows this man Morgan. He's a psychic and is schooled in the Kabala. I'll have him interpret your dream and I'll get back to you as soon as I can."

"Sure, go ahead. I'll write it down for you. Can't hurt."

Victoria figured two people will be interpreting my dream. If the revelations are conflicting, it would be all hokum and I'll charge it up to a nightmare.

Normally, Victoria would talk to her mother if she had a dream that seemed significant, but for some strange reason, she didn't want to talk about this dream to her. Victoria feared her mother might relate it to her impending move to Nutley. She wanted her own home so badly, she didn't want to start their new life off with any negativity. Angela was intuitive. She always seemed to know when things were going to happen. Because her warnings usually came to pass, even Victoria's father, Victor, was afraid when Angela would raise her finger to predict some looming danger. He laughingly and cautiously called his wife "The witch."

Within a week, both Maria and Rita came to Victoria with their respective diagnoses. Uncannily, they were identical. Both had recommended that whatever Victoria was focused on lately should be stopped. "Get out of it immediately...you are in danger and avoid crowds," was the advice of both swamis.

Chapter 6

Long before Victoria and Mark had contracted to purchase the house in Nutley, she had volunteered to help in her friend's campaign run for Councilwoman in Newark. Claire Capasso was a charismatic woman, a pied piper, who was running against the nephew of a local mobster who had ties to organized crime. Victoria didn't have much experience with politics, but her friend, the candidate, knew that Victoria had an exceptional writing ability. She had read some of Victoria's letters to the editor in which Victoria had captured the essence of the issues she was dealing with, her points were easily understandable even by the uninformed, and powerful in their content. Using their friendship, she recruited Victoria as her speech writer and at various political rallies introduced her as such until Victoria asked her not to do so.

"Please don't broadcast that I write your campaign speeches. Thanks for the credit, but my mother-in-law has been receiving some threatening phone calls lately. My phone number is unlisted. She told me the last caller, who thought he was speaking to me said, 'You might have a little accident if you don't get out of the campaign.'"

"I'm sorry to hear that." Claire's eyebrows raised in concern.

"I'll continue to write your speeches, but I don't want to attend all the political events. I gave you my word and I'll stick to it, but I need to protect myself and my family."

How much credence could she put into an interpretation? But, here were two, and both had warned her to stop what she was focused on; and the campaign was her focus. It frightened her some, but not enough to break her word. Victoria continued cautiously with the campaign.

After the machine had won and her friend had lost the election, Victoria would find out that someone in the other camp had arranged to have an accident befall her which was fortunately foiled by a friend of her Uncle Tony. The phone threat was more than simply that.

It was just after the election that Victoria ran into her Uncle Tony at a family wedding held at Tomaso's Villa on Park Avenue. During the cocktail hour, he pulled her to the side and confided, "Get out of politics. The speeches you wrote for your candidate have angered some very powerful people. The fact that you are my niece saved you from having a little accident."

"I'm out of Newark politics for good. We just bought a house in Nutley. Who needs all that work and aggravation? I only helped her because she was a friend. It wasn't as if I was looking for a job."

Her rich Uncle Tony was a doctor who had some powerful and shadowy friends, most notably Bobby "Shoes" Savino, who had a piece of everything that happened in Newark. It was his association with "Shoes" that prevented Victoria's accident. They had attended Barringer High School together. Bobby was nicknamed "Shoes" because he only wore expensive Italian made loafers. In high school. Tony was smart enough not to rebuff Bobby's friendship. Tony knew Bobby's father was connected and a "made man" in the mob. They double dated sometimes, but Tony never got involved in Bobby's business; taking numbers and football bets from the other students at school.

Uncle Tony had the distinction of being the only professional in the family. He had won a scholarship to college and worked at Sears nights to make ends meet. Somehow, he managed to save enough to get into medical school. The family grapevine had it that Great Aunt Ida had helped him financially. When she took sick years later, he hired nurses around the clock until her death. But even Great Aunt Ida would not have been able to give him enough to open his practice, which he did almost immediately alter his residency at Newark City Hospital.

Victoria was now convinced that the dream was a warning of the danger she was in during the campaign, a danger she was totally unaware of. Somebody is looking out for me, she thought. At least now she understood the fear she felt in the dream and could forget about the whole episode. Now she had to put all her energy into their move to Nutley.

Chapter 7

SEPTEMBER, 1971 - NUTLEY, NEW JERSEY

The last four months had gone by quickly. So much packing to do, arranging for a mover and the mountains of paperwork involved in buying a house had just about done Victoria in. She remembered the bittersweet day when she left her parent's house for good.

Her father was out and just Angela was there to say goodbye as Victoria and Diana walked down the stairs. They kissed Angela at the front door as they had so many times before. Victoria could see that tears were welling in Angela's eyes. Victoria hadn't thought about how their move would impact her mother. In an effort to make the moment lighter, Victoria smiled. "Mom, we're only a short drive away, less than twenty minutes. It's better than moving out of state."

"I guess I should count my blessings," Angela grinned halfheartedly. Victoria would carry the mental picture of their parting forever. When Victoria and Diana got into the car to leave, they waved to Angela who was holding onto the front door with her hand to her mouth in an attempt to stifle a gasp that would set off a flood of tears. Her body slumped as she bent her head and sadly closed the door behind her. Her mother's heart was broken. A tear rolled down Victoria's face. It killed her to be the source of her mother's pain.

With all she had to do to set up her new home, Victoria hadn't seen much of Angela during those first few months which made what followed even worse for her. That terrible Saturday when her father called. His voice shook as he spoke,

"You better get down here. Your mother went with the ambulance to the hospital. I rode in it with her. I found her on the floor this morning. She was conscious, but couldn't get up. She had been complaining of a back ache for the past few days. They took her to Clara Maas. I'm in the emergency room. I told the nurse to call your Uncle Tony."

"Dad, I'll be there as soon as possible." Victoria's heart was racing. "Mark, stay with Diana. My mom was just taken to the hospital.

"I have to meet my dad there. I'll call you as soon as I know what's going on."

Victoria grabbed her keys and purse and ran out the back door to the driveway. She jumped into her car and raced off to the hospital. Franklin Avenue, the street that stretched from Nutley to the hospital in Belleville, was crammed with traffic causing more angst for Victoria. The ten-minute drive seemed like an hour by the time she pulled into a parking spot near the emergency room. When she reached the entrance to the emergency room, she saw her dad pacing.

"Dad, what's going on," Victoria questioned, frantic for information.

"I don't know. They took her in and the doctors are examining her now."

She had never seen him so worried before. He looked confused and vulnerable.

After what seemed like several hours, Uncle Tony, whose face showed concern, came out and told Victoria and her dad, "Angela has a stomach aneurysm and needs emergency surgery. I've called the best surgeon I could find. She's scheduled for three o'clock. The surgeon is on his way up from St. Barnabas. You can see her before she goes up to surgery. They're doing x rays right now. When she comes down, I'll take you to her."

"Dad, I better call Mark. Stay here. I have to get to a phone."

Victoria walked to the hospital lobby and found a phone. She had to dial twice; her trembling fingers didn't seem to obey her.

"Mark, my mother needs surgery right away. She has an aneurysm." "I'll drop Diana off at my mother's and I'll be there as soon as I can." "I'm really worried, Mark. I have a bad feeling about this."

"Stay calm. I'm coming." Mark could feel the anxiety building in Victoria's voice.

He arrived just as Uncle Tony came to get them. Tony brought them to Angela's room and told them they had just a few minutes. Victoria rushed to her mother's bed,

"Mom, are you OK?"

"Just this damn pain in my back."

"You're going to be fine mom. Uncle Tony got the best for you. We'll see you when it's over. I love you Mama."

When Mark went to Angela, he bent to kiss her and she whispered in his ear, "Mark take care of my two little girls, promise." "You know I will, mom."

It was the way his mother-in-law looked into his eyes when she asked him to promise that scared Mark. He believed she knew that this was the last time she would see them.

Victoria and Mark kissed Angela before they left the room and then stood outside waiting for Victor. She was crying and leaning on Mark. Victoria could hear her father's voice cracking as he spoke to his wife.

"Cara, te amo. It should be me lying in this bed, not you. I wish I could do this for you."

"Victor, be strong. The kids are going to need you to be there for them. Remember, I love you always."

Victor kissed her lips, then looked into her eyes once again and said,

"Te amo. Come back quick."

Just then, two men dressed in blue scrubs came into the room and pushed Angela's bed out the door and towards the elevator to surgery.

"Let's go down to the coffee shop for something to eat. It's going to be a long day," Mark suggested.

The surgery took hours. The nurses kept coming out for more and more blood. When Mark approached the nurse for news, all she would say was, "She's holding her own."

When it was over, the surgeon came out to speak with Victor.

"We did all that we could. Now it is in God's hands."

Uncle Tony looked exhausted. He told them, "Why don't you all go home and get some rest. There's nothing you can do now. She'll be in intensive care for quite a while."

Victor responded, "I'm not going anywhere until I know she's all right."

"I'll stay with her, Vic. I won't leave," Uncle Tony answered. "No. I'm not leaving. I have to talk to her first."

Victoria could see the look of concern on the surgeon's face - that awful look when there is not much hope. She knew her mother was going to die. She needed to be alone lest her father saw the desperation in her eyes.

"I'll be back in a few minutes," she told her husband and father. They thought she was going to the bathroom. Her head bent and with tears streaming from her eyes, Victoria made her way to the hospital chapel. There she could talk to God and beg him for her mother's life.

When she composed herself, she returned to her father and husband to sit and wait.

Angela died a couple of hours after the surgery, never regaining consciousness. Tony was with her. He held her hand as she slipped away, and then wept profusely.

"She's gone. My baby sister is gone," he murmured.

A nurse tried to comfort him. He knew he had to get himself together enough to be able to tell the family.

"Nurse, my sister's family is in the waiting room. Ask for the Grasso family. Please bring them to the consultation room."

When they arrived, he saw hope in their eyes, and it was too much for him to bear. He began to cry. No words were necessary. They knew Angela had died. Victoria held her dad in her arms. Victor, who had always been so strong in mind and body, had dissolved. Tears flowed unashamedly from both pitiful figures. They rocked back and forth unable to believe that they would never have Angela in their lives again. Mark stood there next to them, his arms outstretched and open enveloping them both as if to shield them from Uncle Tony's words. He loved his mother-in-law very much and tried to fight back his own tears, but he could not.

"She didn't suffer. She never regained consciousness," Tony sobbed. Victoria went to her uncle and hugged him tightly.

"Vikky, we did our best, but her veins were calcified. There was nothing more the surgeon could do."

"I know, Uncle Tony. If God wants you, there's nothing anyone can do."

They composed themselves as best they could and wearily left the hospital, their bodies devoid of strength, their minds disbelieving.

Stone faced and silent, Mark drove to Victor's house. They had to call the family, the funeral director. People would be coming to the house; friends and family bringing cakes and food. That's the way it is in Italian families. They keep you so busy, you put your mourning on hold until the wake and the funeral are over.

When they arrived at Victor's house, Mark called Brown's Funeral Home in Nutley and made an appointment time so final arrangements could be made by Victor and Victoria. Then the countless phone calls to relatives and friends were made.

"Mark, how are we going to tell Diana?" Victoria winced.

"I called my mother. She knows. She'll keep Diana overnight. told her not to tell Diana. We'll tell her together tomorrow after we take care of the funeral arrangements and the flowers."

Family, neighbors and friends filtered into the house bringing pastry and food until late in the evening. Victor was in bed before Mark and Victoria left his house. They drove home without a word passing between them. Exhaustion carried them both into a deep sleep that night.

The following morning Mark picked up Victor and the three made Angela's final arrangements and ordered flowers. Afterwards, they dropped Victor off at his home so he could rest. Victoria and Mark continued on to his parent's home. They both dreaded telling their daughter the sad news.

Diana cried upon hearing that her Nana was gone, but surprisingly took it better than Mark and Victoria thought.

"Nana told me that she might be going to heaven soon. She's been talking to me about it for a few months. She told me it's beautiful there and that she will be able to see her mom and dad. I wish she didn't have to go. I told her I didn't want her to go and that I wanted her to stay with us. She told me not to cry if she went and that even though I won't be able to see her, she'll always be near me."

Mark and Victoria couldn't believe their ears.

"Why didn't you tell me?" Victoria asked.

"Because Nana said it was our secret."

"Mark, my mother knew she was going to die. She tried to prepare Diana. No wonder she began showing me where she had her papers stored. She kept saying, 'Just in case you need to find them. If something happens to me, your father won't know where to look.' I joked, 'You're not going anywhere, I didn't take her seriously."

Chapter 8

It was the night after they had buried Angela, Victoria, lost in an exhaustive sleep, bolted upright from her pillow. Her heart raced as she glanced at the digital clock on the nightstand which proclaimed it was three thirty once again. She woke cowering from something unknown and unseen, an instinctive fear rather than one produced by the events revealed in the dream. It was as if she had watched a scary movie that she had seen many years ago, one that she had forgotten the ending of, but her body reminded her with each unfolding scene of the absolute terror of the film's climax.

The second- floor passageway, which squared and overlooked the great room in the brownstone mansion, was the scene of this night's installment.

In anguish, and as if she would no longer have need for beauty in her life, a blonde woman wearing a lavender silk ball gown was hurling a large rose-colored crystal luster candle holder over the railing to the great room's marble floor below. Tears streamed from her eyes in a macabre harmony with the crystal as it crashed into thousands of glistening shards.

Victoria never sought advice after the first dream. She had kept the subsequent dreams to herself, only revealing the details of each to her journal. Her silence ended this morning when her husband Mark awoke to find her scribbling down the events of this latest dream in the dimness of the nightlight.

"What's wrong?" Mark inquired. "Can't sleep?"

Shuddering and afraid to go back to bed, she decided to tell him of the secret place she had seen in her dreams.

"I've been having dreams that frightened me when I woke up. They take place in this big brownstone mansion. I've been writing them down every time I have one. They are not like anything I've ever experienced."

Mark listened patiently, but desperate for sleep, coaxed her back under the covers reasoning, "It was just a nightmare. We'll talk about it tomorrow."

Secretly he hoped she would just forget about it. Mark was still haunted by the fact that Victoria had located his father's stolen car some years before when they were dating. She said the car would be found on Fifth Street and when Mark went down Sixth, she insisted, "Not here. I said Fifth Street."

"It's all a waste of time. That car is probably in South Carolina by now," Mark grimaced.

He grudgingly indulged her fantasy to prove her wrong, but to his amazement, there was the old station wagon with two flat tires. He had a tough time explaining to his old Sicilian father that his girlfriend had pulled the car's location and recovery out of the air.

If Mark could see it, feel it, hear it and smell it, he could deal with it. If it belonged to the ethereal world or any shadowy realm, it did not exist and he would not discuss it.

"You make your mind conjure things when you watch those scary movies," he lectured Victoria whenever she wanted to talk about ghosts or unexplainable happenings. He could not accept the fact that sometimes Victoria was psychic. He liked nice and normal in a woman, but that's not what he got in Victoria.

Chapter 9

The sun was high, but not too warm and everything was right with the world. It was the first time since her mother's passing that Victoria and Mark had a chance to relax and spend the day together. Mark's parents had picked up Diana that morning and were taking her to Turtle Back Zoo.

"Vikky, are you ready to go?"

"Just have to get my purse. What store do you want to try first?" "There's a couple of discount places I thought we might go to. I'm looking for a set of Hogan's."

They spent the morning bargain hunting for a new set of clubs for Mark's birthday. After visiting several stores, Mark found just what he wanted. On the ride back, he talked incessantly about golf and how the new clubs were going to make all the difference in his game. He talked so much that he missed his exit and had to get off the highway in Paterson. They found their way to Valley Road, where Victoria noticed a sign for Lambert Castle Museum.

"Mark, let's stop in. I never knew this place existed...and so close to home."

Still on a high from buying his new golf clubs, he smiled, "I can't deny you anything today."

She was excited about finding a new place to explore. Victoria wanted to stretch this beautiful carefree day out as long as she could. Museums were not usually places of interest for Mark, but he wanted to please Victoria. Since Diana was spending the day with Mark's parents and there was no rush to pick her up, Mark agreed and swung up the driveway and parked in the museum's lot.

As they walked down the stairs leading to the museum's entrance, Victoria thought to herself, What an unhappy place. She didn't know why she felt that way; she hadn't even entered the building yet. The grounds were stark and lifeless. No flowers or shrubs were in bloom to brighten the brownstone structure. It looked like an old sepia photograph of the 1 930's.

They were greeted by a museum employee who took their $3.00 admission fee and greeted them warmly saying, "Welcome to Belle Vista." The first floor was not very impressive; dark and without life. It was as if a great magician had taken all traces of residual life force from it. Dusty and sterile, it left the visitor feeling no one had ever lived there. One room housed a spoon collection; another an antique piano. The few pieces of furniture in the dining room were dark, ugly and brittle. The great room housed a twelve-foot elaborate Cornu' conical pendulum clock made in France circa 1867.

A little bored since the second and third floors were off limits to visitors, they had decided to leave when Victoria noticed an archway to the right of the entrance. As they made their way through, they found themselves on the veranda. Immediately Victoria's body tingled with fear and discovery. It was the veranda in her first dream. Victoria gasped and grabbed Mark's arm crying out, "This is the scene of my first dream. I can't believe it's a real place. I found the mansion."

"Impossible," he frowned, "You must have come here as a child and just forgot."

"I know I've never been here", Victoria insisted. Pointing to her left she remembered, "See there's the sunlit grassy knoll, but the stairs are missing and that ceiling inside, the one above the great room, it shouldn't be there!" recalling the dream of the blonde woman hurling the luster to the floor of the great room.

"Vikky, it's getting late. We have to pick up Diana at my mother's."

She got the hint. As usual Mark didn't want to hear about unexplainable things, so the ride home was silent. Victoria knew in her heart that there was an untold story in the walls of that sad place and somehow the truth was trying to get out through her. She vowed to find the connection between her dreams and this strange place and what it all had to do with her. She felt it would be the only way to stop the dreams and the unexplained terror they brought.

When they arrived home after collecting their daughter, Victoria retrieved her journal from the nightstand and recorded her visit to the museum. I have to find out where the Paterson Library is, thought Victoria. She wanted to know everything about Lambert Castle.

Chapter 10

Due to a death in her boss' family, Victoria had the day off and thought she would take this opportunity to visit the Paterson Library to do some research on Lambert Castle. While having her morning coffee and with a street map of the Paterson area laid across her kitchen table, Victoria traced the route she would take from her home to the library, writing down all the rights and lefts.

With directions in hand, she grabbed her purse and made her way out the back door to the driveway. When she got in her station wagon, it started right up. Old but dependable, she thought as a little smile crossed her face. Victoria was excited about what she might find.

Carefully following her directions, Victoria pulled up to the stark gray building. Graffiti marked the lower stone walls. The neighborhood looked like so many she had seen in Newark that were in varying stages of decay after the race riots of the late 60's. She quickly made her way into the defaced edifice and walked to the librarian's desk. The place looked deserted from what she could see.

"Hello," Victoria smiled. "Can you please help me find anything you have on Lambert Castle and the Lambert family."

"We don't have very much, but I will show you what we do have. Follow me."

Victoria trailed the librarian to the reference section where the librarian pulled a large folder from one of the shelves and handed it to Victoria.

"Have a seat here," the librarian said, while pointing to a small desk and chair in the corner. "You can review what we have. It's surprising that we don't have more considering Lambert was one of this city's most prominent men during the turn of the century."

Victoria put on her glasses and began to read. Paterson was called the "Silk City of the New World" and Catholina Lambert was one of its most distinguished mill owners. In 1892, he built his mansion on Garret Mountain in Paterson which he called Belle Vista.

There was a small book detailing Mr. Lambert's life, his family and his silk mill entitled "Silk and Sandstone," written by Flavia Alaya. Victoria discovered a newspaper account of a sort of "housewarming" gala when Lambert opened Belle Vista to his friends. There was an article by the Passaic County Historical Society on the opening of Belle Vista as a museum which stated that Lambert's silk mill and mansion were purchased by a New York financier, Walter L. Woodsworth, from the Lambert Estate in 1938. Belle Vista was subsequently sold to the Historical Society upon the death of W. L. Woodsworth in 1965. When Belle Vista was opened to the public as a museum, the Society renamed it Lambert Castle after the original owner. Victoria could not find anything of importance on the Woodsworths except an archived newspaper article on the mill's opening under Woodsworth ownership. In the social pages, she found announcements of the weddings of the Woodsworth sons, James and Frederick. James had married an Elizabeth Stanhope and Frederick a Winifred Teasdale.

Not wanting to spend any more time in the library and in this unfamiliar neighborhood, Victoria copied most of the information on the library's coin operated copier, thanked the librarian and left the building.

Chapter 11

HONESDALE, PENNSYLVANIA - MARCH, 1938

"Pull!" shouted Walter Woodsworth as he lifted his shotgun. His aim was true and his shot smashed the puck to smithereens destroying the peace of the misty Pennsylvania morning. The shotgun's kickback barely jarred his portly five-foot ten-inch frame. Walter was a deliberate man, never lifting his gun nor his power unless he was sure he would get what he aimed at without unintended consequence. He was all about control. His once strawberry blond hair had darkened with age to a nondescript color and the spectacles he wore magnified his piecing black eyes that could easily trespass deep into a person's soul.

Smiling, with a face red from the cold weather, Walter boomed with a look of self-satisfaction,

"How's that for shooting! I always get what I aim at."

"You sure do, Walter. Great shot."

Ever conciliatory, Richard Miller, Walter's attorney, feigned interest. Actually, he hated hunting and thought,

Why would anyone want to hunt and kill any creature in this beautiful place?

An astute business man with a superior knowledge of contractual law, Richard cultivated wealthy clients with one of his best assets, fierce loyalty. If he took you on as a client, and he was very selective, he dedicated his life to your interests. His boyish benign appearance belied the legal tiger within.

Just as Walter and Richard were rounding the lake nestled in the center of this tranquil sylvan compound, Walter stumbled. His shotgun discharged hitting a white swan lingering at the lake's edge. As they neared the dying bird, Walter, whose face showed no sign of emotion, raised his shotgun, pulled the trigger and put the bird out of its misery. Walter, always so precise, was guardian of this thing of beauty and without intent had killed it. It had to be the bird's fate," he thought, and I was just a tool used to accomplish the will of the gods. His reasoning had suddenly given him pause. He felt vulnerable to a force greater than himself. It made him think, Who then, will be the instrument of my demise. It frightened him enough to quickly push the thought away. Staring straight ahead he commented without emotion, "The bird was in the wrong place at the wrong time."

Richard lowered his eyes and did not reply, but he could feel the atmosphere change around them. His tall thin body stiffened in his down filled olive drab hunting attire. A normally quiet, contemplative man rooted in reality, he could not understand why he felt this was a bad omen. An ominous foreboding came over him that sent a shiver up his spine. Richard hated the squandering of life in any form. Sickened by the bloody mess and disturbed by feelings foreign to him, he could not wait to conclude his business.

"Let's get on these contracts, Walter. I need your final OK on them so we can set a closing date with the heirs."

Walter, sensing that the bird's death had made Richard uneasy and knowing that his attorney had little use for guns and hunting, acquiesced, "Let's get to the lodge. I could use a hot cup of coffee," dismissing his own sense of unease.

Because Walter was paranoid about competitors overhearing and getting a jump on some good piece of business he had uncovered, the two men met at The Thicket, Walters's log cabin hunting lodge.

The lodge sat about a hundred yards from a crystal-clear lake frequented by all manner of birds. A thick forest surrounded the lake and lodge creating an aura of isolation. The first floor encompassed a spacious living room dominated by a large stone fireplace which sported a heavy oak mantle. The room was decorated with English and German weaponry, steins and the like which celebrated Walter's heritage. There was a rustic beer hall type dining room which held a long oak table with as many as twelve chairs. The kitchen and caretaker's quarters were at the back of the lodge. On the second floor were six bedrooms and several baths. On occasion, business associates were hosted there for a weekend of hunting, drinking and grand venison dinners.

Today's business at the lodge was to finalize arrangements for Walter's acquisition of the deceased Catholina Lambert's silk mill and his mansion Belle Vista, located in Paterson, New Jersey.

Their heavy boots trudged through the damp earth as they walked back to the lodge, each inhale and exhale emanating from the men visible in the cold air.

"I'm buying the mill for my sons, you know. I want to see what they're made of. It will be a proving ground, and their handling of the business will give me a better feel as to who I will leave in charge to replace me at the helm of Boar's Head Investments. James will run the operation of the mill and Frederick will do the accounting, purchasing, etc. With a war looming and my State Department connections, there will be money to be made in government contracts for the manufacture of parachutes, ribbons for military medals and uniform trimmings. If the war comes, and I know it will, my sons will not be drafted because the mill will be producing material necessary for the war. I have no intention of losing my sons to Europe's lack of spine. That madman in Germany will take nothing from me."

"I wondered why this purchase was so important to you."

"I'm moving my family out of New York because it will be the prime target of any aggressor and it will always be that way. It is a symbol of what this country is all about...money. Destroy the stock market and win the war.

"As for Belle Vista, my wife Harriet will be installed as mistress. You know, Richard, they say that place was modeled after Warwick Castle in England. It sits high atop Garret Mountain overlooking the silk mill."

Part of Richard's cultivation of trust was to listen attentively to all of the non-business conversation spewing from the client. This was the hardest part of his job. He was all business; hated the minutia, and that gave him his edge - his ability to focus on what was important, protect his client and deliver the goods, no matter what.

As they walked through the door of the lodge, Hank, the caretaker had a fresh pot of coffee brewing; its aroma was the first comfort Richard had felt all morning. The tall, thin, weathered looking man lived at the lodge year-round free of charge in exchange for protecting the property and cooking services when Walter had guests. He more or less came with the deal when Walter purchased the place. The previous owner had told Walter that he bought the property from Hank on condition that he would be retained as caretaker. He had lived there all his life and could not adapt to city life. Walter agreed to the stipulation.

They hung their heavy jackets on the pegs just inside the entrance, then walked to the oversized stone fireplace in the living room to warm themselves before the glowing fire. Their faces still red from the bone-chilling cold, Richard retrieved the contracts from his briefcase while Walter poured two glasses of brandy, handing one of them to Richard.

"This should warm the cockles of your cold heart." "Thank you, Walter," Richard replied sarcastically.

Richard took a sip and then handed the contracts to Walter who motioned for Richard to sit at the long, rustic, rough-hewn table in the dining room on which a platter of sandwiches had been placed. Walter, chomping on one of the sandwiches, studied the documents for quite a while and then gave his approval.

"Richard, as always you write an iron clad contract. Good job. See if you can set up the signing for Wednesday next."

"Glad you're happy, Walter," Richard replied confident in his ability.

Their Spartan lunch eaten and their business concluded, the pair changed back into their suits and entered the waiting Miller and Weiss company limousine for the return trip to Manhattan.

As they were driving away from the lodge, Walter could not help but brag about his special gift to Harriet for consenting to move to New Jersey.

"I have commissioned two statues - one of Apollo and one of Venus, to flank the front entrance of Belle Vista."

Walter thought of himself as Apollo, the god of prophecy, to represent his uncanny, almost clairvoyant, ability to know which people were best suited to head his various projects. That special ability had brought him much success. Venus, goddess of love and beauty, was to represent Harriet as she was when he first met her. Although time and children had taken some of the bloom from Harriet's cheeks, he still cared for her deeply and had no trouble making love to her, but she no longer gave him the thrill that only a new sexual conquest can give.

"Belle Vista will be a fitting frame for the woman who gave me two sons to continue my dynasty and without whose inheritance, I might add, I would not be in the kingly position in which I find myself today. But I didn't marry her for the money she would someday inherit, I married her because she was the most beautiful blonde-haired, blue-eyed girl I had ever seen and her figure was outstanding. The inheritance was a fortunate bonus. It's ironic isn't it? Her parents thought she married down because I was not flush with money. Wish they were around now to see the fortune I've turned Harriet's inheritance into and what I've become."

Walter cared as much as he was able for his wife and children, but he viewed them more as possessions; everyone else was collateral, not worthy of care or sympathy. His life had been devoted to the accumulation of wealth, and his family and possessions were to be a showcase for his accomplishments.

That night Walter had a dream in which he was driving a car on a smoothly paved road. Then, suddenly, the road was no longer there. The car floated in the air above a deep canyon. He no longer had control. Just before the car plunged, he woke with a start.

Chapter 12

THE MILL

STRAIGHT STREET, PATERSON, NEW JERSEY

It was June 1938 when the mill opened under Woodsworth ownership. That morning, Walter gave his new employees a celebratory breakfast of coffee, tea, cakes and juices in the mill's lunchroom. It was not so modern a workplace as to have a cafeteria. The lunchroom had been a drab place aged by time and use. It was gray and typical of an old factory, with large dust laden pipes crisscrossing the high ceiling. Scattered about the room were six-foot-long wooden tables and benches at which the employees ate their bagged lunches. The room had been freshly painted by Walter's order.

He thought A fresh coat of paint for a fresh start. He wanted the employees to see that things were going to be better under Woodsworth leadership.

There were yellow chrysanthemum bouquets strategically placed to make the stark white room seem festive. At one end, a table covered with a white cloth faced the rows of tables where the employees sat. Walter and his sons were seated behind it. It was from this table that Walter would rise to address his employees and to introduce his sons.

Adjusting his spectacles, Walter rose. The room, which was a bit noisy with the men's chattering, grew quiet.

"I hope you all enjoyed the refreshments this morning in our recently renovated lunchroom. This is a family owned business and I would like to take this opportunity to welcome you all into the Woodsworth family. With your hard work we can make this silk mill the most efficient in the nation producing the best quality goods. There will be bonuses for better than average production and we look forward to a mutually profitable partnership. 1 would now like you to meet my son James at my right hand, who will run the day to day operation of the mill and my son Frederick at my left hand, who will be doing the accounting and purchasing for the mill. James would you like to say a few words?"

James stood, and with an open and friendly tone, addressed his audience. "Over the next few weeks I will get to know you all. Your advice will be important to the success of the mill and will help me to do my job better. If you have any suggestions or complaints, I want to hear them. Thanks."

He sat down to a rousing applause. It was easy to see he was a man's man; big, muscular and plain speaking. The men connected with him easily.

Walter rose again and asked Frederick to say a few words. Frederick stood stiffly erect and with an air of authority spoke: "I will probably not have too much contact with you, as my office is above the mill and my work will keep me there. I will, however, be taking special care that your paychecks are done correctly. If you ever have a question on your wages, please speak to the payroll clerk who will bring your concerns to me."

The applause from the crowd was polite, an indication by the workers that they knew he really did not want any contact with them.

When the work whistle sounded. Walter stood and raised his arm and with an energizing cheer shouted, "Let's get to it." The employees filed out of the room to take up their tasks. Quietly, they shared their opinions of their new bosses.

As Walter and his sons rose to go to their offices, Walter put his arm around James and took him to the side, deliberately excluding Frederick from the conversation,

"I don't want to lose any key people, James. I want a smooth transition."

"Don't worry, Dad, I'm on it." replied James.

Seething with envy and anger at his exclusion, Frederick's pale face pinched, distorting his features. He loathed them both.

For years Walter had pitted his sons against each other thinking that if his boys competed against one another, they would strive harder to excel. Walter thought, Competition is what the world is all about, and he had to groom his sons for that reality; but his games brought out the good and evil inherent in each of his sons.

James had caught on early to his father's manipulations and confident in his own ability, ignored Walter's ploys focusing only on doing the best he could and taking the lumps for his own missteps. James was a man of his word, replete with integrity and a sense of fair play.

Frederick, on the other hand, took the bait and was driven not by personal accomplishment but to best his brother. Never forthright, Frederick always had an excuse for his mistakes, usually blaming circumstance or others. Walter had created a monster. Frederick would never measure up in his father's eyes. He did not like his younger son very much and at times his feelings toward him bordered on hatred.

Chapter 13

NOVEMBER, 1938

From his vantage point on the veranda at Belle Vista, Walter surveyed the landscape and his mill on Straight Street feeling smugly self- satisfied. I'm king of all I survey, he thought.

Several months had passed since he had asked James for a smooth transition, and that is exactly what James had delivered to him. The mill was running at top efficiency and the employees were actually smiling and enthusiastic about their work. Walter knew that James had earned the respect of the mostly Polish and Slavic immigrant workers by making it his business to know them on an individual basis. James had kept the old ones on the payroll, respected their opinions, shared their lunches and had a beer with them when they had to work late into the night. Walter was so proud of James' accomplishments, he gave him a sizable increase in salary knowing that James would now be able to afford a wife.

Walter had sent Frederick a memo asking him to increase James' salary. When Frederick received the memo, his animus was palpable. Furious by this obvious slight, he stood and slammed his fist on his desk. His head was beginning to pound and the light coming from the window only compounded his pain. He went to the window to adjust the blinds and there he observed James' interaction with several employees in the mill yard. Look at that pissant that my father rewards, he thought to himself. The sight of James with rolled up shirtsleeves, incensed Frederick. He could feel the hatred reddening his pale face and yanked the cord plunging his office in darkness. He thought that James, by never carrying himself as a man of privilege, did not manifest his birthright. 1 have to make father see that James, with his common manner, can never be taken seriously when negotiating with gentlemen sharks in the boardroom. James is better suited to beer and bad jokes with riffraff rather than with the polite company of the affluent.

When James returned to his office, Frederick burst in and with an acrimonious tone chided, "You are a Woodsworth. Why do you idly pass the time with those foreigners? You should keep an authoritative distance; and wash those dirty hands. One would think you a laborer."

Frederick used the argument of class to denigrate his brother and disguise the real issue; his brother was well-liked and better at doing and accomplishing than he. Frederick felt he had nothing in common with those he worked with and chose not to engage in banal conversation with them. The only time Frederick spoke to an employee was to give an order. Frederick was reticent and secretive not open and inviting like his brother.

James smirked, "Fred, when the hell are you going to get off that high-horse you're on? I do what I have to in order to get the job done. Want to get some lunch? I'm hungry."

James was seldom offended by what his brother said. He had no time to play childish games. He knew his brother had a grand opinion of himself.

As they walked out of the office, the women swooned as James passed them. James was a tall, six-feet two-inches, big-boned and square jawed with black hair and blue eyes, He had a confident stride and made eye contact with each employee that passed him.

Fred was not quite as tall as James and his slight build moved catlike, unlike his brother's confident stride. Rarely looking people in the eye, Frederick's downcast gray eyes were barely visible above his long thin nose. When they reached Frederick's car in the lot, he said to James, "Let's take your car, you're not dressed well enough to ride in my Cadillac."

"Aren't you afraid you'll get some dust on you if you ride in mine, you stuffed shirt?" James retaliated.

The pair drove to a local slightly upscale tavern near the mill. A waitress came to take their order.

"I'll have a roast beef sandwich on rye and a beer," said James.

"I'll have the blue plate special and a glass of white wine," ordered Frederick in a condescending tone.

"Have you been dating anyone special yet, Fred?"

"Too busy playing the field."

"Haven't met someone with enough money I gather."

"Well, if they can't bring anything to the table, they're only good for one thing. You haven't done so bad for yourself. Elizabeth's got a nice trust fund. She'll not come to you empty handed.

"I'm not marrying Elizabeth for her money. I love her. Haven't you ever been in love?"

"I don't allow myself that weakness. It's a base emotion and it makes fools out of men. I'm looking for a merger."

"Fred, you have a rock where your heart should be. I hope someday you'll find someone who can penetrate that coldness and bring some warmth into your life. Elizabeth is the best thing that has ever happened to me."

"Have you gotten into her pants yet?”

"No, she's not that kind of girl."

"How are you getting your rocks off if not with her?"

"Never mind about me and my rocks. Lunch is over. Time to get back to work."

"Well, I'm taking a long lunch today. I've got a sweet little thing to munch on until I find the girl of my dreams. You know, the girl with the heavy pocketbook."

"Who is it?"

"Now that would be telling, and as you well know, I am a gentleman and a gentleman never tells."

Frederick and James drove back to the mill. When James got out of the car, Frederick with a lecherous look in his eyes waved, "See you later brother. I have to take care of some rocks."

James shook his head and as he walked through the yard, the gatekeeper approached him. "Jim, can I speak to you a minute."

"Sure thing, Ralph. What's up?"

"I don't know how to begin. You know Anna Kovak?" "Yes, I do. Real nice lady. A hard worker."

"You see, she's was widowed last year. Got a beautiful daughter. Poor kid had to quit school to take care of the house and her kid brother so Anna could work. I saw her daughter Stella getting into your brother's car a few months ago and then a few times after that. I think something is going on with them. Hate to see Anna have more trouble than she's already got."

"I promise I'll take care of it, Ralph. I don't want to see Anna hurt either."

"Thanks, Jim. I knew you'd understand."

Chapter 14

Several months earlier, as Frederick was walking from the mill, he had spied a beautiful flaxen-haired girl rushing towards the building. She had a lunch pail in her hands. As she neared him, he smiled slyly. "Why the rush beautiful?"

Not expecting a voice to question her, the girl blurted the cause of her hurry, "My mother forgot her lunch and I have to get it to her."

Fred grabbed the lunch pail from her hand, thinking what a lovely diversion she would make.

"What is your mother's name? I'll have the gateman deliver it for you.

"Anna Kovak, sir."

"- and your name is?"

"Stella, sir."

"Come with me."

They walked to the gatehouse and Frederick ordered, "Guard, see to it that this is delivered to Anna Kovak."

"Right away, Mr. Woodsworth."

"You're the owner?" Stella stared.

"Not yet. I'm Walter Woodsworth's son, Fred, and for doing such a good deed for your mother, I'll reward you and take you to lunch."

"Oh, sir, I couldn't. I have so much to do at home," she replied nervously.

"But I insist. A beautiful girl like you shouldn't have to work all day. Think of it as a little vacation and it will make me so happy not to eat alone again." His eyes downcast, he hoped she would take pity on him. "We'll go to a little place I know; its not far and it's just for a sandwich."

"I'd hate to have you eat alone, sir, but my mother...! don't think she would approve."

"I'm sure it will be OK. We're all family here at the mill. It's just for a sandwich."

Before she could protest further, he took Stella's arm, walked her to his car and opened the passenger door. She hesitated. She didn't want to offend her mother's boss, but she liked being called beautiful.

Oh well, it's just for a sandwich, she thought. Putting her apprehensions aside, she got in.

Frederick was careful not to bring her to a local place. He drove to a small Italian restaurant in Montclair, just a short drive from the mill. When they pulled into the parking lot, Frederick made a mad dash around the car to open Stella's door. He knew that a young innocent girl would be greatly impressed by gallantry. Her skirt raised slightly when he helped her out of the car, causing Frederick to salivate over the creamy white, flawless skin that covered her long legs. He held her elbow close enough to him to smell the freshness of her hair and guided her into the restaurant and to a table in a darkened comer. Frederick could see that Stella was uncomfortable. Her eyes looked downward. After they had ordered their lunch, Fred lifted her chin with his long, thin fingers, stared into her eyes and asked, "Tell me about yourself, Stella."

Nervously fiddling with her napkin, Stella began her story, "Not much to tell. I had to quit high school to take care of the house and my little brother after my dad died so my mother could work. My brother is in school and I have to pick him up at three o'clock. Do you know my mother?"

"No, only by name. My work is in the offices above the mill. I make sure your mother's pay check gets to her on time. I handle the mill's money. Since our move here from New York, I haven't had time to make many friends."

"Oh, I'm sorry."

"Don't be. I've met you. You can be my friend." He wanted her sympathy; this was his hook to break down her defenses. He knew she was young and inexperienced and would respond to his flattery.

Stella blushed averting her eyes from Frederick.

"Thank you, sir, for the lunch and the nice conversation."

"Please call me Fred, and you are quite welcome. Do you think we can do this again next Wednesday?"

"Oh sir, I mean Fred I don't think so."

"Please. I really enjoyed your company and am quite alone here. Don't say no now. Think about it and if you want to have lunch again, meet me at the gate on Wednesday at noon."

"I'll think about it."

Frederick dropped her off a few blocks away from her home at Stella's insistence because she didn't want the neighbors gossiping. As she walked away from his car, he stared at the back of her and thought, That's a big dumb blonde with huge knockers. It shouldn't take me long to get in.

Stella's whole life had crumbled when her dad died. Her mother had to work and she was consigned to be the house drudge; washing, cooking, cleaning, ironing. She longed to be back at school with her friends. She was young and wanted some fun in her life. When Wednesday rolled around, Stella was there waiting for Frederick. They went back to the same Italian restaurant each time they met, where Frederick encouraged Stella to talk about her dreams, her cares. He listened intently making her reveal herself to him, to drop her guard. Each time Frederick would get a little more familiar.

First, he put his arm around her shoulders as he led her into the restaurant, then a good-bye kiss building to long lingering kisses which raised the young girl's natural passion. She thought they were falling in love.

Soon the lunches turned into petting sessions and finally into sex. Stella didn't want to give in to him, but he assured her that they would someday be married, as soon as his cheap father gave him a raise. He promised that her mother's job would be secure if ever there was a layoff and he would see to it that there was more money in her mother's envelope.

Chapter 15

When Frederick arrived back at the office, James was waiting for him. Frederick walked across the room, sat in his chair, leaned back and put his feet up on his desk. Smirking and thinking how far he had gotten with Stella, he cleaned the bits of lunch left in his teeth with a toothpick.

James opened the door and made sure it was closed behind him. In a stern voice and looking directly into Frederick's eyes, he asked, "Fred, it has come to my attention that you are dating Anna Kovak's daughter. Is that true?”

"So, what if it is! It's none of your business," replied Frederick cockily.

"Like hell it isn't. I know what you think of women who have nothing to bring to your table as you so eloquently put it. You're only using that kid and her mother works here. I want it stopped now."

"It's over, but not because you're ordering me to end it. I broke it off today. The bitch actually thought I would marry her," he lied.

"Fred, I'm warning you. Don't do this sort of thing again or you and me will have it out and I don't mean with words."

James stormed out of Frederick's office furious with his brother. When he got back to his own office he tried to calm down and thought of Elizabeth. She always made him feel better.

Chapter 16

James had been engaged for a year to Elizabeth Stanhope, the daughter of his dad's best friends, Senator and Mary Stanhope. Both families were pleased when the couple announced their engagement. Now, with his large salary, he could well afford to make her his wife.

James leaned back in his chair, closed his eyes and remembered when he first realized he loved Elizabeth. They had known each other for years but he thought of her as a kid. She was seven years younger than him and he hadn't seen her for quite a while. It wasn't until he attended her eighteenth birthday party at the Senator's country club that he realized she was no longer a child. She had blossomed into a beautiful young woman. He stared at her not believing his eyes. She was wearing a gown of pale green, cut low enough to reveal an ample breast. The green of her gown complimented her auburn hair and happy green eyes. No one had ever had such an effect on him. He was so struck by Cupid's arrow that when he congratulated her on her birthday, he stuttered, a malady he was totally unfamiliar with.

"Hey Liz... ah hap happy birthday. You, ah look real really nice," he stuttered. When he bent to kiss her cheek, her perfume enchanted him. He whispered, "Would you care to..." Just then another suitor whisked her away.

While James waited for the right time to approach Elizabeth, he noticed her sister Helen sitting alone. He knew she was too young for her sister's friends and too old to play with the children. James sat next to her and asked, "How are you, Helen? How's school going? "

"Fine, Jim," she responded timidly.

James thought that drawing conversation from shy little Helen might be difficult so he invited her to dance.

Flustered, Helen said, "I don't know how."

"Well, I'm not a very good dancer either. Maybe we can practice together. Come on."

James took Helen's hand and brought her to the dance floor. As they were gliding to a waltz, Frederick, who was dancing nearby, whispered to James, "Can't get a real woman? You, pedophile."

"My brother's a jerk," James said. He hoped Helen had not heard his brother's remark, but she had, and responded, "Yeah I know. He never acknowledges me even if I'm in a room alone with him. You never know what he's thinking. He kind of gives me the creeps. I'm sorry to say this to you. I know he's your brother. Thank heaven you're not like him."

When their dance was over, he brought her back to the table and offered to fetch her some punch. Her mother Mary approached them.

"Hello James, nice to see you again. Helen, please come with me. want to introduce you to my friends, the Johnsons."

As Helen left with her mother, James surveyed the room looking for Elizabeth. He spotted her on the dance floor. Tired of waiting to get her alone, he tapped the fellow she was dancing with on the shoulder.

Obviously annoyed, the young man graciously gave up Elizabeth. "You certainly are in demand tonight." he smiled.

"It's been a long time, Jim." she answered. "I've grown up." "How did I miss that?" he replied.

"I guess you were busy with college and co-eds." "Not me. Had my nose in the books all the time." "I'll bet." Elizabeth smiled.

James had all he could do not to kiss her right there, right on the dance floor. Elizabeth fit into his arms as no other had and he knew then that he would never let her go; but alas, some young man had tapped his shoulder. Grudgingly, he handed her over to him, but his eyes never left her. They followed her gaiety all evening, but suddenly when he turned his head for an instant, she had vanished. James anxiously surveyed the dance floor. Unable to spot her, he thought she might have walked out to the terrace for some air and meandered out there to look for her. He stopped short behind a potted palm when he saw her talking to a young man who would not be satisfied with just conversation. In moments the masher's mouth was on hers and his hand grabbed at her breast. Struggling to free herself, she pushed her attacker away recoiling.

"No, don't." But he was not so easily put off. As he went at her again,

James stepped forward and with a loud booming voice bellowed, "So there you are!" immediately halting any further advances from the young man who, upon seeing James' towering stature, made a hasty exit.

"I'm so glad to see you, James. I don't know what came over him."

"I do. You look amazing. Will you marry me?"

His proposal broke the tension and made her laugh. The words just flowed from him naturally. He felt he would die if any other man laid hands on her. Beautiful, young and naive, a dangerous combination, he thought. She was prey for any unscrupulous trolling male looking to satisfy his lust. From that night forward, he monopolized her; and she knew she was safe with him. Like a delicate flower, he cultivated her with his kindness and gentle manner, never forcing her any further than she was willing to go.

Sadly, just before Elizabeth's nineteenth birthday, while James and Elizabeth were having dinner with his parents, a call came for Walter. The maid announced, "There is an urgent call for you, Mr. Woodsworth."

"Excuse me. I'll return in a moment. Continue eating." "Walter Woodsworth here."

"It's Helen," her voice shaking. "There's been an accident, mother and father have been killed. Elizabeth needs to come home."

"Helen, we'll be there as soon as we can. Is someone there with you? "Yes, the staff."

"Stay calm. We're on our way."

It took Walter a while to compose himself before he could return to the dining room. James could see something terrible had happened. His father's eyes were red and swollen. He had been crying.

"What's wrong father?"

Walter walked to where Elizabeth was seated. Seeing the look of horror in Walter's eyes, she rose out of her chair, her dinner napkin falling to the floor.

With eyes widened, she looked at Walter and whispered, “What's wrong?"

"I have some terrible news child. There's been an accident in Cape Cod. Your parents.”

Walter's voice trailed off as tears choked off his voice.

James held Elizabeth. She was in shock and looked as if she would faint. Harriet ran to Walter and all dissolved into tears.

"My sister Helen," cried Elizabeth.

"It was Helen who called," answered Walter. "The staff is with her and we shall be there shortly."

When he had composed himself, Walter ordered the limousine which took them to Westchester.

The Stanhope's were killed in a boating accident off Cape Cod, leaving Elizabeth and her sixteen-year-old sister orphaned. Since neither the Senator nor his wife Mary had any living relatives, guardianship of the girls was left to Walter, their best friend, who would manage the sisters' inheritance and provide for their care. They would be maintained in their parents' home in Westchester, until Elizabeth's marriage to James. Afterward they would all come to live at Belle Vista. The Westchester house would then be sold and Helen would be enrolled in a private girls' school in Montclair to complete her last year of high school.

That was over a year ago, and it would be just a few more months and Elizabeth would no longer be an orphan, she will be my wife, James smiled.

In fact, Elizabeth had gone to Manhattan that day to meet his mother. They were going to St. Patrick's to finalize some wedding plans.

Chapter 17

The move from New York City's upper east side to Belle Vista in Paterson, had been difficult in only one respect for Harriet. She missed going to St. Patrick's Cathedral in New York City every morning. For years she had daily occupied the first seat in the first row on the right side of the center aisle at the 8:00 AM mass. Most especially, she missed her priest, Father Jerome, to whom she confessed weekly. He was not only her confessor, but her friend as well. She and Elizabeth had come to the church today to make final arrangements for Elizabeth and James' wedding. Harriet easily stepped into the role of mother to advise and help Elizabeth plan the wedding. She loved her intended daughter-in-law for her kindness and for making James so happy. Harriet thought Elizabeth was the epitome of what a lady should be and wanted the best for her.

Months earlier, Harriet had asked Elizabeth if she would like to be married in St. Patrick's. Elizabeth knew it would make her future mother-in-law happy, so she consented. It was an easy concession because she knew her small church in Westchester would never be able to accommodate all the important guests that Walter would invite. Elizabeth really didn't care where the wedding was, she just wanted James.

Since Walter controlled the purse strings, he would have preferred the wedding and reception be held in New Jersey, but

Harriet insisted, which she rarely did, that James and Elizabeth be married in St. Pat's. Harriet and Walter worked together on the wedding, planning each detail. Walter made the arrangements for special railcars to bring their guests from New York City to Paterson after the ceremony. A fleet of limousines would await the train's arrival at the Paterson station to transport their guests to the festivities at Belle Vista. Walter made sure that most of the wedding costs were taken from Elizabeth's inheritance without informing her, reasoning that the responsibility for the wedding's expense would normally be the Stanhope's. He never informed her about her assets and she was too much in love with James to care.

Harriet had ordered the west wing of Belle Vista be prepared for James and Elizabeth when they returned from their honeymoon. Elizabeth's younger sister Helen would have a room in that wing as well. Harriet made sure that Helen's room would be an appropriate distance from that of the happy couple.

Vivienne, Harriet's sister, would be attending the wedding. They had not seen each other in a few years. Growing up they were never close. Harriet was five years older than Vivienne. They were as different as day and night. Years ago, after receiving her inheritance, Vivienne Worthington had seen the world, rarely contacting Harriet. Her excesses were legend. Rumor had it she was almost out of funds. Taller and more vivacious than Harriet, she was a stunner who had a penchant for picking up penniless Counts.

Vivienne would be staying at the Plaza Hotel in New York City for the wedding. Harriet was cordial to her sister, but she didn't want her staying in her home and had not offered her an invitation of a room at Belle Vista.

Walter's sister Agatha would be attending the wedding as well. Harriet had never had a close relationship with her. She had tried, but they had nothing in common except their love for Walter. Harriet felt Agatha resented her for taking her brother. Walter arranged to have a limousine pick up Agatha from her Newark home and return her to it when she wanted to leave the wedding reception.

Chapter 18

APRIL, 1939 - WESTCHESTER, NEW YORK

The months of preparation flew by and all of a sudden it was the night before the wedding. Harriet had offered to rent a suite in Manhattan for the girls so they would be closer to St. Patrick's, but Elizabeth and Helen wanted to spend their last night together at their family home in Westchester.

Unable to sleep, Helen dressed in her pajamas, knocked on Elizabeth's door.

"It's me, Helen."

"Come in." Elizabeth, in her nightgown, was seated at her vanity table brushing her hair.

"I'm sorry. I just need to have a little more time with you before you belong to James. It was such a busy day we barely had time to talk. I want to say how happy I am for you. James is a great guy. I know you'll be happy."

"I wish Mom and Dad were here. I so wanted Dad to walk me down the aisle."

"Missing them is all I seem to do. I'll miss this house and the life we had here."

"Promise we will always be close. Not like Harriet and her sister Vivienne. They hardly ever see each other."

"I promise. You are all I have, Elizabeth."

The verbalization of those words brought home their reality. She had never felt more alone in her life. Elizabeth was to be a wife and someday a mother. What am I to be? she thought.

" I love you, Elizabeth."

"And I love you. Nothing will ever change that, not even my marriage."

They hugged each other tightly and said, "Good-night."

Chapter 19

Early the next morning, the limousine arrived to pick up Elizabeth and Helen. The ride to St. Patrick's would take about thirty minutes. Helen lovingly straightened Elizabeth's dress when she seated herself in the back of the limousine.

"Elizabeth, you look beautiful. Does James know how lucky he is?"

"We're both lucky. I love him so much it hurts and I hope someday you will feel the same way about your man. After you're married, we'll buy houses near one another and raise our families together."

"Look we're nearing the church. Not nervous are you?"

"No, I'm ready."

The limousine pulled up to the front of the church. As they emerged from the car, the photographer's flash bulbs nearly blinded them. The two sisters climbed the stairs to the vestibule. Helen walked behind Elizabeth holding her train. Walter and Winifred Teasdale, Elizabeth's maid of honor, were waiting there for the sisters' arrival. It was a perfect day for a wedding that early spring morning. After an early morning rain, the sun came out and the temperature was a comfortable 72 degrees. St. Patrick's was filled with flowers; the candles with their golden hue created an aura of solemnity. Then the organ sounded and everyone took their places. Helen was first down the long aisle, then Winifred.

Walter held Elizabeth's arm, looked into her nervous eyes and said, "Elizabeth, be calm. You are the most beautiful woman in the world today and are a most welcome addition to our family."

"Thank you, Walter."

As Elizabeth made her way down the aisle on Walter's arm, it was as if good and evil had personified. The French lace veil loosely laid upon her auburn tresses framed her angelic face. Her gown made of the same lace, ever so lightly jeweled with seed pearls at the bodice, captured the beauty and purity of the treasure within, giving Frederick something else to be jealous about.

Walter looked fairly distinguished in his black tuxedo. Walking slowly down the aisle he remembered the thrill of conquest at his deflowering of Harriet on their wedding night and wished he could witness Elizabeth's undoing that evening. There is nothing like that first time with a woman you have been hungering for, he thought to himself. Walter, never a religious man who had serious doubts as to God's existence, didn't look upon the marriage ceremony as anything other than a necessary evil to get what he wanted. Walter's credo was, "The world was all about money and power, and religions were just some of the players out to grab as much money and power, as they could."

Elizabeth's first choice for Maid of Honor was her sister Helen, but always seeing the resentment toward James in Frederick's eyes, she thought she would pair up her friend, Winifred Teasdale, with Frederick, the best man. She hoped that sparks would fly and maybe, just maybe, Frederick would loosen up and be happy.

There was also another reason. Ever since they were children, Elizabeth knew Frederick had a cruel heart. Whenever he wasn't winning or was not the leader at some game they were playing in the yard, he would go off by himself, sit on the ground and pull the legs off spiders or the wings off any flying insect unlucky enough to cross his path. When Elizabeth asked him why he did this, he would smile ghoulishly and say "l want to hear them scream." Elizabeth had never seen an act of kindness from Frederick. She thought he was missing a soul.

Unlike Winifred, who could take care of herself, her sister was young and vulnerable and she didn't want Frederick hurting Helen's tender ego or cause her pain in any way. Elizabeth had told Helen when the date for the wedding was set, "I've asked Winifred to be my Maid of Honor. Frederick is going to be James' best man. I really wanted you to be my Maid of Honor, but I know how much you loathe Frederick. Maybe Winifred can break through Frederick's icy veneer and turn him into a human being."

"I'm glad not to be in the limelight. I will be much happier as a bridesmaid and relieved that Frederick will not be my partner. I hate being in the same room with him."

Helen had come to puberty late and was quite shy. Her body, thin and childlike, had yet to develop fully. The small mounds that resided on her chest had to be padded to fill out her bridesmaid gown.

James stood nervously waiting for his bride, his heart bursting with joy. Finally, she's all mine, he thought. Several of the young single invitees were overheard commenting how sad they were that James was now out of play. "He is as handsome as it gets," one girl remarked.

When they got to the steps below the altar, Walter lifted Elizabeth's veil and kissed her on the mouth which startled Elizabeth a bit. He then took her hand and placed it in James' hand. They walked up the stairs to Father Jerome as Walter took his seat next to Harriet. When James and Elizabeth exchanged their vows, their eyes locked and each found paradise in the other's soul. They were one.

As a tear made its way down her cheek, Harriet put her hand into Walter's. He lifted her hand to his mouth and kissed it tenderly and quietly assessed his union with Harriet.

She is a good wife, receptive to my needs; sexually and in every other way valuable to a man in my position.

He was always proud to have her on his arm. Her parents had opened many doors for him professionally and socially. He knew he married up and perhaps that gave him the impetus to best Harriet's parents in the accumulation of wealth. They had given their daughter a privileged life, but he had made her a queen in a castle.

Chapter 20

Belle Vista was brilliantly dressed to receive its guests. Spring flowering bulbs of every variety lined the driveway. Flowers of all colors were in profusion everywhere. Upon the happy couple's arrival, the band on the veranda played "Here Comes the Bride." Cocktails in hand, the guests milled about admiring the grandeur of every part of the mansion open to them. Wonderful works of marble statuary abounded in the mansion as well as in the gardens. Precious artwork hung in the great room and in the one-hundred-foot marble colonnade gallery wing.

At the bottom of the grand staircase, there was a large oak picture frame carved with fruit and flowers that had been installed by Catholina Lambert, Belle Vista's previous owner, to frame his wife's beauty as she descended to the main floor. It left one to wonder if Lambert used the phrase "You are as pretty as a picture," to compliment his wife. Installing the frame made words unnecessary as it would be a permanent reminder of how beautiful his wife would always be to him. The story about why the frame was installed had come to Walter when he had a conversation with the heirs at closing. It had prompted Walter, who was not to be outdone, to commission the statues of Apollo and Venus.

Winifred was deeply impressed by the lavishness of the reception and of the Woodsworth fortune. Not that her family wasn't well off, but the Woodsworth money seemed endless. She remarked to Frederick, "This is the grandest wedding I have ever attended and I have gone to some of the best."

"My dad never does anything half way. It's all or nothing with him. Would you like to take a walk in the garden and get away from the noise?"

Frederick wanted to know all about Winifred to see if she was worth his time.

"What business is your father in?" he inquired.

"Have you heard of Cheshire Foods? That's one of daddy's companies."

"Yes, an English Company."

They parried assets back and forth for a while then Winifred, batting her blue eyes, quickly interjected, "I came out last year." She thought mentioning she was a debutante would impress Frederick. It did. With an aristocratic air she added, "You must come out to our little place in the Hamptons this summer."

Although not as lovely as Elizabeth, Winifred was from a prestigious family; an asset more important to Frederick than beauty. Winifred was attractive in a different way. Not as natural as Elizabeth, her dirty blonde hair was expertly coiffed and her makeup gave her thin lips some fullness and her cheeks roses, which her very white skin denied her. Her blue eyes did not soften the sharp angles of her face.

When they reached a more secluded area of the garden, Winifred swung around and impetuously French-kissed Frederick moving her hand dangerously close to his zipper, stimulating him to distraction. He moaned, "Don't start something you can't finish," prompting Winifred to grasp his rising manhood. Sex came easy to Winifred. From an early age, she knew what most men wanted and she knew how to use it to get what she wanted. In her circle, how not to become pregnant was a life course. If you accidentally did become pregnant there was always a recourse for the rich...an accommodating doctor.

Frederick's breath quickened as he pulled her behind a large Rhododendron clumsily groping her. As his passion rose, he bent Winifred's lithe body beneath him, but in his mind's eye it was Elizabeth he held in his arms. She did look so beautiful, he thought with envy, and probably a virgin besides? Voyeuristically, he was stealing James' prize. Frederick always wanted what his brother had. Growing up, he even resented that James had a larger bedroom than his. He would steal James' candy, even though he had the same, because somehow it was always sweeter when it belonged to his brother. Frederick's hand was quickly under the heavily crinolined full skirt of Winifred's gown. It glided over her garter belt hook that held her silk stockings to the sweet spot between her thin thighs; his fingers groping so hard, it caused her pain - a pain she didn't mind. Their little tryst was thwarted when they heard some wandering guests approaching.

Straightening their clothing, they continued their walk as if nothing had transpired. They were inseparable for the rest of the evening. When her parents decided to leave, Frederick offered to drive her home so she could stay until the party ended.

It was a gala event and the revelers stayed late into the night. When they had wished the last of their guests farewell, Walter congratulated Harriet, "You did a magnificent job. You have made me proud, my dear." As he kissed her good-night he told her, "I do not want to be disturbed. I have some very important papers to sign in my study."

"You work too hard," she scolded. "All this has to be paid for dumpling."

"I'll be up to bed as soon as I speak to the caterers and the cleaning people." Harriet wanted to make sure that all the bathrooms would be sanitized and that the house be placed back into pristine condition. She told the wedding manager she wanted every scrap picked up and disposed of.

"Please have the staff be as quiet as possible. My husband will be working late and does not want to be disturbed."

Chapter 21

Exhausted from the day, her feet sore and swollen, Harriet decided to use the servants' steps rather than the grand staircase to reach her bedroom. As she looked up, she saw her sister Vivienne descending the stairs visibly disheveled.

"I thought we said goodbye a while ago."

"I'm out of funds, darling, and your husband has demanded his interest," Vivienne said nonchalantly as she adjusted her clothing.

"You, money grubbing whore!"

Harriet tore at her sister knocking the blonde wig off her head. Vivienne's excesses had extracted their price. All those men, all that liquor, those opiates; they had left her beautiful raven hair a mousy mess.

"Get out and stay out," bellowed Harriet as she pushed Vivienne through the doorway to the great room. "Forget you ever had a sister!"

Harriet, forcing back her tears and with a renewed energy that only anger can produce, ascended the stairs with such speed that her feet barely touched the wood.

Walter stepped from the study into the hallway to see what the commotion was about. Harriet ran towards him screaming, "My sister, my sister! How could you? Can't you get enough? I could tolerate your discreet little forays into Manhattan disguised as overnight business meetings so you can get what I won't do. But my sister! Have you no honor Walter? You animal! Sleep wherever you want, but not with me...ever!" her words reverberating throughout the expanse above the great room.

To emphasize her resolve, Harriet, nostrils flaring and blind with anger, seized the rose-colored crystal luster on the hall table and hurled it over the railing down upon the great room's marble floor. The servants ran out to see what had fallen. Raising their eyes upward they saw Walter, who in an attempt to hide his embarrassment, waved his hand at them and angrily shouted, "Just clean it up."

His face twisted as he walked back to his study. Walter's body shook with fury. He poured himself a large glass of scotch. She didn't even let me explain. She believed the word of her harlot of a sister. Hadn't I given her everything her heart desired?" I have made her a queen in my castle and now I am repaid by such behavior. Cut me off will she?

*   *   *

Vivienne had tried to get Walter's attention all evening, but he was in constant movement, shaking hands and conversing with the guests. Remembering one of her conversations with Harriet that Walter always had a bit of brandy he kept in his study before retiring each night, she decided on a plan.

When just about all the guests had departed, Vivienne saw Harriet saying her good-byes to a group that was leaving. Knowing that her sister would be occupied, she ran to Harriet quickly and kissed her saying, "I have to rush. I'll call you tomorrow." Quietly, Vivienne slipped up the servants' steps and hid in Walter's study.

Some minutes later, Walter entered. He could see the back of Vivienne's blonde head. She was sitting in one of the leather chairs facing his desk.

"What are you doing here? I thought you left."

She stood and walked toward Walter. Standing almost toe to toe, she stared at him seductively and touched his tie.

"Walter, darling, It seems I've gotten into a bit of a financial bind and I can really use your help. I've been waiting here for you because I don't want to worry Harriet with my problem."

Walter broke away from her and walked to sit behind his desk.

With his hand to his temple, he sighed, "Vivienne, Vivienne. When are you going to learn? You have ample coming in from your trust to live very well, but with all those lavish parties you throw and keeping penniless royalty... don't you think I've heard?"

"Don't tsk, tsk me Walt. You and I are cut from the same cloth. You have an appetite for forbidden things just as I do."

"Yes, I do, but I control my appetite, as you so nicely put it. It never interferes with my family or my business."

Vivienne pouted. "I'm just not as sneaky as you."

"You're too old to play the coquette," he smirked. "I'm tired Viv.

How much do you need?"

"$50,000,' she answered stoically.

Walter pulled his checkbook from the desk drawer and wrote the check. Ripping it from the book with a flourish, he walked around the desk to hand it to her.

Noting the look of disdain on his face she asked, "Are you afraid I won't give it back with interest?"

Grabbing his lapels for leverage, she kissed him pushing her tongue into his mouth.

Walter shook her and then pushed her away.

"You're my wife's sister. I don't crap where I eat. You'd better go."

With her hand on the doorknob, she glared back at him, "We all make mistakes Walt, and even though you think you can control every minute of your life, someday you'll fail and it will cost you more than money."

Not since he was a child had anyone spoken to Walter as Harriet had that night. His mind was afire with anger. My father would never take this from his wife. She knew her place.

Walter remembered one night when he was a very small child. It was when he first learned that fathers and husbands should never be questioned. He lay asleep in his bed when he heard the shouting. His mother was questioning where Walter's father had been so late. He heard a slap and then the sound of a chair being knocked over in the kitchen, then everything was quiet. The next day he saw that his mother's eye was blackened. Walter asked his father at breakfast,

"Did you hurt mother's eye?"

His father's response was quick and violent, slapping Walter's face so hard he fell off his chair. As he lay on the floor, he kicked Walter and screamed, "Never question your father again."

Walter had come too far to put his hands on Harriet, but he would not allow her actions to go unpunished.

Chapter 22

OCTOBER, 1971 - NUTLEY, NEW JERSEY

Victoria wasn't feeling well lately. Her energy had declined and she was lightheaded and dizzy. Between work, cooking, cleaning, taking care of her daughter, and helping her widowed father, she had pushed herself too far and could barely get through the day. Victoria always worked beyond her capacity and had a cadre of family and friends who counted on her continually. She never said "no" to anyone who asked for her help. It seemed to Victoria that she was fatigued all the time and decided to call her Uncle Tony for a checkup. Minnie, her uncle's receptionist, answered, "Dr. Russo's office."

"Hi Minnie. It's Victoria. Do you think I could get in to see Uncle Tony today?"

"Sure Vikky. Let me see. I've got a four o'clock open."

"That's good for me. I'll come in straight from work."

Victoria hung up the phone to disconnect and picked it up again to call her neighbor Pam. Pam had been the first neighbor to welcome Victoria when she moved from Newark to Nutley. They had become good friends and helped each other out whenever there was a need. Diana and Pam's two girls attended the same school.

"Hi Pam. It's Vikky. Could you do me a favor. I've got a doctor's appointment at four today. Could you pick up Diana from school and keep her with you until I get home?"

"Sure Vikky. No problem. She can have dinner with us. Take your time."

"Thanks Pam. I owe you one. See you when I get home."

Three o'clock couldn't come fast enough for Victoria. She finished her day at the office with a yawn and waved goodbye to her co-workers as she left them. On the subway ride to her car she tried to close her eyes, but a bunch of students at the back of the car were making such a racket it made it impossible for her to rest. The subway delivered her across the street from the lot where her car was parked. She paid the attendant and drove to the Professional Building a few blocks away from the subway in Belleville. Victoria was still yawning when she entered her Uncle Tony's office.

"Hi Minnie. I'm here for my four o'clock appointment."

You're early, but in luck. The three-thirty didn't show so I can get you in right now."

Victoria had barely sat on the examining table when her Uncle Tony came in with a flourish. Peering over his half glass readers precariously perched on the bridge of his nose, he looked at her file and remarked, "How's my beautiful niece? I see you haven't had a physical in quite a while. What's going on?"

"I've been fine, but lately I feel like hell. I'm always tired and lightheaded."

"You better slow up. When are you and that husband of yours going to take a vacation?"

"When you pay for it Uncle Tony."

He coughed and smirked. Uncle Tony was known for his frugality. He strapped the blood pressure cuff to her left arm and after some pumping announced, "Well your blood pressure is low. It's 90 over 60. I'm surprised you're able to walk."

He listened to her heart and chest and said, "Well that sounds good. We'll take a vial of blood and we'll know more in a week. Your iron is probably low."

After drawing her blood, Tony told her, "Come see me next week, OK? Give your dad my regards."

"Love you Uncle Tony. See you next week."

After she left the room, Tony stared at her file for a few minutes. It always made him uneasy when he saw Victoria. It brought back that horrible night. That rich son of a bitch thought he could pay me to kill that kid. Animale. he angrily thought in Italian.

Victoria stopped by the front desk,

"Minnie, Uncle Tony wants me to come back next week. He took some blood and said he'll have the results when I come back."

"Here you go. Four o'clock next Monday," Minnie replied as she· handed Victoria her appointment card.

"See you next week Minnie. Have a good day." "Bye Vikky. Get some rest."

Chapter 23

Victoria walked to her car, put the key in the ignition leaned on the steering wheel for a while and rubbed her eyes. Boy am I beat, she thought. What can I make for supper? Diana's eating at Pam's. I'll order Chinese for me and Mark. I'm too tired to cook.

She started the car and drove back to Nutley. When she arrived back home, she dropped her purse on a kitchen chair, called for the food and then called Pam,

“Hi. I'm home.”

"Is everything all right Vikky?"

"My Uncle Tony thinks my iron is low. I'll know in a week."

"I'll walk Diana home at eight o'clock. It will give you a chance to rest."

"Thanks Pam. I'm going to lay down for a while."

At 6;30 Victoria heard the back door open. She called out, "Mark I'm in the living room."

With his briefcase still in hand, Mark walked through the kitchen to Victoria. Puzzled to find her on the sofa, he asked, "What's up?"

"I went to see Uncle Tony today. I've been really tired lately. He took some blood and thinks maybe my iron may be low. I've ordered us some Chinese. It should be here soon. Diana's at Pam's. Pam picked her up from school and Diana is having dinner there."

"I'm sure Uncle Tony will get to the bottom of it. Try to go to bed early tonight. You know you stay up too late."

"I'm a night person. It's hard to change, but I don't think I'll have a problem tonight. I'm beat."

"Let me change out of this suit and I'll be right down."

The doorbell rang just as Mark came down the stairs. "I've got it Vikky. Stay put."

Mark paid the delivery man and brought the little brown shopping bag to the table. He set out the dishes and forks. After they had eaten he ordered Victoria back to the sofa, "Go lay down and I'll clean up."

"I won't argue with that," Victoria smiled.

"I'll bring you some Chamomile tea."

Victoria smiled-and kissed him, "I love it when you take charge."

At 8:00, Diana opened the back door and as she entered called, "Mom, dad, I'm home."

Mark walked to the back door,

"Hi sweetie. Did you have a good time at Pam's?" He grabbed Diana, swung her around and gave her a big kiss.

"Yeah. It was good. I did my homework there. Where's mom?"

"She's in the living room lying down. She's really tired."

Diana ran to Victoria and after giving her a kiss asked, "Mom are you OK? Pam said you had to see Uncle Tony."

"I'm fine kiddo. Just a little tired. Uncle Tony is checking my blood to see if I need more vitamins. Dad will check your homework. Take your bath and get your PJ's on, OK?"

"Don't worry mom. I can take care of myself. You rest."

Mark had cleaned up the kitchen, checked Diana's homework and got her off to bed. When he went into the living room he saw Victoria dozing on and off.

"Let's go to bed Vikky."

"OK."

Half asleep, she walked to her bedroom, took off her clothes and put her nightgown on. Uncharacteristically, she left her clothes on the bedroom chair and decided she was too tired to brush her teeth. She was out cold before her head hit the pillow.

Chapter 24

Suffering from fatigue, the last thing Victoria needed was another dream to deprive her of the rest she so needed, but come it did.

"I don't want to know." Victoria blurted out, still in a half sleep. Adrenaline running, her heart was beating wildly. "Oh God, not again," she shuddered. Victoria looked at the clock. It was 3:00 AM. With shaking hand, she opened the drawer of her night table and took out the pad and pen she kept there. As quickly as she could, she made her way to the bathroom and turned on the light. Seated on the toilet lid she began to record the night's installment.

She was in an underground storage place, not a cellar but similar to where one would store hay or gardening tools or such. The stone block room was damp, dark and dank. There was another door to another storage area opposite the door to the one Victoria was in with about ten feet of cobblestone separating the two doors. Victoria had found statues there but could not discern what they were. All of a sudden, she heard a voice she instinctively recognized as that of her aunt Mim who had passed away when she was a child. The voice said, "I have come to tell you what you want to know." An overwhelming fear engulfed Victoria. "I don't want to know," she screamed ... then in an instant, she summoned the courage to change her mind: but it was too late, the dream was broken.

What a coward I am, thought Victoria. I want to know so badly what this dream means and when I'm about to find out, I don't jump at the chance.

Fright and anger collided within her. Damn it. Damn it. God help me. If you're trying to tell me something through these dreams, be plain. I'm not good at deciphering symbols. These dreams are driving me crazy. You took my mother before I could tell her about them. Now there's no one to help me. She always made it better.

Victoria had not thought about Aunt Mim in years. All she could remember about her was a warm tender hug. She was married to her mother's brother Nick and had died in childbirth when Victoria was four. Uncle Nick was never the same after Mim's death according to Angela. Although he did remarry, he would never know that kind of love again. He was the saddest man Victoria ever knew.

The first and only time Victoria had ever had a dream of Aunt Mim was when she was about nineteen years old. She dreamt she was in a cemetery carrying a pot of pink flowers searching for Aunt Mim's grave, but could not find it. When Victoria related the dream to her mother, Angela told her, "Aunt Mim loved you very much. She probably is just trying to tell you to visit her grave so you will remember her. She's buried in the Protestant cemetery in Belleville."

Victoria remembered that she was working for Wallace and Tieman in Belleville at the time. She went on her lunch hour to the only Protestant cemetery she knew of in Belleville, stopping first to pick up flowers to plant on the grave. She would soon find out there were two Protestant cemeteries. She had gone to the wrong one and her dream was fast becoming true. There she was carrying a pot of pink flowers and not finding Aunt Mim's grave. She called her mother who was more specific about where Aunt Mim could be found. The next day at Calvary Cemetery, she found her aunt's resting place.

Victoria knew this latest dream of the storage room brought to her by her long dead aunt meant something. She decided to make another visit to Lambert Castle. She knew it was not one of Mark's favorite places to take her so she traded off letting him play golf on Sunday for coming with her to the Castle on Saturday. He was almost happy about the deal because it let him off the hook from his promise to clean out the garage on the weekend. Diana would be at a birthday party with some of her classmates.

Chapter 25

Mark and Victoria drove Diana to her birthday party and then proceeded to Lambert Castle. He could see there was a bit of urgency in Victoria's stride from the parking lot to the building. He could tell she was on a mission. As soon as she could, Victoria got the ear of a museum guide, a nice young man barely in his twenties, Victoria told him about her dreams. He didn't make fun of her, but took what she said seriously. Mark was making faces in the background. He couldn't understand how she could be so open about things like that to a perfect stranger. He pulled her aside and whispered, "Vikky, this guy is going to think you're nuts."

"So, what! It won't be the first time someone thought I was nuts. It's not like he's got a net or anything."

Mark responded with a look of frustration and thought, She never listens to me. If it peaks her curiosity, she's like a dog with a juicy bone. All you can do is get out of her way.

Victoria motioned to a closed door and told the guide, "In my dreams, the servant steps were just beyond that door."

"Yes, they are. Come with me and I'll bring you back there. That area is off limits to the general public, but I'm sure it will be all right."

Victoria whispered to Mark, "See, he doesn't think I'm crazy. He's intrigued."

They were just as Victoria had pictured them. Then they proceeded towards the great room. Victoria looked upward and commented, "By the way, the ceiling over the great room...it was not there in my dreams. The space above it rose up two floors to a glass dome in the roof."

"You're right," the guide said with a look of surprise. "That ceiling was added sometime after the Woodsworths occupied the house. I think in 1939 or 1940. The dome is visible from the second and third floors, but they are off limits."

"Gee, that's the year I was born."

Then Victoria told him about her last dream and of finding the statues in the underground storage area.

The guide's eyes widened. "Have you been to the front of the castle yet?"

"No, why?"

"We did some excavating and found two underground storage areas that we were unaware of. We found two statues in them, one of Apollo and one of Venus."

"Oh my! Mark, let's take a look."

They said goodbye to the helpful guide and walked through the archway near the front entrance to the veranda. Victoria looked over the railing to her left and there they were. Two doors facing each other about ten feet apart.

By the time they left the building, Mark's eyes were as big as saucers. He was speechless and had enough of this weird stuff for today.

"Let's go Vikky. The ball game is on," he said in a pitch higher than his normal tone of voice.

From the look on his face, she knew he wanted out of this place.

“I'm done, Mark."

"Thank God for that," he said with relief as he grabbed her elbow and escorted her out.

The Yankees were his escape from the world and anything else he didn't want to think about. The few times he had dragged her to the game, she would have preferred to be home staring at a blank wall then to endure the screaming, beer swilling fans.

Walking to the car, Victoria commented, "So what do you think? I'm not nuts. The servant steps were there. The ceiling in the great room shouldn’t be there. They even uncovered the statues from my dream. This stuff is all from another time. I wonder why I'm tapping into it."

"Well, I can't give you an answer. I think the best thing you can do is to forget about the dreams. If you think too much, you'll only get more of them and you know what they do to you."

"I don't think about them when I go to bed, they just happen. I have no control over them. You must admit this whole situation is mystifying. Someone or something is trying to tell me something. I just can't figure out who or what. Do you really think I want this happening to me? I don't," she said sharply.

Mark didn't answer her. They drove toward home without exchanging another word. He could tell she was a little miffed at his "Just forget about it," comment. As he drove Mark thought, Things like this happen in scary movies. They don't happen to real people. There has to be a logical explanation for all this. The best thing I can do is just to drive. No matter what I say it's going to be wrong. Mischievously, he snickered to himself, If I tell her to look up "Swami" or "Witch Doctor" in the yellow pages. I won’t get any for a month. Best keep my mouth shut.

Mark broke his silence when he asked, "What time do we have to pick up Diana from the birthday party?"

"Four o'clock," Victoria answered mindlessly.

"It's three-fifteen now. I'll buy you a cup of coffee and a piece of pie at the diner before we have to get Diana."

"OK," she smiled. Guess he realized he ticked me off, she thought.

When they arrived at the diner, Mark was grateful that they had run into some old friends and the conversation had nothing to do with the castle. The time passed quickly and soon they were on their way to get their daughter. Mark went to the door and Diana came running out.

"Hi Dad."

"Did you have a good time. I see you've got a big goodie bag." "Yeah, it was fun. What did you and Mom do?"

"She dragged me to a museum." "No fun, huh?"

His face said it all: an exaggerated grimace.

"Don't tell your mother," Mark smiled.

When they arrived home Mark and Diana watched the game and Victoria made sausage and peppers for dinner. The excitement of the day had left her drained and she couldn't wait till Mark and Diana went to bed to have a quiet hour to herself. When they did, she recorded all that happened at the castle in her journal. Tomorrow is Sunday, she thought, I'll make a lasagna in the morning and bring it to Dad's. Mark will be golfing and he can meet us there afterwards and we can all eat together. The fatigue was still with her and she was a little apprehensive as to what the blood test would reveal. Monday couldn't come fast enough.

Chapter 26

Victoria hoped her Uncle Tony had something good to tell her as she waited for the last patient to leave his office. Minnie had shown her into the examining room and she was sitting there perched on the table when Uncle Tony came booming in with her file in hand,

"Well, nothing too bad Vikky! I was right, your blood is low in iron so you'll have to come in for B-12 shots a few times. That should keep you going for another 100,000 miles."

"You know how much I like needles, but OK, I'll be brave and close my eyes."

"Don't give me a hard time. You know I give the best shots in town," he laughed.

Victoria grimaced as her uncle plunged the B-12 into her arm. "That didn't hurt, did it?"

"You're the best, Uncle Tony."

Victoria jumped off the table, kissed him good-bye and gave him a big hug.

"Thanks, Uncle Tony. I don't know where I would be without you."

Tony smiled almost sardonically. He thought to himself, dead probably, if that animal had had his way.

As Victoria was leaving, Minnie called to her, "Vikky, here. This is a type card the lab sent. Keep it in your wallet just in case you ever need blood." "Thanks Minnie. See you soon." Victoria mindlessly put it in her purse as she left.

On the way out to her car she thought about all she had to do this week and hoped she had the energy to accomplish everything. Her schedule was full.

Her dad needed knee surgery and she had to take him to the lab for blood work tomorrow. Victor had been complaining that he found it very difficult to walk and that he had a lot of pain in his right knee. The orthopedist that Uncle Tony recommended suggested a knee replacement. If all was well, they would do the repair to his knee in a week.

Mark had a business dinner in New York City on Friday night which Victoria had to attend. What am I going to wear and who can I get to sit? she groaned to herself.

Victoria also had to visit Diana's teacher, Ms. Thaler. Diana had had an altercation with a classmate that needed to be discussed.

Her life was a blur of responsibility. She felt as if she was lost in a gigantic maze, but at the back of her mind the castle loomed large and it was still there waiting for her to explore its secrets.

Chapter 27

MAY, 1939-BELLE VISTA

Two weeks after James and Elizabeth's wedding and still everyone of importance was talking about Walter and Harriet and how they really knew how to throw a wedding. Every whim was catered to that night. In some circles the reception was referred to as the Cecil B. De Mille Epic. In others, it was said to rival a royal wedding. The gaiety and joy of that day seemed like a distant light in the darkness that had now enveloped the mood at Belle Vista.

Walter, rankled that Harriet was punishing him by locking him out of their bedroom, decided to use symbology again to express his feelings toward her. He would make sure that she would never throw anything over that railing again. No one punished Walter and got away with it. I'm the king in this castle, he thought to himself.

Vindictively, he hired workers to install a ceiling over the great room.

Symbolically and literally, he stopped the sunshine from entering Belle Vista through the magnificent glass dome in the roof. In another act of revenge, he had the statues of Apollo and Venus removed and put into the underground storage rooms; locked away and buried as their love and trust now was.

Meanwhile, James and Elizabeth were honeymooning in a Spanish style coral-colored villa on one of the Keys in Florida, complete with cook and staff; a wedding present from Walter and Harriet. James was more than gentle with Elizabeth on their first night. Since they had never been together in an intimate way before, he wanted to make sure there would be no fear. They were truly soul mates and could not have been more in love. Many nights, they could be found hand in hand walking along the beach, counting the stars and planning their life together. When their time there was over, it was difficult for them to leave their paradise. They were unaware of the coldness they would encounter between Walter and Harriet upon their return. Helen and Harriet anxiously awaited the arrival of the honeymooners.

When their car entered the driveway from the airport, they ran to the door to greet the happy couple. After kisses and hugs were exchanged, Harriet announced, "I thought you would be hungry so I've had a lunch prepared for us. Come into the dining room and we can catch up."

A lively conversation about the beauty of the Florida Keys ensued over lunch. After he had eaten, James, anxious to see how the mill fared in his absence, excused himself from the table and said he was going over to the mill.

Harriet responded, "Just like his father, work, work, work."

James blew them all a kiss and rushed to the door.

"Come, Elizabeth," Harriet said. "I want to show you what I've done with your rooms. I hope you like it."

The three walked to the West Wing. With a bit of a flourish, Harriet opened the door and announced "Ta Da," allowing Elizabeth to take in the newly decorated rooms.

"Mother, I cannot thank you enough. Everything looks wonderful." Elizabeth said excitedly.

It was the first time Elizabeth had called her mother-in-law Mother and it only endeared her more to Harriet. After living in the house with Walter and the two boys, Harriet enjoyed having females around to converse with. She had come to love both girls.

Harriet had had Elizabeth and James' bedroom papered in a pattern of vined roses. The huge four poster walnut bed was covered by a rose patterned white on white silk bedspread. The sitting room had been papered in a white and burgundy stripe. There was an overstuffed sofa of burgundy mohair and coordinating easy chairs. A carved antique desk made a statement in the comer.

When Harriet had left the room and the sisters finally had a private moment, Elizabeth and Helen reclined back on the bed. With her sister lying next to her, Helen asked, "So how is it being married? Do you feel any different?"

"It's wonderful." Elizabeth blushed.

Seeing her sister's reddening face, Helen shyly said, "Did it hurt?"

"A little, but it got more enjoyable with practice," she giggled." "But enough about that. What's happening with you since I left?"

"Well, my art instructor told me I have real talent and suggested that I study in Paris for a couple of years after I graduate high school in June."

Elizabeth had never seen Helen so enthused about anything before, Helen's eyes literally danced with excitement. Elizabeth's mind drifted back to when they were children. She remembered how Helen would rather color with her crayons than play. When she outgrew crayons, her sketch book was her constant companion.

"Should I do it?" Helen asked, barely able to contain herself.

Elizabeth wanted to tell Helen that she would miss her too much, but she was so happy with James; how could she deny her sister anything?

"Of course, you should do it." she smiled.

"My professor said he knows of a wonderful school in Paris that he is sure he can help me get into."

"I'll miss you, but you have to follow your heart." "I love you, Elizabeth."

"... and I love you. How about a nap before dinner."

"Sounds good to me. I didn't sleep a wink last night waiting for you to come home."

Chapter 28

That evening at dinner, to Elizabeth and James' surprise, Frederick showed up with Winifred on his arm. Frederick had been dating Winifred since his brother's wedding, showing up together at parties and family dinners. They were seen at all the fashionable clubs in Manhattan.

James whispered to Elizabeth, "Well looks like your little scheme worked. Frederick almost looks happy, at least happier than I've ever seen him."

"Love does that to people," she sighed as she squeezed his hand. James thought to himself, Well he found one with deep pockets.

Guess her old man has enough dough to satisfy Fred.

Winifred planned an "opening of the season party" at her parents' place in the Hamptons on Memorial Day weekend for some friends and had invited James, Elizabeth and Helen, but at breakfast the day of the party, James told Fred, "I don't think we are going to be able to make it to Winifred's party. Elizabeth must have some sort of bug. She threw up this morning and is feeling nauseous."

"Winifred's going to be so disappointed." Turning his gaze towards Helen, he invited, "Helen, you can drive with me."

Fred anticipated her refusal. He was well aware that Helen disliked him.

"No, no thank you," she replied averting her eyes in her usual shy way. "Elizabeth may need me," recoiling just enough not to be offensive.

"You're going to miss a good time. Lots of young, rich boys on that beach."

"Thanks anyway Fred, but I think I better stay with Elizabeth."

Helen hated to be near Frederick. She had a dark feeling of foreboding whenever he was near her.

Chapter 29

JUNE, 1939 - BELLE VISTA

Elizabeth's sickness soon turned to joy when she visited the doctor. She was pregnant. She had conceived on their honeymoon. Dr. Fitzgerald had told her she would have the baby in January. What a surprise for James, she thought, and could not wait to tell him. Elizabeth telephoned her husband at work as soon as she returned from the doctor's office.

"James, I would love to go to Mario's tonight. Do you think we could?"

"Anything for my beautiful wife."

James could deny her nothing. He called Mario's and made a reservation for their favorite table in the corner.

As they were sipping their wine, her eyes were downcast and she made her voice ominous, as if she had something terrible to tell James,

"I've been to see Dr. Fitzgerald today..."

Her demeanor raised his concern. He held her hand and asked, "Is there something wrong?"

She hesitated until his facial expression looked pained to finish her sentence.

"and he told me that you are going to be a father," covering her mouth as she giggled.

James' eyes flashed with excitement. He jumped from his chair to kiss her. "Mario, Mario wine for everyone. I'm … we're going to have a baby!" The whole place lifted their glasses in a toast to the baby and the young lovers.

"We have to tell my parents," James beamed.

"We can tell them over dinner this weekend. It's your father's birthday on Sunday and everyone will be there."

"My Dad will be bowled over with this present and Mom will be as over the moon as I am."

Chapter 30

The family had all gathered at Belle Vista for Walter's birthday. Helen, Winifred and Walter's spinster sister Agatha were there as well.

Agatha, a quiet woman, not readily given to conversation would speak only when spoken to. She was quite tall, five-feet, eight-inches, with a straight sturdy back, and had come from a strict working class background. Her role in life had been servile to her parents and to her brother Walter. The highlight of her week was Walter's phone call. She lived a very austere life even though Walter provided for her handsomely.

Just before the birthday cake was to be served, James stood, lifting his glass to Elizabeth. Sheer joy beamed from his face as he said, "Elizabeth and I have an announcement to make. His gaze then shifted to his parents, "Dad, Mom, I would like to inform you that in January you shall be grandparents."

For a moment, Harriet and Walter were joyous together and even exchanged a kiss. Walter raised his wine glass. "You could not have given me a better gift," and swallowed heartily. Frederick and Winifred as well as Aunt Agatha congratulated the happy couple. Helen was so overjoyed, she cried.

Damn him. thought Frederick. James had bested Frederick again by announcing his news before Frederick could announce his own. He and Winifred had become engaged over the weekend. Unhinged, Frederick stood and said, "I also have an announcement to make. Winifred and I have become engaged and will be married in late March next year."

Walter rose. "This is the best birthday I have ever had. Congratulations son, Winifred. Good things come in threes; my birthday, the baby and the engagement. I am a fortunate man."

Everyone wanted to see Winifred's ring. It was a beautiful solitaire diamond in a platinum setting; not quite as large as she would have expected, but nothing she would hesitate to show off.

Everything was falling into place, thought Harriet. It doesn't matter so much about me and Walter. My children are happy.

That evening, encouraged by Harriet's spontaneous kiss when James announced that they were to be grandparents, Walter attempted to accompany Harriet to their bedroom, but the answer was "No." He thought she might give him a present too, but that damned ceiling was too much of a reminder of all his unfaithfulness and lechery.

Chapter 31

Shortly after the announcement of Frederick and Winifred's impending marriage, the Teasdales discussed inviting the Woodsworths to their home in Westchester. The two families had been introduced at James and Elizabeth's wedding, but had never met prior to that. Now that their families were to be joined together by marriage, Laura wanted to know the Woodsworths better.

"Larry, we should invite the Woodsworths to dinner. We really don't know very much about them."

"I've done some checking, Laura. No lineage, but there is a whole lot of money. The wedding was a vulgar display of it. Heard he made it big on his wife's inheritance. He had nothing to speak of before that, but turned it into a fortune. Walter is a force to be reckoned with in the business world. guess our little princess could have done worse."

"I'll call Harriet tomorrow to set a date. Maybe next Sunday, if that's convenient for you."

"It's fine with me."

Laura placed the phone call to Harriet the next morning,

"Harriet, it's Laura Teasdale. Larry and I would love to have you and Walter to dinner next Sunday. Would that be convenient?"

"I'll check with Walter, but I'm sure it will be fine with him. He never conducts business on a Sunday."

Walter and Harriet accepted the Teasdale's invitation.
When their limo drove up to the eight-foot-high black wrought iron entrance gate to the estate, Walter's chauffeur got out and spoke into the intercom "The Woodsworths have arrived." The gate which was inscribed Sunnydale in large gilt lettering swung open allowing the Woodsworth's limousine to proceed.

The white columned southern style mansion was set back about one quarter of a mile from the gate. Shasta daisies lined the driveway which contrasted with the deep green lawn, creating a picture postcard of simple elegance. As the car neared the mansion's rhododendron and azalea shrubbed entrance, Larry and Laura came out to welcome their guests and escort them into their home. Unlike the dark feudal colors of Belle Vista, the color scheme of the Teasdale's home was pale greens and blues with some yellow. Harriet was impressed and expressed this to Laura.

"Your home just lifts one's spirits. It's lovely."

Fluttering her pale blue eyes, Laura beamed.

"I have a wonderful decorator. I'll give you his card. Larry makes it and I spend it." Both women laughed.

After drinks, canapes and some light conversation, Larry invited, "Walter, would you like to see my stables? I have a prize stallion out there."

"I'd be happy to, Larry."

"Let's leave the girls to talk and get better acquainted."

Both men entered Larry's golf cart and proceeded about a half mile to the stables. It was an immaculate brick building with a cobblestone floor and very well maintained. Larry led Walter to a middle stall and proudly announced, "This is my prize Arabian, Windsong. He is as black as the night is around here and runs like the wind."

"Magnificent beast," replied Walter raising his eyebrows to suggest that he was impressed.

Larry then took Walter to the tack room to show off his collection of antique English riding saddles. Tall and physically strong, Larry easily lifted one of the saddles out of its storage case to show Walter.

"Look at the quality of the leather and the silver workmanship on the saddle's fittings. Can't get this quality anymore."

"Impressive." Walter deliberately allowed Larry to do most of the talking. If the Teasdale's were to be associated with his family, he wanted to get a feel for who they were, what they thought and how they spent their money.

"I haven't had much time for hobbies," Walter offered. "I do a little hunting when I get a chance, but even that is mixed with business. Do you hunt, Larry?"

"I did years ago, but haven't in a long time."

"Well then, you must come to The Thicket sometime. It's my lodge in Pennsylvania. The grounds are just crammed full of duck and deer."

"I look forward to it. Well, I guess we had better get back to the girls. Dinner should be ready."

Harriet and Laura were deep into wedding conversation when the men arrived back at the house. Just then the butler announced, "Dinner is served." The dining room table was set with Laura's best crystal, bone china and antique English silver flatware.

Harriet remarked "This silver pattern is beautiful."

"It belonged to my great grandmama, Lady Whittingham. Grandfather married an American and now the only royal blood runs through the veins of Larry's horses."

Laura's remark brought a smile to all their faces. The dinner was sumptuous and the atmosphere most cordial. The Woodsworth's, sated with food and conversation, thanked their hosts and departed for home.

Now that they were alone, Laura remarked, "I think that went well."

"It certainly did dear. Dinner was wonderful. Did you have a nice conversation with Harriet?"

"She's a lovely woman, poised and elegant. We talked about Winifred's wedding dress and where we would shop to find our own gowns for the big day. How did you fare with Walter? I hope he wasn't too much of a bore."

"I guess I did most of the talking. He invited me to his hunting lodge in Pennsylvania. Not something I really would look forward to."

"Did you talk to Walter about the wedding reception?"

"Not yet, but I think I have an angle. I'll play to that big ego of his." "Harriet has invited us for Thanksgiving. You can do it then."

Chapter 32

AUGUST, 1939 - BELLE VISTA

At breakfast Helen announced she was going in to Manhattan to buy clothes for her trip to France.

Walter suggested, "Why don't you come in with me. The car is dropping me off for a business luncheon; then the driver can take you to the shops. We could meet at my office around seven o'clock. Then if you wish we can go for some dinner."

"Thank you, Walter. That is very kind of you."

Walter could be quite charming when the mood struck him. Helen, young and filled with dreams, amused him.

When Helen returned to Walter's office, he had the driver take them to The Plaza for dinner. As they ate, the conversation was light and entertaining for both. Feeling invigorated, he asked Helen, "A friend of mine is having a party this evening. Would you like to go? I am sure there will be plenty of single young people there." He smiled.

"I'm not really dressed for a party," Helen replied.

"You look fine. It's Friday night and most of the guests will be dressed in their business attire," he countered.

In an air of gaiety, she fluffed her hair, straightened her little black suit, widened her beautiful green eyes and said, "OK. Let's go."

Belle Vista was a lovely place to live in, but lonely; Helen longed for friends of her own age.

Jonathan Hayward owned one of the most prestigious art galleries in New York and always gave the most lavish parties at his Park Avenue penthouse. He invited all the right people; artists, literati, and those who could afford his wares.

As soon as Walter and Helen arrived, someone put a glass of champagne in their hands. Not accustomed to drink, Helen took small sips. With the powerful Walter on her arm, several people came up to them and introduced themselves wanting to know if Walter had a new "niece". They quickly engaged Helen in conversation, and, in minutes, her whole story was before them. They thought her a child, unsophisticated, and soon abandoned her. Walter had somehow wandered off and was talking to a blonde woman on the other side of the room.

Left on her own, Helen wandered around the smoke-filled room looking at the art work. Her eyebrows raised when she saw that some of the women in the room were dressed in very provocative clothing and there were couples practically fornicating in the corners and alcoves. The suite was so jammed with people she could hardly breathe. A little overwhelmed, she asked someone where she could find the powder room so she could get her bearings. When she entered the unlocked door she found a woman on her knees retching in the toilet, obviously drunk. Helen stammered, "Oh, I'm sorry," and quickly closed the door. Helen thought this was definitely not where she wanted to be.

Her life had been somewhat sheltered as a senator's daughter and her strong Catholic upbringing did not prepare her for this type of life. She looked around the room for Walter, but he was nowhere in sight. She managed to get through the night listening to a middle-aged artist talk about her work.

Finally, around midnight, Walter emerged from what looked like a bedroom with the blonde woman Helen had seen him with earlier. On the way home Walter asked, "Did you have a good time? Did you meet anyone interesting?"

Not wishing to offend him, Helen replied, "I certainly learned a lot about art and artists."

They arrived back at Belle Vista at 1 :00 AM. The house was eerily quiet. Everyone was asleep. Helen kissed Walter on the cheek and thanked him for the dinner and party and went off to her room.

Walter walked to his study. He needed a brandy, as he always did before retiring. Sitting behind his desk staring at the glass in his hand, he wanted to go to his wife and tell her the truth of what had happened that night with Vivienne, but she had believed her sister. His pride had been bruised. She never let him explain. Just threw him out of her bed. He couldn't deny her accusations to him that night about seeking a certain kind of gratification when he was supposed to be working late in Manhattan. How could she have known? I never showed her less affection, he grimaced guiltily. She should not have made the leap that I would be so hungry, I'd have gone after Vivienne. He swallowed the rest of the brandy and slowly walked out of his study toward the room he had been exiled to.

Chapter 33

Because of morning sickness, Elizabeth had stopped having an early breakfast with the family. Helen, having slept in due to the lateness of her arrival home last night, joined Elizabeth at the table around 10:00 AM.

Elizabeth asked, "Helen, how did the shopping go? You were out pretty late last night."

"Well, ·· I shopped all day and then met up with Walter at his office...then we had dinner at the Plaza. His friend was having a party and he asked me if I wanted to go. I was having such a good day, I said I would. There were a lot of strange people there, but I did get to see some interesting artwork."

Helen was discreet and did not tell Elizabeth about Walter's disappearance that night and how uncomfortable she felt at the party.

"The good news," Helen beamed, "is that I have found some wonderful clothes for Paris. Come, let me show them to you. In another two weeks, I'll be in Paris. I can't wait."

The time went by more quickly than Elizabeth would have wished. Both Harriet and Elizabeth accompanied Helen to the airport. Harriet put five hundred dollars in Helen's hand as she boarded the Air France plane. "Just in case. It's a little mad money." Harriet forced a smile. She was going to miss Helen.

Excited and sad at the same time, Helen kissed them both goodbye and promised that she would write often.

Walter had set up an account for Helen at a Paris bank, but he had put her on a budget. Knowing how green Helen was, he did not want any French scam artist taking advantage of her.

Chapter 34

JULY, 1972- MOUNTAINSIDE HOSPITAL

All the pre-admission tests had come back fine and Victoria's dad had the surgery on his knee. He was very groggy when he came out of recovery and was in and out of sleep. Victoria was hoping he would be more alert today. She had taken the day off from work to tend to all the arrangements for his care when he returned home from the hospital. With a cigarette and a cup of black coffee in hand, she completed the many phone calls to accomplish this. She had recently gone back to smoking. I'll quit again as soon as my life eases up, she thought as she butted it out. With the last call made, she grabbed her purse and set out to visit her dad. Her mind and body were in overdrive.

It was a short ride to Mountainside Hospital in Montclair. When she arrived, the parking lot was full as usual. Victoria circled until, at last, she found someone leaving and quickly pulled her station wagon into the spot. It was a hot humid day and she hated the heat. By the time she got to the hospital entrance, she was sweating. Thank God for air conditioning, she thought as she stopped at the desk to pick up a pass. Crammed into the back of the elevator when it reached the third floor, she extricated herself from the tight quarters and walked to her father's room.

"How are you feeling Pop?" she asked as she kissed him hello. Victoria noticed her dad looked bewildered. His round face seemed almost childlike.

"Why did you sell my house?"

"Dad, I didn't sell your house. Where did you get that from?"

Her father looked back at her with an even more puzzled look than that on her own face.

"I'll be right back," she said anxiously as she went scurrying off to the nurses' station.

"My dad is in room 3421. What's the matter with him?" "What do you mean?"

"My dad is not right in the head. He seems disoriented."

"It's OK. Some older people have that response to the anesthesia. He will be back to normal in a few days. By the way, we had to give him a unit of blood. His count was down, but that is not unusual either."

"There's nothing to worry about?"

"No, don't worry. He's going to be fine."

Comforted by the nurse, Victoria went back to the room and tried to have as coherent a visit as possible with her dad, but he was really out there. He told her he was seeing animals climbing trees in his room. Normal conversation was out of the question. She had brought some lavender oil with her. She hated the way hospitals smelled and knew its essence was good for healing. Rather than just sit there she tried to be useful. Victoria wet a cloth and put some of the oil on it and cooled her dad's face and hands. Just then the beeper went off on the machine dispensing the blood.

She noted that the bag was labeled 0-Positive, and called the nurse who promptly came in and removed the apparatus. Her dad's blood was the same type as her mother's. She knew that because her Mom had received over ten pints the night she died of an aneurysm. The hospital was short of blood that evening and had asked for O-Positive donors.

When her father looked like he was going to drift off again, Victoria kissed his forehead and told him she would see him tomorrow. She dreaded the long walk back to the parking lot in the heat.

Chapter 35

Since Mark had to work late and then would be having dinner with a client that evening, Victoria decided to treat Diana to dinner at her favorite place, Dales Pancake House. Diana was due to get out of band practice at 4:30. Victoria drove from the hospital to the school to pick her up.

"Hey kiddo, how was practice?"

"It was good." Diana played the glockenspiel.

"Dad's not coming home for dinner tonight. Want to go to Dales?" "Yeah, I'm in the mood for a cheeseburger."

She always was. Victoria had a hard time getting her to eat anything else when they went out.

Diana ordered her favorite cheeseburger concoction. Victoria had the pot roast. Knowing of her mother's visits to Lambert Castle Museum and for no apparent reason, Diana asked, "Mom, what's so interesting about that castle museum. Didn't you and dad visit it a few times?"

"I've been having dreams of the place for quite a while and I don't know why. Your father and I ran into the Lambert Castle by accident when we were coming home from some shopping. Why do you ask?"

Suddenly Victoria witnessed the color drain from Diana's normally rosy complexion and her big brown eyes became fixed and trance-like.

Victoria reached across the table and shook her daughter's shoulders in an effort to bring her back from wherever her mind had taken her. When she saw the light return to Diana's eyes, Victoria, in a panic, asked, "What happened to you? Are you all right? You went spacey on me."

"Mom, Mom, Nana was behind you on the paneling. She even had those old gray glasses on and she was moving back and forth. Boy that was weird. Why would I see Nana after I asked you about the castle?"

Diana did not seem upset by what had just occurred, but seemed to be in awe. Angela was a seer and Victoria could not explain her own 'knowings'." What is going on here? Victoria thought. Has Diana inherited some sort of psychic gift, or is the castle now insidiously reaching for my daughter. Whatever was giving Victoria her dreams had now given Diana a vision. To ameliorate any upset the vision might cause, Victoria tried to give her daughter a logical reason for her mother's appearance. She had to convince Diana that it was just a trick of the mind and not an extraordinary event. This psychic stuff was driving Victoria crazy and she didn't want it to affect her daughter.

"You miss Nana so much that maybe your mind made her appear. You know how you can picture things in your head when you are imagining? Well your imagination just went one step further. Your question about the castle had nothing to do with the vision."

Victoria didn't buy her own story, but she hoped Diana did. She didn't want Diana to dwell on what had just happened. Victoria changed the subject which allowed them to finish their dinner and leave.

Knowing that Diana was everything to her mother Angela, Victoria reasoned, It had to be the discussion of the castle and my dreams that prompted my mother's appearance to Diana. She would only appear to protect her only grandchild from something she did not want Diana to know...something that could hurt her. It was obvious she didn't want me talking to Diana about the castle.

If the truth of the dreams chose to reveal itself, it would do so to her alone. Victoria swore never to discuss the subject with Diana again.

When they arrived home, Diana began her homework and Victoria did some laundry. Evidently, Victoria's explanation of why her mother appeared to Diana seemed to work; she was sleeping soundly when Victoria went upstairs to kiss her goodnight.

Mark had come home late. "Vikky, I'm home," he called as he came through the back door.

"I'm in the kitchen."

Mark came to her and kissed her hello. "So, what did my two girls do today?

"I made all the arrangements for my dad's care and then I went to the hospital. The anesthesia made him nuts. He was seeing animals climbing trees in his room. The nurse said it should wear off in a few days. Scared the hell out of me. Then I went to school to pick up Diana from band practice. From there were drove to Dale's for something to eat."

"Diana ordered a cheeseburger, right."

"As usual. I guess I had better tell you before Diana does. She asked me about the castle over dinner and then went spacey on me. She said she saw my mother. I had to shake her to bring her out of it."

"What's your mother got to do with that castle. You shouldn't talk to her about this stuff."

"I don't know what my mother has to do with it, but I didn't bring it up, she did. Don't worry. It scared me enough that it will be the last time I ever say anything to her again even if she asks."

"I'm tired. It was a long day. I'm going to change my clothes and watch the game."

"OK. I'm going to finish the laundry."

When the last of the clothes were folded, Victoria went into the living room to talk to Mark and found him snoring. She nudged him,

"Go to bed Mark, you're sleeping."

"I'm not sleeping. I'm just resting my eyes."

Groggy, he let out a big yawn, raised himself from the sofa and walked towards the stairs leading to their bedroom.

"Coming?" he asked,

"In a few minutes. I have to get a couple of things ready for tomorrow; then I'll be up."

As Victoria set her clothes out for work, she was grateful that the next day was Friday. Tired but not sleepy, she thought she had better clean out her purse; the weight of it had been hurting her shoulder. She felt as if she was carrying around a bowling ball. Sitting at the kitchen table, Victoria was amazed at how much her purse could collect in two weeks.

In the midst of receipts and coupons, she came across the blood type card that Minnie had given her when she was at Uncle Tony's office. Before slipping it into her wallet as Minnie had suggested, she noted that the card indicated her blood type to be B-Negative. That can't be right, she thought. Mom and Dad had 0-positive. I'll have to tell Uncle Tony his lab made a mistake. She was to see him soon for another B-12 shot.

Chapter 36

NOVEMBER, 1939 - BELLE VISTA

Harriet, overjoyed at the expectation of a first grandchild and Frederick's impending marriage, was happily looking forward to Thanksgiving. She had been planning the event for weeks. Winifred's parents, Larry and Laura Teasdale, were invited and Harriet was hoping they could talk more about the wedding.

Walter's sister Agatha would be in attendance for Thanksgiving dinner as well. His dark spinster sister lived alone. She and Walter had inherited their parent's home in Newark and she had lived there by herself ever since. Walter wanted her to hire a maid, but Agatha wouldn't hear of it. The dutiful daughter had taken care of her parents' every need until their death. Grateful that he did not have to deal with the sickness of his parents, he kept his sister very comfortable financially.

Agatha adored her younger brother almost in a sick way. She was trained by her mother to cater to the men in her family. Walter and Agatha had a more than special relationship. He knew her devotion to him was unflinching. Sometimes he even discussed his business ventures with her, something he never did with his wife.

Harriet always envied their closeness, but felt pity for her sister-in-law who never knew romance or children.

Helen would not be coming home for the holidays. Paris had her in its spell. She was excited to be young and alive and thrilled with the prospect of discovering all life could offer.

Belle Vista was ablaze with the reds and golds of autumn when the Teasdales and Winifred arrived. It was a beautiful crisp sunny day. After cordialities were exchanged, Walter rang for cocktails. He had had the Teasdale's investigated when Frederick had announced his engagement. Although they were old money, Larry did not have very much of it and Laura spent it as if they did.

After she had become engaged to Frederick, and because she was so impressed by Elizabeth and James' wedding reception, Winifred nagged her father to find a way to have her wedding at Belle Vista. The nuptials were to take place in late March. Larry, who adored his little princess, had a strategy to get her what she wanted. Thanksgiving Day, as they were driving to the Woodsworths, he told Winifred how he would get Walter to offer Belle Vista.

"I'll tell Walter that we're planning a small intimate wedding at our country club in the Hamptons. I know that will not sit right with the grandiose Walter. That ostentatious showoff will gladly offer Belle Vista. He needs to impress with excess. A great failing of new money," Larry stated in a most condescending manner.

"Daddy, you sure can read people. I think I have the smartest father in the whole world."

After dinner during coffee, Larry, who was sitting to Walter's left volunteered, "We're looking into having the wedding at my club in Westchester. I'm sure it will hold about one hundred and twenty-five guests. We will try to divide that amount evenly of course."

"Why should we be held to any limit? Why not have the reception here at Belle Vista?"

Larry smiled smugly and said, "If that is what my little princess wants then I guess it would be fine with Laura and me."

"Oh, I'd love that father... I know it's a little early, but do you mind if I call you father, Walter," Winifred said excitedly.

"Not at all my dear," Walter replied, inwardly wincing. He knew what Winifred was all about.

Thinking her father, a genius, Winifred smiled at him and then turned to kiss Frederick who seemed more than a little amazed at his father's generosity.

Walter, a master of manipulation in his own right, knew he had been played and decided to use it to his advantage.

"I would like to show you my study, Larry." Winking, Walter added, "I have a rare Napoleon Brandy there."

Built-in English walnut bookshelves covered the walls of the study. A brass ladder gave access to the higher shelves. Walter's desk, a massive structure that dominated the room, had a boar's head carved just below the surface at each corner. Walter took his key ring from his belt and unlocked the glass doors of a cabinet and took out the Napoleon Brandy which he poured into crystal snifters.

"Here you go, Larry."

"Thanks, Walter. Here's to our kids and the grandchildren we hope they'll give us."

Walter raised his glass in assent and heartily swallowed the rare nectar. They sat in the study's comfortable leather chairs, Walter in the one behind his desk, Larry in the chair that faced Walter. As they sipped their brandy, Walter seated in the power position, stated, "Larry, I will be happy to make all the reception arrangements. Do you have a budget or caterers in mind?"

Quickly responding to Walter's obvious ploy to see if he could match the extravagance of James' wedding, Larry said, "Winifred was so impressed by James, and Elizabeth's reception, just use the same people and send the bill, whatever it is, to me. My little princess deserves the best."

Walter sensed that Larry's quick answer and bravado was an attempt to hide his anxiety about the cost. He was a proud man and wasn't about to be bested by someone he thought was beneath him. Larry did not want to let on by any hesitation that he was financially weakened from some recent business losses. Finishing their drinks and conversation, they rejoined the family. A little unnerved from his talk with Walter, Larry suggested, "It's getting late. We really must leave."

As they were putting on their coats, Laura said. "You all must come to Sunnydale for Christmas."

"Oh Laura, Elizabeth will be in her last month. I don't think that it would be prudent with the uncertainty of the weather at this time of year," Harriet answered.

Walter was happy that Harriet, in her caring for Elizabeth's safety, had given him an out.

"My first grandchild you know. I think Harriet is right. Can't have the car slip-sliding on ice if the weather's bad. You are more than welcome to come here."

"I'm sorry we have other family and guests coming," Laura frowned. "Well I'm sure after the wedding we can look forward to sharing many holidays together." Walter smiled with relief.

Laura hugged Harriet, "Thank you for the most sumptuous meal and the good company. We'll get together soon."

"We enjoyed having you. I'm so happy my family is growing."

Winifred kissed Harriet and Walter. "Thank you, father, mother for a most enjoyable day."

Larry put out his hand to Walter. Walter shook it and laughed to himself, A little clammy for November. He's nervous. His business maybe isn't so good.

On the drive home to Westchester, Winifred hugged her father for getting her what she wanted.

Winifred cooed, "Daddy, you are the best. Walter played right into your hands. You knew exactly which buttons to push."

"Princess, you should always have your heart's desire, and daddy will see that you have it always. If it doesn't work out with Fred, I'm sure my lawyers can get a chunk of that Woodsworth money for you."

"Money is important daddy dear, but power is just as nice. I've got plans for Freddy. You're not the only strategist in this family."

"You are daddy's little girl, aren't you," Larry laughed as he tickled her stomach just like he did when she was a little girl.

Walter quietly made a late-night phone call to his attorney, Richard Miller. He didn't trust Larry's promise to pay him, nor Larry. He's a snob who skates on his pedigree, thought Walter.

"Richard, Walter here. I want you to check out my son Frederick's intended father-in-law, Larry Teasdale and his business. One of his ventures is Cheshire Foods. Find out if there is a parent corporation. If it serves us, start buying stock in it under a dummy corporation untraceable back to me."

"Of course, Walter. I'II start on it tomorrow."

Walter thought he would need leverage over Larry and his daughter in the future just in case the marriage did not work out.

Chapter 37

JANUARY, 1940 -BELLE VISTA

The winds of winter blew cold. Icicles draped the trees around Belle Vista. Inside, the warmth of two bodies entwined was disturbed by a gush of wetness. Elizabeth woke and in a frightened little voice stirred James with, "I think it's time. My water broke."

He jumped from the bed and ran around to her side, "Are you sure? Oh my God."

"Yes James, calm down. Help me to the bathroom."

He took Elizabeth's hand and got her seated in the bathroom: "Don't move. I'll get my mother."

Panicked, James ran to his mother's room and rapped loudly on her door before bursting in.

"Mom, Mom, come quick. Elizabeth's water broke."

"I'll be right there. Go back to Elizabeth and calm down," Harriet smiled from ear to ear.

Then he ran to his father's room, again rapping loudly before opening the door, "Dad, have the car brought round. Elizabeth is going to have the baby."

"Right away, son." Walter replied in sleepy hoarse voice.

Harriet, hastily dressed in her robe and slippers, hurried to Elizabeth and James' room. She giggled a little when she saw her confident big strapping boy totally undone.

"I'll take care of Elizabeth. You go call the doctor and get dressed.

“You can't go to the hospital in your underwear."

Harriet rubbed Elizabeth's shoulders and tried to calm her. She could see a bit of panic and the pain of labor on her daughter-in-law's face. It brought back memories of her first time. As she helped Elizabeth dress. Harriet murmured, "You'll forget all about this when you see your beautiful baby."

Elizabeth hugged Harriet, "I love you mother."

With Elizabeth safe in his mother's care, James called Dr. Fitzgerald, who said he would meet them at the hospital.

When James appeared in the doorway to their bedroom, his dress was haphazard and his hair was spiking randomly. He looked as if he just stuck his finger in an electrical outlet. The sight of him gave both women a laugh when he nervously yelled, "We have to go."

Elizabeth's eyes fell to his pant zipper, "Not till you zip up, Jim."

Embarrassed, he turned his back towards them and zipped. Red faced, he replied, "Now can we go?"

Walter put his arm around Harriet's shoulders as the car left the driveway. "Want a little brandy my dear?" he smiled.

"That's a good idea. I don't think I've ever been this excited."

"Well, we don't want to put a damper on that now do we," he leered. She glowered at him.

"Can't blame a guy for trying," he smirked.

She raised an eyebrow. "Trying. Yes, you are Walter."

Harriet didn't take the bait. She wasn't about to forgive him yet. He handed her the brandy and smiled.

That evening James called Belle Vista to tell his parents that Elizabeth's labor was long and hard, but finally at seven thirty that evening, Mary Harriet Woodsworth was born weighing seven pounds three ounces and measuring twenty-two inches long. She was pink, perfect and beautiful.

Minutes after Elizabeth was placed in her private hospital room, James was there holding her hand and admiring their little girl. Without warning, Elizabeth suddenly went into a seizure. James, unable to comprehend what was happening, yelled for the nurse. She came scurrying into the room. Seeing Elizabeth's condition, the nurse called for Dr. Fitzgerald then quickly jammed a tongue depressor in Elizabeth's mouth. When Dr. Fitzgerald entered the room, he asked James to wait outside. Upon his examination, he found that Elizabeth was hemorrhaging and her uterus had collapsed.

As he and the nurse wheeled Elizabeth's bed out of the room, Dr. Fitzgerald told James, "We have to take Elizabeth to the operating room and try to stop the hemorrhage," Several doctors were called in and they worked feverishly to stop the bleeding, but it was not going well.

It seemed like hours had passed before Dr. Fitzgerald came out of the operating room. He told James he would have to sign consent forms so the doctors could perform a hysterectomy to stop the bleeding if it became necessary.

James had been pacing franticly in the waiting room since signing the form. After several hours, Dr. Fitzgerald emerged from the operating room and told him, "Your wife is going to make it, but I'm sorry to say that Elizabeth will never have another child. We tried not to, but we had no choice; we had to remove her uterus in order to save her life."

James, in tears, replied, "I don't care that we can't have more children. Will my wife be OK? "

"Yes, James, we expect a full recovery. You can see her as soon as she comes out of recovery." Dr Fitzgerald put his arm around James trying to comfort the distraught man.

"Thank you doctor for saving Elizabeth. Thank you and God." James sighed in relief.

When James had composed himself, he called his parents this time with the bad news. Walter was beside himself. He was relieved that Elizabeth and little Mary Harriet were out of danger, but he had so hoped for a grandson from James. He knew that was no longer possible. His estrangement with Harriet left him alone in his sorrow. He retired to his study and drank himself to sleep. Harriet took to her room and her crocheting. She mindlessly stitched whenever she could not bear the cruel realities of life.

When James entered his wife's room, he was glad that she was asleep and could not see the shock on his face. Elizabeth's beautiful auburn hair was matted with sweat. There were intravenous lines running to both her forearms. He moved out of the doorway and leaned his head upon the wall and wept. When his emotions were spent, he sat quietly by her bed until she woke up. She tried to speak, but James cautioned her, "Darling don't. You need to preserve your strength."

Elizabeth looked at him, nodded her head and closed her eyes once again.

Frederick easily put on a mask of concern when James returned from the hospital to Belle Vista. He said all the right words to his brother. "I'm really sorry. Bad break old man. I'm sure they are going to be fine." Frederick's mind was already calculating that James could never give Walter what he wanted and expected, a grandson. He was now the only son who could provide that prize for his father and intended to work on it as soon as he and Winifred were married.

Elizabeth and baby Mary Harriet arrived home from the hospital two weeks after her ordeal. She was delighted with their new little bundle. James had reassured her that they could always adopt later if she wanted.

"You are the most important person in my life and the thought that I could have lost you that night almost killed me," he murmured as he lay their precious child into her crib.

"Jim, you and Mary are my life."

James kissed her tenderly and ordered, "Into bed with you. Take a little nap. You're still a little weak."

Chapter 38

JULY, 1972

Victoria's dad was home from the hospital recuperating from his knee surgery, and thankfully was no longer seeing things. She had arranged for a live-in to attend to his needs until he was on his feet, giving her a bit of a break.

It was Saturday and Diana would be spending the weekend down the shore with Mark's parents. They owned a bungalow at Seaside Heights near the bay. Her grandfather loved to take Diana crabbing. Mark and Victoria thought they would spend the day doing some chores around the house. When they were having lunch, Victoria said, "I have this weird feeling that the castle is deteriorating and that the facade is falling off in pieces. Maybe an evil that was committed there had so saturated its structure that it has now reached the facade and is causing the brownstones to fall apart. Sounds crazy doesn't it, but that's what I feel."

"There's one way to find out; let's go there."

"You'll do anything to get out of mowing the lawn, even go to a place that creeps you out. I know you hate it there."

"We don't have to go if you don't want to. Afraid you're wrong about the brownstones?"

"I'm not afraid of being wrong! Let's go."

"You certainly do come up with the damnedest things."

If she's wrong, maybe she'll forget about that place; but suppose she's right. I'll have to hear more about this stuff, Mark thought. Me and my big mouth!

They got into their old station wagon and drove to Paterson. Victoria chattered all the way trying to make sense of this latest "feeling". Mark just listened half-heartedly. He pulled the car into the driveway and up to the parking lot. They walked to the stairs and down towards the castle.

"Mark, there's yellow tape in front of several sections around the castle," she said excitedly in a high-pitched tone.

Victoria quickly walked to the cordoned off area. "Oh my God, look Mark!"

Brownstone debris littered the area within the yellow tape. Mark thought he was in a horror film and quietly said to himself, Feet don't fail me now.

"Let's go inside," he muttered.

Victoria rushed to the first guide she could find and asked, "What's happening to the building? Are you doing repairs?"

The guide replied, "The brownstone has been deteriorating and pieces are now falling off. Those areas have been cordoned off to protect the public. The stone will be treated to stop any further erosion."

Mark listened, but could not believe what he was hearing. My wife must be some sort of psychic. How did she know pieces of the brownstone blocks were falling? For that matter, how the hell did she know where my dad's car could be found after it was stolen all those years ago? He really did not want to know. Her ability to pull things out of the air was incomprehensible to him.

Mark interjected, "When did the facade start to fall?"

"It's been happening for months, but very little. In the last two weeks it happened so much that we had to put up the yellow tape to prevent the public from getting hurt by the falling pieces."

Visibly shaken, Mark's body language uncharacteristically showed his nervousness. He almost seemed to lose his balance and with a look of wonder asked Victoria, "How did you know? It was in the paper, wasn't it?"

"Like I have time to read the paper. I don't know. I just get this feeling about things. It comes out of the blue. I don't even have to be thinking about it. Remember when I told you your boss was going to get fired after being with the company for over twenty years and it happened two weeks later. It was one of those feelings. I can't explain it. My mother had it too. She knew things would happen before they did."

Every time one of her "feelings" was proven, she would be more stunned than Mark. She reacted by getting hyper, her eyes would enlarge and her body would tense and she would talk about it to anyone who would listen.

He knew once they left, she would be talking about it non-stop in the car. Mark really didn't want to relive what had happened. On the way home, he put the ball game on the car radio a little louder than usual. This was his signal to Victoria that he didn't want to talk. He needed to get grounded and forget about that place and the effect it was having on them. Helpless to do anything about it, he employed his ability to put anything out of his mind that bothered him by thinking about the Yankees. They were his touchstone.

Chapter 39

Monday and reality came quickly and it was time for another B-12 shot. Victoria's energy had started to come back and couldn't wait to tell her uncle what a good doctor he was, when he came rushing into the examining room.

"So how's my niece today.? I'll get your shot ready. I'm really busy. Seems like there is a stomach flu going around."

"By the way Uncle Tony, my mom and dad had 0-Positive blood. Minnie gave me a card from your lab stating that I had B-Negative. I think they made a mistake. Shouldn't I have the same type as my parents?"

His face was ashen just enough to give her pause. Victoria was a Scorpio and not much got by her. She could tell just by his body language that her question bothered him. He recovered quickly and stammered, "When you were born there was something wrong with your blood and we had to give you an entirely new blood supply."

"Gee, Mom never told me that."

"She was just so happy you were OK, I guess she never wanted to think about it again. You know she miscarried three times before you were born. "

Knowing how little Victoria knew about medical things, Tony hoped she would not question him further; but Victoria sensed he was not telling her the truth.

She laughed, "Hope you didn't mix me up with another kid the night I was born."

"You were the ugliest kid I ever delivered. Couldn't have mixed you up with the cute ones. Too bad that hospital closed. It served North Newark. Now they have to go to Belleville or the other side of Newark. Nothing close anymore."

Victoria got her shot, kissed her Uncle Tony goodbye and left with her suspicions. As she was driving home Victoria wondered if any other girls were born on the same day that she was in the American Legion Hospital in Newark. A switch at birth wasn't impossible by an overworked nurse. She would check with the Hall of Records the next day.

Chapter 40

Leaving work an hour and a half early to do her research, Victoria walked down Halsey Street to Market and took the bus to the Hall of Records. When she arrived at the records room, she asked the girl behind the counter if there were any females born in American Legion Hospital on November 22, 1940 other than herself. The clerk took a while to access the information, but finally responded to Victoria's inquiry.

"I've got the information. There was one other female delivered at American Legion on November 22, 1940, but it appears she was stillborn, born to a Helen Stanhope of 9 Forest Street."

That's a few blocks away from my parents' home, Victoria thought to herself then she blurted, "Would you happen to have a death certificate for the mother?" Why did I ask that? she thought. Where did that come from? The words came out of my mouth, but I never formed the question in my mind.

"I'll check." replied the clerk.

When the clerk returned, she asked, "Do you want a copy of the death certificate?"

“Yes, I would.”

Victoria paid the $4.00 fee. The cause of death was hemorrhage from childbirth at 3:30 AM. The certificate was signed by Dr. Anthony Russo. Oh my God! Uncle Tony was her doctor. Victoria gasped. My mother did have all those miscarriages. Uncle Tony could have done this! I can't even check with the hospital; It's closed. She was so rattled that she cautioned herself, Calm down Victoria. This all could be coincidence. Don't go off half cocked. You have a lot more investigating to do.

Victoria's next step was to find out who owned 9 Forest Street, where Helen Stanhope had lived before her death. She checked her watch not wanting to be late picking up Diana from school. I think I have enough time to get to the tax assessor's office, she nervously thought as she quickly walked down Market Street to Broad then to City Hall. She took the elevator to the second floor. The tax assessor's office was the third door down on the right. Almost out of breath she asked the clerk,

"Can you tell me who owned 9 Forest Street in 1940."

“I have to go to the file room. Have a seat. I'll be back in a few minutes."

Impatiently, Victoria alternated between sitting and pacing, until finally the clerk came back carrying a slip of paper. She called Victoria to the counter and read, "An Agatha Woodsworth up until 1959, then Boar's Head Investments, then it was sold to a Robert and Ella Anzovino in 1963." She handed the paper with the information to Victoria.

"Thank you," Victoria answered, mindlessly lost in thought.

She left the room staring at the paper. When she reached the daylight of Broad Street, she slipped it into her purse and caught the bus back to the subway. It was getting late and she had to run down the subway stairs to catch the next car. It was just pulling in when she arrived. She sat in the first vacant row and pulled the paper the clerk had given her out of her purse. One of the owners of that house was Boar's Head. Victoria had an instant flash back to her first dream on the veranda when a boar's head appeared next to her, became frightened of her and vanished. This was too creepy, she thought.

I can't get weirded out by this. I have to think logically. Uncle Tony gave me a cock-and-bull story about my blood being transfused at birth. There was one other girl born that night at American Legion Hospital delivered by Uncle Tony. The mother, Helen Stanhope. died and her child was stillborn. She lived with an Agatha Woodsworth at 9 Forest Street. What was their connection? Who owned Boar's Head Investments? The Woodsworth's purchased Belle Vista from the Lambert estate and I think a Stanhope was married to one of the sons. I have to mull this over for a while and decide what my next move will be. Maybe I'll call the American Medical Association and ask if it's possible to transfuse a baby with a B-negative blood when the mother and father have O-positive. Yeah. I'll do that tomorrow.

Chapter 41

Victoria had taken the next day off from work to get some things done for her dad. She had brought him some food and did a little house cleaning. While checking his medication bottles, Victoria noticed Victor had only two heart pills left and called Liss Pharmacy on Mt. Prospect Avenue to renew his prescription. While waiting in line at the drug store, she spotted an old friend.

"Ed Byrne! What are you doing here?" smiled Victoria.

"Hey Vikky, long time no see. There was a robbery here a few days ago. Just tying up some loose ends with the manager. Our old neighborhood has sure changed. Remember when we could walk anywhere at any time of day or night in the North Ward without worrying that someone would mug you?"

Ed had followed in his dad's footsteps and was a sergeant on the Newark police force. He had put on some weight since the last time Victoria had seen him; a stark contrast to the skinny blond, blue eyed kid who had played ball with her. His imposing six-foot two-inch uniformed frame exuded strength and authority.

There were twelve kids in the Byrne family. They lived across the street from Victoria's family on Sylvan Avenue. As close friends, they played together, got in trouble together, and when they grew up attended each other's weddings. After each had married, they moved away from their old neighborhood and, busy with their own lives and families, lost touch. Their parents had been part of the hard-working poor in Newark's old North Ward. They had shared each other's homes and food and had cemented relationships that would last a lifetime.

After they caught up for a few minutes, Victoria asked, "Hey Ed, if I wanted to get some information on someone who lived in Newark in the early 40's how would I do it?"

Ed didn't question her. It was enough that Victoria asked. She would not impose unless it was important to her.

"I have a friend, a guy named A. K. He's a private investigator. He owes me a few favors. Give me what you have and I'll see what I can get for you."

"Got time for a cup of coffee, Ed?"

“Sure, I'm done here."

"Let me pay for my dad's medications and I'll meet you at the Woodside Diner on Broadway."

"See you in a few minutes Vikky."

Victoria paced until the druggist called. "Victoria. Your father's prescription is ready."

Victoria walked to the counter and paid for the prescription. "Thanks, Mr. Liss."

As she exited the pharmacy, Victoria crammed the bag into her purse. She was lucky enough to have gotten a parking spot right out front. She got in and drove as fast as she dared down Montclair Avenue to Broadway and turned into the diner's parking lot.

Ed was waiting for Victoria in the second booth from the entrance so he could see her when she came in.

"Over here, Vikky," he waved.

She sat down across from him on the torn faux red leather bench. They both ordered coffee and English muffins. Ed took out his pad and asked, "What do you want to know, Vikky?"

"Take these two names down. Agatha Woodsworth and Helen Stanhope from 9 Forest Street in Newark. They lived there in 1940. Anything you can find out about them will help."

"Anything you want to talk about, Vikky?" "I'm not sure about anything right now."

Victoria gave him her home and work phone numbers. When they had finished their coffee, Ed walked Victoria to her car.

Thanks, Ed. This means a lot to me. My regards to your family." "Sure thing, Vikky."

That night, Victoria had another dream of the castle.

She was on the stairs coming up from the basement of the mansion when the walls began to compress around her. She managed to reach the landing and opened the door, but then everything went black. She had lost her sight. She held on to the walls of the hallway and reached a room where, in her mind's eye, she could see a large plush burgundy sofa and a fringed lamp and heavy drapes. She felt the wall for the light switch, but was surprised that the switch was push buttons, a fixture that had not been used for years. She pushed the buttons furiously, but she still could not see. Suddenly, the dream shifted. She was driving a black car on a highway; the mansion on its mountain visible to her left; then without warning, she went blind again.

Her heart pounded so violently it woke her. The terror she felt was off the chart. Throwing the covers off her, Victoria moved as fast as she could in the dark to the living room and turned on the night light. She could not go back to sleep and lay shaking on the sofa for the rest of the night. Sleep had become an unsafe place for her. She was afraid that one night the fright from a dream would kill her.

Mark's alarm went off. He swung his legs out of bed and rubbed his eyes trying to get them to focus. While walking through the living room on his way to the bathroom, he was surprised to see Victoria in a fetal position on the sofa.

"What are you doing here?"

"I had another dream. It scared the hell out of me. I was afraid to go back to sleep."

"You think about that place too much. That's why you are always having those scary dreams."

"That was a blow-off remark. The dreams started long before I knew that place even existed. You think it's that simple? Just stop thinking about it and it will go away. Well, it won't."

"I need to take my shower. I have to get to work."

From the tone of Victoria's voice, Mark knew he said the wrong thing. I won't dare eat breakfast this morning, he thought. The look she just gave me could kill.

Chapter 42

He that troubleth his own house shall Inherit the wind.

Wisdom of Solomon

Proverbs 11:29

FEBRUARY, 1940- PASSAIC, NEW JERSEY

Frederick had planned to break it off with Stella just before his marriage to Winifred. Today would be the last time he would meet her in the second-floor room he had rented in Passaic for their trysts. After James had warned him to stop seeing Stella, Frederick looked for a place at which they both could meet without being spotted. He had found the room while driving through the downtown section of Passaic. He noticed a sign, ROOM TO LET BY DAY OR WEEK in Benny's Pawn Shop, a store front on the street level of an old brick, three story building. The room was sparsely furnished with a double bed against one wall covered by a threadbare blue hob nail chenille bedspread. A small dresser with a milk glass lamp was against the opposite wall facing the bed. A drape of multicolored material, which could be closed to block out the light, hung over the lone window.

He'd tell Stella after he had pleasured himself. Why waste the cost of the room, he thought. The sex was unusually rough and took longer, causing Stella to whimper a bit. Afterwards, while they were getting dressed, Frederick announced, "I have something important to talk to you about."

But before he could begin, Stella incorrectly divined, "You got your raise! Wonderful, but we have to be married quickly. I think I may be pregnant."

"Have to! Married!" he laughed. "You must be kidding. You haven't told your mother about us. You hid our relationship. You knew what you were getting into. I can't marry you. You have no breeding or education. My father would never agree to such a union and If you're pregnant, that's your problem. You better get rid of it if you are. Tell anyone it's mine and your mother won't have a job."

With a look of horror and disbelief, Stella gasped as if a light bulb had gone on. "You just used me. How could you do this to me?"

"Easy. A couple of lunches, a little flattery and you laid down."

"Now I know what you are. You're not capable of love. You're dead inside... evil. Well a curse on you. Nothing in your life will ever bring you happiness."

"It was nice while it lasted," Fred laughed as Stella stormed off toward the door, but he had reached the door before she could open it. He held it closed and said, "My dear, allow me." With eyes fixed and glaring, he grabbed her arm opened the door and walked her to the stairs. The look in his eyes scared her. She was like a deer caught in the headlights. She feared that pain was imminent but was too dumbstruck to do anything about it. Just as she placed her foot upon the first step, Frederick pushed her and Stella went tumbling down the stairs. Dazed, she lay there in a heap, like so much garbage.

"Hope that helps you with your little problem. Your little trip down these stairs is only a taste of what will happen to you and your family if you make trouble for me." Frederick snickered.

Stella looked up at him from the black and white tiled floor and with a strange calmness said, "One day, Fred, you will regret what you did to me. That's a promise."

She didn't know where the words she had just spoken came from. Poor as she was, she could never make a rich man suffer or regret anything. God will have to deal with him, she thought with anguish.

As soon as Stella composed herself, she wiped the stinging tears from her eyes, raised herself up from the floor and left the building. Her body aching, she limped to the bus stop. She had to get home.

Chapter 43

MARCH, 1940

A new Helen emerged from the Air France plane that had carried her from Paris to Newark Airport. Living on her own had certainly changed her. She no longer was the shy, thin and shapeless girl who had left the states six months ago. With an air of independence, the young sophisticated woman walked confidently to the baggage area where the waiting limousine driver held a card with the name Stanhope spelled in large black letters.

"I'm Miss Stanhope," she told the man holding the card. "I'm Albert, ma'am. I'll see to your luggage."

Helen handed him her claim checks.

After retrieving her two pieces of luggage, the chauffeur escorted Helen to the car. Helen was coming back to Belle Vista for Frederick's wedding and to see her new niece, Mary Harriet. Could life be any better? she thought.

Elizabeth was on the veranda at Belle Vista enjoying the mid-day sun and anxiously awaiting Helen's arrival. When she spotted the long black car entering the driveway, she quickly ran to the entrance. Helen had barely made it out of the back seat when Elizabeth hugged her sister so tightly that Helen thought she would lose her breath.

"Let me take a look at you!"

Helen twirled around in her navy-blue suit with a navy polka dot and white blouse. Her shapely legs looked beautiful in her white and navy leather sling back pumps. "How do I look? I feel wonderful."

"Where is the little girl, I saw off to art school? You certainly have filled out. Guess it's all that French food. Come inside. We're alone except for the servants. We will have plenty of time to catch up."

Elizabeth barely recognized her sister. Her beautiful green eyes were wide and happy with a certain glint that was not there before. Her whole being seemed to shine. That look in Helen's eyes was familiar to Elizabeth. She had seen it before in her own eyes when she fell in love with James. As they walked toward the west wing, Helen impatiently asked, "Where's my niece?

“1’ll let you have a peek at her; then we can talk in your room. James hired a nanny to help me with Mary. 1 was so weak otter her birth."

Elizabeth opened the door to her rooms and tiptoed over to Mary Harriet's crib. She mouthed to the nanny seated in a rocking chair, "This is my sister." The nanny acknowledged them with a nod and put a finger to her lips to warn them not to wake the baby. Helen's face lit up with joy at seeing her niece. I have one more piece of family, she thought. Little Mary, her mother's namesake, was like having a bit of her mother back. They tiptoed back out of the room, and giggled all the way to Helen's room. They plopped themselves on Helen's bed and talked as they had when they were kids.

"She's so gorgeous and she looks just like you." "Thank you. 1 knew you were my favorite sister. " "Are you hoping for a little boy next time?"

"There won't be a next time." Elizabeth sighed sadly. "l didn't write you because I didn't want you to worry, but something went wrong when Mary Harriet was born. 1 hemorrhaged and the doctors had to remove my uterus in order to stop the bleeding and save my life; so I can't have any more children."

"Oh, how horrible. Why didn't you call me? I would have come straight home."

"That's what I didn't want. You would have missed your art classes and I know how important they are to you."

"You're more important to me than anything."

"I guess now you will have to be the one to populate the Stanhope blood line. Have you met any good prospects? Tell me all about Paris."

"It's so beautiful, so alive. I've met some very interesting people." "Anyone special?"

"Well, a girl named Colette, the one I wrote you about. We met at art school and became best friends. She showed me all of Paris. One evening she took me to a cafe where many of the art students meet after class. It was there that I met Jacques. He's so handsome and so attentive. We've been dating for a while now." Averting her eyes, a little flush appearing on her face, Helen confessed, "I think I'm in love."

Freedom, Paris and love had transformed her shy little sister into a woman, men would lust for. With a motherly instinct rising in her, Elizabeth wanted to tell Helen to beware and warn her how deceptive men could be when they were on the hunt to satisfy their baser instincts, but her exuberance was so refreshing, she decided not to say anything to dampen it.

"Are you ready for Frederick's wedding on Saturday. I hope the weather will be good. It's the end of March and anything could happen. Religious Harriet put a statue of the Blessed Virgin in the window to assure good weather, so I guess we won't have to worry about that." Elizabeth giggled.

"Harriet must be busy with all the preparations?" Helen inquired.

"She's not as involved as she was with my wedding. Of course, Winifred has parents to handle the major details, so she wasn't needed in that capacity. But what is strange is that Walter is handling everything to do with the reception. Walter and Harriet's relationship has not been the same since we came back from our honeymoon. They barely speak to each other.

Elizabeth continued, "The big story was when Frederick told Harriet that he agreed to be married by Winifred's uncle, an Episcopalian minister, Harriet was devastated. She threatened Frederick with her absence if he persisted with the Protestant nuptials. He changed her mind by saying, 'If the marriage doesn't work out, I could be married in the Catholic Church the next time, since the Church does not recognize a Protestant ceremony.' When Harriet questioned Frederick's love for Winifred and his thinking, he responded 'Mom, you never know what the future will hold. Later, when she's my wife, I might be able to convince her to convert.'"

"Well, since we are on the subject of the wedding, let me show you the gown I'll be wearing," Helen said with excitement.

When Helen tried the gown on for her sister's approval, Elizabeth again felt a swell of pride. Helen was a vision. She is too beautiful, Elizabeth thought anxiously. As she bit her lip, all Elizabeth could say was, "You're going to turn a few heads in that."

Helen had just changed back into her clothes when the nanny knocked on Helen's door to inform Elizabeth that Mary was awake and was ready to be fed. Even though Elizabeth could not breast feed because of what happened the night Mary was born, she insisted on doing the bottle feeding herself. Today, she would let Helen have the honor. Helen seated herself in the rocking chair in Elizabeth's room and held her arms out so Elizabeth could give Mary Harriet to her.

"A baby becomes you," Elizabeth smiled.

"She's so precious. I can hardly wait to have one of my own."

"Well, let's get you married first. You'll make a wonderful mother. Don't stay in Paris too long. I want you to see Mary Harriet grow up. She'll need some cousins to play with." Elizabeth winked.

With Mary Harriet fed and played with, she was given back to the nanny's care. Both sisters were tired and decided to nap before dinner when the family would be back from their various appointments.

That evening, with all assembled around the dining room table, everyone noticed the change in Helen. They kept her busy answering questions about school, Paris, the Parisians, etc. The mood over dinner was lively and cordial. Walter could not keep his eyes off her. Lasciviously, he thought, I wonder if she has tasted a bit of forbidden fruit and that is the reason for the change in her? She is ripe for picking. Walter could not understand why she had this effect on him. He was usually excited by more garish women. Must be the wine, he thought.

Chapter 44

Due to coincidence or Harriet's faith in placing the statue of the Blessed Mother in the window, the weather on Frederick's wedding day was beautiful...sunny and in the 60's. The nuptials took place in the marble colonnade wing which was profusely decorated with white lilies and orchids. A white lattice arbor had been placed at the far end of the room under which Frederick and Winifred were married. Rows upon rows of white upholstered chairs filled the long room on either side of the aisle. In the house where the reception would take place, tables were scattered throughout the great room, dining room and music room. Fountains of cocktails were strategically located in each area.

Once again Walter had exceeded his guests' expectations. The wedding was another super-duper, Walter Woodsworth extravaganza impressing all in attendance.

While the cocktails were being served, Tony Russo approached Frederick. "Congratulations ole buddy," he smiled putting his arm around Frederick's shoulder.

Frederick surveyed his old college friend and thought, Still big and strong and rough cut. Tony's black wavy hair, deep brown eyes and olive skin made him stand out in this crowd. Fred knew that Tony had graduated medical school. He had been invited to Tony's party, but didn't show. He gave some excuse that he would be out of state on business for his father. Frederick sent a card with $50 in it. He really didn't want to spend much time with the poor first-generation Italian folk that would be at the party. Slapping him on the back Frederick asked, "When are you going to open your own practice?"

Tony was putting in long hours at Newark's City Hospital. "I'm working on it," he answered with embarrassment.

Never afraid to throw a punch or two, Tony saved Fred several times from getting the stuffing knocked out of him because of his snobbery and underhanded dealings with the other guys at college. He looked after Frederick because he felt sorry for him. Frederick had told Tony that his father favored James and that he always had .to play second fiddle to his brother.

Seeing Tony again reminded him how much he owed his friend. "Maybe I can help get you started. Let me talk to my dad." Frederick hated to be in anyone's debt. He liked it the other way around. Fred managed to get Walter's ear, knowing it would be hard to refuse him a request made on his wedding day.

Walter knew Tony had kept his quisling of a son alive in college. He made it a practice to always have people who associated with his children checked out. Tony was a sure thing; hard-working and honorable. Tony would pay his debt with interest; of that he was sure. Walter always had a second sense about who to lend to and what to invest in. He knew a winner when he saw one. Walter approached Tony with a smile, extended his hand, and told him, "Find an office. My lawyer will draw up the papers next week. I'll give you a favorable rate; below market by a half point."

"Thank you, sir. You won't be disappointed."

Tony could not believe his ears or his good luck; but instinctively, the hair rose up at the back of his neck, almost as if he had made a deal with the devil himself.

Walter had been watching Helen out of the corner of his eye all day. Her emerald green velvet gown caressed her lithe little body in all the right places. She looks so appetizing, he thought. The sight of her stirred the savage in him. He thought of the passion his son Frederick would soon experience with Winifred. Fred won't have to be as careful as James on his first night with his bride. Unlike Elizabeth, he was sure that Winifred had been around the block many times. Grabbing another drink from a passing waiter, he thought to himself I have to put this fire out. Control yourself Walter. Just then Helen passed him. Walter could see that she was a little unsteady on her feet and was walking toward the west wing.

Helen was a bit flushed and a little dizzy from the champagne and decided to leave the festivities for a while and recuperate in her room until she felt more in control.

Walter waited a while and told himself, I'll just see if she is alright. As he neared her door, he could see it was slightly ajar. Pushing on it, the door opened to reveal Helen on her bed; her eyes closed, her hand upon her forehead.

He walked over to her and asked "Are you ill, child?"

Turning on her side to answer him, the scoop neckline of her gown bowed revealing her pink breast, the brown of her nipple just in view. "The wine made me a little dizzy," she groaned.

When Walter leaned down to kiss her forehead, he caught her scent. He had to have her. It was as if a great beast had possessed him. Passion obliterated reason. He abandoned all control and in an instant, his mouth was on hers firmly muffling any sound she could attempt to make. His hand quickly probed under her dress pushing over her undergarments and then he was on top of her. Helen's eyes pleaded for him to stop. Her arms were too weak to move his great mass. She could not breathe. Realizing what was happening, she lost consciousness.

Walter completed his vicious attack, zipped his pants and fled down the servant's steps. As he entered the great room, he told Harriet, who was standing there, that he had been checking with the caterers to see if there was a sufficient supply of wine. Harriet noticed that her husband was unusually nervous. She rarely saw him this way and wondered what could have caused it.

When Helen regained awareness, she realized what had happened. Her mind screamed Why did he do this to me? She wanted the comfort of her sister, but how could she tell Elizabeth. It would destroy her and her marriage. I can't tell Harriet. It will kill her. There was no one in Belle Vista that she could go to. She was trapped at the scene of the crime against her. Still groggy and sore, she lifted her pain racked body and bolted the door. Elizabeth will come looking for me if I'm gone too long, she thought, I can't speak to her tonight, she'll know something horrible has happened. Helen quickly undressed. Barely able to step into the tub, she let the warm shower run over her painful body, cleansing the blood and Walter's sap from her.

Knowing that she had to return to the reception, she summoned all the courage she could and redressed herself in another gown she had brought as a spare. If anyone noticed my absence, she thought, I can tell them that I dropped something on my dress and had to change. She quietly slipped back to the party keeping well away from Walter. Moving constantly, she took refuge in any nook or cranny. She was visible, but avoided engaging in a conversation. She wanted to just scream and run into the night, but Elizabeth and Harriet's happiness was at stake.

The next morning Helen told Elizabeth she would be leaving for Paris earlier than expected; in fact, that afternoon. Elizabeth noticed the change in Helen's eyes. They were no longer young and happy, but filled with anxiety. Elizabeth asked, "Helen, is something the matter?"

Avoiding her sister's eyes and attempting to control the trembling inside her savaged body Helen replied, "No, I must get back to my studies and to Jacques. I miss him terribly."

"I thought we would have more time to spend together."

Elizabeth knew something was wrong. Helen always looked her in the face. She must be hiding something. Maybe I can find out when we correspond. It is obvious that Helen doesn't want to talk now," she reasoned. With an uneasy feeling, Elizabeth accompanied Helen to the airport.

Strangely, as the plane took off, Elizabeth sensed she would never see her sister again.

Chapter 45

SEPTEMBER, 1972

It had been several weeks since Victoria had seen her friend Ed Byrne. I guess he still hasn't gotten in touch with the private investigator. When it's for free, you just have to wait, she reasoned. Since patience was not one of her strong suits, she decided to do a little snooping on her own.

Victoria made up a very official looking dummy petition to register the Old Methodist Cemetery on the historic preservation list. She thought that using the pretext of getting signatures on a petition was a good foot-in-the door ploy to canvas the houses on Forest Street. She could then engage the residents in conversation to see if there was anyone old enough to remember an Agatha Woodsworth and the girl who was living with her in 1940. Unfortunately, after walking her feet sore, no one knew much about the old lady who had lived at Number 9 Forest St.

The neighborhood had changed and most of the people she talked to were new arrivals. What a waste of a sick day, she thought.

Having put it off until last. Victoria was more than a bit nervous when she pushed the bell at 9 Forest Street. A short, gray haired woman answered the door. Victoria introduced herself,

“Hello, 1’m Victoria Valentino. I'm trying to track down part of my family who lived here during the forties; the Woodsworths and Stanhopes."

Victoria had changed her foot-in-the door story because she thought that if the woman knew anything about the Stanhopes or Woodsworths, she would be more apt to divulge to a relative than to a petitioner. The neighbors on the other hand, would have been hesitant to talk to a relative if they had some gossip to tell.

"I've never heard of the Woodsworths, but Stanhope rings a bell, but I don't remember from where. We didn't buy the house from anyone with the Stanhope or Woodsworth name. We purchased the house through a realtor who was acting on behalf of a Boar's Head Company. Miller and Weiss were the attorneys. I believe they were from New York. They handled the closing for Boar's Head. Wait a minute! I found a box in the attic with some art books and some letters addressed to a Helen Stanhope. I haven't thrown them out yet. I keep meaning to, but never seem to get around to it. Bad habit of mine. I never throw anything away. Would you like to have them?"

"Yes, I would. I don't know how to thank you."

The woman invited Victoria to sit on her porch while she went to the attic to retrieve the box. Victoria was excited that finally something tangible had fallen into her lap. When the woman returned with the box, she also gave Victoria a Miller and Weiss business card, explaining she didn't have further use for it.

"Thank you again for being so kind."

Victoria raced to her car. She couldn't wait to open the box. She pulled at the string that secured it, lifted the lid and found a sketch pad inside. On the cover of the pad was written "The art of Helen Stanhope." There was a drawing of a sinister looking elderly woman; the eyes of whom were so cold and vacant, they brought chills to Victoria's skin. She turned the pages and there were drawings of trees and houses and one of a man who looked like Uncle Tony whose eyes were filled with compassion, but it was the drawing on the last page that brought her to tears. It was of a mother gazing at her infant. Helen's artistic genius was capturing the soul of a person in their eyes. She could see that Helen poured all the love she had into the eyes of the mother, and all the sweetness she could, into the face of the infant. It took her a few minutes to compose herself. Under an art book she found letters from France addressed to Helen. She couldn't read them now, her eyes were clouded with tears.

She sat in her car for a while unable to move. Then she thought, If I look on the outside what I'm feeling on the inside Mark will see that something has happened. Can't go home like this. Have to look normal. She started the car and drove down Forest to Summer Avenue. She decided to stop in at an old Italian grocery store, De Marzi's, to pick up some provolone cheese for Mark. It was his favorite.

She hadn't been in the store for years; not since her mother had sent her there for cold cuts. Mr. De Marzi had been there for fifty years. His son now ran the business. The old man more or less sat around these days just giving his son orders. He was happy to talk to Victoria.

"Hi Mr. De Marzi. Do you remember me; Victoria. My mother was Angela Grasso."

"Sure, I remember. Where you been. It's a long time."

"I moved to Nutley. I just happen to be in the neighborhood so thought I'd stop in and get a pound of your good imported Provolone."

"Sure thing. Antonio, get Victoria a pound of imported Provolone." "Did you ever deliver to a lady who lived at Number 9 Forest Street in the 40's."

Thinking for a while, the old man remembered, "Yeah, the old lady, Agatha Woodsworth; a good customer. Those were the days before all these big supermarkets. There was a young widow living with her; she was pregnant. I didn't believe she was a widow. You know how things were then. Now being pregnant and unmarried means nothing, but then it was a big deal. After the big snow storm in November of 1940, I never saw the young woman again. Could never ask that old lady anything. She never shot the breeze with anyone. Real secretive that one. I used to send the old woman's bills to her brother Walter in Paterson. Once in while he would send a company check...Boar's Head something."

Victoria's body stiffened. Boar's Head again/ This is more than coincidental. Her eyes began to hurt. Damn I'm getting a migraine. Got to stop.

Antonio motioned to Victoria that her cheese was ready.

"Thanks Mr. De Marzi. Stay well," she said as she paid for her cheese. "Come back soon, Victoria."

Now she knew that Agatha had a brother Walter who had something to do with a Boar's Head Company. She looked at her watch and realized she was out of time. Victoria rushed to her car and then to the school to pick up her daughter. While they were driving home, Diana told her that the English teacher was handing out random topics for an essay, and guess what Mom, she gave me Lambert Castle! I wanted to give it back, but then I would have had to explain why and no way was I going to do that. I know you said that my vision of Nana was just my imagination, but I didn't believe you. I know it has something to do with that castle."

Victoria's heart sank.

"No, I'm sure the castle has nothing to do with Nana. But let's look at the positive, I have all the material you will need on the subject from the Paterson Library. I'm sure it will help you with your report and you won't have to go to the library."

Victoria had promised herself she would never talk about the dreams with Diana after she went spacey on her at Dale's. She couldn't chance it happening again.

"Sounds good to me." Diana replied.

Another coincidence. I don't think so, thought Victoria. What force managed to get Diana selected to do a report on Lambert Castle. It's a wonder I'm not losing my mind.

The material Victoria had gathered on Mr. Lambert had come in handy. Diana got an "A" on her report. Victoria was happy that some good had come from her research.

Chapter 46

April, 1940

Back in Paris, Helen buried herself in her art in an attempt to obliterate what had happened to her. She didn't sleep well any more. Jacques had noticed the difference in her; she seemed less vibrant. They had never engaged in sex, but had gotten close before her trip to America. Now, when things heated up between them, Helen would push him away and begin to cry.

"You don't love me," he would chide.

"Of course, I do, but I can't, not until we are married."

When this happened, Jacques would get angry and walk out, leaving Helen in tears. The last time, still aroused, Jacques went to a cafe to pick up another to finish what he had started with Helen. Jacques' hubris and enormous ego forced him to continually return to Helen. He enjoyed the challenge. He confidently told himself, I know I will eventually break down her resistance. She's American, so it will take me a little longer. He was a man on a mission; no woman could resist him forever, or so he thought.

Helen, unnerved by the pressure Jacques was putting on her, confided in Colette. "Jacques is pressuring me for sex. I just can't give in to him."

"Sex is a natural part of falling in love. He's a man. You are a woman. C'est la vie. Just be careful not to get pregnant." "Oh my God. I never thought of that."

Her pent-up secret could no longer be contained.

"I was raped when I went to America for Frederick's wedding. It is too terrible."

"Oh, you poor angel. You can trust me. Tell me what happened. Does your sister know?"

"I couldn't tell Elizabeth. It was her father-in-law who raped me. I had too much to drink and went to my room to lie down. He came to my room to see if I was ill and the next thing I knew, he was on top of me and then I passed out. When I woke up, I realized that I couldn't say anything. It would destroy too many lives."

After telling Colette all the gruesome details, Helen sobbed in Colette's arms for hours. In the morning Helen found herself on the sofa covered with a blanket. She had no idea when Colette had left the apartment.

Helen dragged herself to the bathroom. She splashed cold water on her face when the thought hit her. Trying to recover from the emotional pain of being raped, she hadn't noticed that the time for her April period had come and gone. Now it was the end of May and she still did not have her period. Panic set in. She quickly showered and dressed and rushed off to school.

Between classes she cornered Colette. In a hushed voice she confessed, "I haven't had my period in two months. What should I do?"

"I have a doctor. I'll write his phone number down for you." "Oh Colette, suppose I'm pregnant. What will I do?"

"Let's wait and see what the doctor has to say. It may be that your blood is low. You have been very tired lately."

When her classes were over for the day, Helen walked rapidly to her apartment and called Dr. Fermi. He was able to see her late that afternoon. She nervously paced back and forth thinking What will I do if I'm pregnant? The question reverberated constantly in her brain until she thought she would faint from exhaustion.

Helen called a cab to take her to Dr. Fermi's office. She would have walked, but her legs felt like rubber. When she arrived, she was shown into a small examining room. Outside of a black knob here and there, everything was white; the walls, the storage cabinets, even the small wooden table and chair in the corner was painted white.

"Hello. I am Dr. Fermi. What brings you here today?"

"I'm a little light headed and nauseous," Helen answered with downcast eyes. Her eyes avoided his in fear that he would suspect the truth. She could not bring herself to tell him that she had been raped.

"Let me take your blood pressure." He quickly strapped the cuff to her arm. "Ah, it is a little low," he smiled. Then, he put the stethoscope to her chest and then to her back." I will take a vial of blood and that should tell us more. Please bring me a sample of your first morning urine tomorrow. We should know something in a few days."

Helen's body language was familiar to Dr. Fermi. He had seen so many other young women in similar circumstances and had a second sense about her condition.

"Thank you, doctor," was all Helen managed to say as she left his office.

Helen hoped she had caught some mysterious foreign bug; not wanting to face the awful truth of what she suspected. I can't be pregnant, she thought; Walter is too old. He must be in his sixties.

She mindlessly moved through the next few days like a robot. She ate, she dressed, she talked, but was not really there. It was as it she had left her body and it was moving around while she was on hold in some sort of nether world.

Her naivete' was ripped from her when the doctor informed Helen that she was two months pregnant and that the child would be born the end of December. The news was more than her mind could handle. The white room became a vortex spinning her down and down in an unending spiral. Dr. Fermi caught her limp body before it could fall to the floor. He laid her back on the examining table and strapped her to it so she would not fall. He opened the door and anxiously called, "Nurse." The starched white figure came in and adjusted the table to set Helen upright while Dr. Fermi put smelling salts under her nose.

Helen moaned something unintelligible as consciousness came creeping back.

"Dr. Fermi, her girlfriend is in the waiting room," the nurse offered. "Ask her to come in. The girl will need someone to help her."

Helen came out of her faint sobbing, "What am I to do?" Colette was holding her hand.

"Don't worry Helen, we will find a way. I will help you." Colette told Dr. Fermi that Helen was raped. He had heard that story so many times before and did not comment, but handed her a small paper envelope containing some tablets.

"She is to take these twice a day. They will help her gain strength. Make sure she eats. She is very frail."

They took a taxi back to Helen's apartment. Helen fumbled with the key, missing the hole several times before she could open the door. With her arm around Helen, Colette deposited her on the sofa. Immediately, she went to the sink and filled a glass of water and gave Helen one of Dr. Fermi's tablets. Retrieving a frying pan from the cupboard, she put it on the stove top added a little olive oil and adjusted the flame to low. Quickly, she took some eggs, cheese and spinach from the refrigerator and began whisking the ingredients together in a bowl.

"I'm making you an omelet and you will eat it. You have to get strong."

"I can't eat. I want to die."

"You think you are the only girl in the world who ever became pregnant. I told you we will find a way."

"But what will become of me and the baby? I can't tell my sister it was her husband's father who raped me. It would kill her. How am I to tell Jacques. I have put him off so many times. He will think I cheated on him with someone else and that I don't love him."

"Too bad you didn't have sex with him. You could have told him he was the father," Colette quipped as she flipped the omelet.

"Colette, I could never do that. I love him too much to deceive him that way. I think I should tell Jacques the truth. It's the right thing to do."

"The right thing may not be the right thing for you." Colette knew that Jacques would never marry Helen. "Don't tell him yet. Let's see if there is another way."

"I can't go home. I must tell Jacques."

"First things first," Colette smiled, presenting Helen with the omelet and some toasted and buttered French bread. "I'm not leaving here until you finish."

After Helen had eaten enough to satisfy Colette, she drew up her knees in a fetal position on the sofa and drifted off from pure exhaustion. Colette cleaned up and then locked the door behind her.

It was the first good sleep Helen had had in a few days. She woke minutes before Jacques was due. Helen decided to tell him that very evening reasoning, He loves me. He has said so many times. It is not my fault I was raped. He will understand. She tried to convince herself that Jacques would be more of a man than he actually was and that he would marry her and save her from scandal.

When he arrived at her apartment, he kissed her passionately before she could close the door behind him. Smiling and lifting the bottle of wine he brought with him, he motioned for her to get some glasses. Nervously Helen put out some cheese and bread as he poured the wine. Maybe tonight will be the night, he thought. Helen was trying to find the right time and words to begin. After they had eaten and drunk a bit, he held her hand and led her to the sofa. He kissed her lips, her neck and ever so lightly brushed her breast, not grasping it, but just enough to raise her breathing. When she felt passion rise within her, she wriggled out of his arms. her voice strained.

"I can't. I have something to tell you."

Tearfully, she related the crime against her innocence. When she finished, Jacques held her in his arms kissing her forehead.

"I want to keep the baby." she cried.

"Mon Cheri, I cannot marry you. I have no money to support a family. I must peruse my art and so must you. I can find you an abortionist and we can go on as before."

"How could you ask me to do that? I thought you loved me. Get out! Get out!"

"Mon Cheri, it is the only way."

"It is not my way," she screamed slamming the door behind him.

Are all men the same? Do they all just want what is between woman's legs? she agonized. Alone, desperate beyond reason, Helen finished the bottle of wine and cried herself to sleep.

When Helen did not show up for class the next day, Colette went to her apartment to see what was wrong. She knocked on Helen's door, but there was no answer. She knocked harder.

"Helen, it's Colette. Are you ill?"

There still was no answer. Colette turned the knob and found the door was unlocked. She made her way to the bedroom. Helen was still in bed. She was hung over and blind with a headache. When Colette called her name, Helen opened her bloodshot eyes.

"What's wrong?"

"I threw Jacques out. He wants me to have an abortion. I can't do that." Her statement opening a new floodgate of tears.

Colette sat on the bed rubbing Helen's back. "I'm sorry. All men are pigs." Then as if a light bulb went on in her head, Colette asked, "Is the father of the child a rich man?"

"Yes, but what has that got to do with It?"

"Helen, in France your situation is very common. I have a plan to help you keep your baby. You must go back to New York and confront the father. I'm sure he doesn't want his family to know. Tell him to put you up somewhere until the child is born and that he should find you a discreet doctor. After the child is born you will return to Paris and he can support the two of you without anyone knowing. You will promise him never to return to America. His secret will be safe. I will move in with you to help raise the child. While you are there you can send me the letters to your sister so she won't be suspicious and I will forward them to her from Paris. Later, if your sister should come here, I can always say the child is mine."

Colette cared for Helen, but she took care of herself as well. Moving in with Helen would give her more money in her own pocket. She was a poor starving artist from the countryside and needed every franc she could get her hands on.

Helen thought about the plan and said, "I have no choice. I can't go back to school pregnant. I'll make arrangements to get back to the States in the morning."

Chapter 47

JUNE, 1940

The taxi Helen hired at the airport carried her to the Algonquin Hotel in New York City. Her heart was heavy with the chore set before her. She would go to Walter's Manhattan office unannounced the next day. She knew he was always there early on Mondays before the staff came in, but tonight she needed a good night's sleep to face the ogre that had put her in such a desperate condition.

She arrived at Walter's office at 6:30 AM and let herself into his room.

When he looked up from his paperwork, he was stunned to see her. "What are you doing here?" was all he could manage to say. "I'm pregnant and you must help me," she blurted.

"Yes, yes, where are you staying? I can't speak to you here. I'll call you at lunchtime and we will meet to discuss the arrangements," Walter nervously replied.

She hurriedly gave him the number for the Algonquin and ran out of the room in tears.

Walter was dumbfounded. Frederick had come into Manhattan with him that morning and was in the next room working on some ledgers, He had overheard everything. Frederick walked into the room, looked at his father, and said, "The little slut. It was probably some prick in France and she wants us to pay for it."

"Shut up, Frederick! You won't lose a penny of your inheritance. I still manage Helen's accounts until she turns twenty-one. Her accounts will show she is taking funds out monthly for living expenses. She'll pay her own way.

"Frederick, you will keep your mouth shut. I'll handle this. I warn you, if James or Elizabeth should find out, I will cut you off without a dime. Understand?"

Fred nodded his head and walked back to his ledgers. That old fuck. I wonder if it was him.

Later that afternoon Walter met Helen in the hotel's bar; she was too afraid to be alone with him in her room. Walter asked for a table in the remotest part of the bar. When they were seated, he began, "Helen, I'm sorry. I don't know what came over me. I have never done anything like this. What can I do to help you?" Knowing first hand of her virginity, he never suggested that the baby was fathered by someone else.

Quietly tears fell from her eyes, "You must put me up someplace where I will not be recognized. When the baby is born, I will go back to France and raise our child with your help financially. My sister must never know."

He apologized profusely again and agreed to all her terms. "I don’t know what came over me. I never meant to hurt you."

He was truly contrite, but could not take the chance of letting Helen live on her own where no one could report on her comings and goings. His sister Agatha came to mind. She was the only one he could trust to control Helen's movements. He could make sure that Agatha kept Helen in the house and behind the tall, heavily shrubbed grounds. That way he could control any unexpected circumstances that might arise.

"Arrangements can be made for you to live with my sister Agatha. believe I know of a doctor who will care for you until the baby is born. Neither you nor the child will ever need for anything. I will take full financial responsibility. After the child is born and you return to Paris, your account will be credited each month with enough money so you will be well provided for, but I must hold you to your promise; you must stay in France."

"If I am to live with Agatha, she might slip to Harriet."

"Agatha always does what I ask. Harriet is not in the habit of calling Agatha and never visits. They've never had a close relationship. As long as you are there, I will not go to my sister's home. There is less of a chance you will be recognized at Agatha's house in Newark than any place else."

Realizing that if she stayed in Manhattan someone would eventually recognize her, Helen reluctantly agreed.

That evening Helen called Colette to say that her plan had worked. Colette asked Helen if she could live in her apartment while she was in America so she could intercept the mail and forward it to her. Colette was always working an angle for her own benefit. Helen was surrounded by serpents. If evil was a hunter, it had Helen in its sights.

Walter telephoned Agatha and told her he would be there for dinner that evening. It was when she served him coffee that he began.

"I have a delicate matter to discuss with you. Without your help, a great shame would befall the family. Helen has become pregnant in France. The boy was killed in an accident before they could be married. The child will be put up for adoption when born. The poor girl came to me for help. No one must know of this. It would kill my daughter-in-law Elizabeth, who is in delicate health since her baby was born. Helen will go back to France when it is all over. I must have your promise that you will never discuss the situation with anyone, including Helen."

"Of course, Walter. Haven't you always been able to count on me?" She knew better than to question him, but was gratified that he still needed and trusted her.

Walter sent a car for Helen the next day. Helen trembled with anticipation of what her future would be at Agatha's as she entered the black car that would deliver her to her fate.

Tony Russo was surprised when Minnie told him a Walter Woodsworth was on the phone. The hair on the back of his neck raised a little. The devil always collects on his debts, he thought.

"What can I do for you, sir?"

"I would like you to have dinner with me tonight. Can we meet around seven o'clock at Bum's Country Inn in Montclair?"

"Of course, sir. I look forward to seeing you again."

Since Walter held the note on Tony's practice, he accepted Walter's invitation graciously. Tony could not reason why Walter wanted to see him. He had made his payments on time. He had no idea what favor would be asked of him, but he knew that one would be asked.

As they ate their steaks, Walter, not mentioning his role, revealed to Tony Helen's plight,

"My daughter-in-law's sister has gotten herself in a family way by a young man in Paris who has deserted her. She has come to me for help and does not want her sister to find out or cause the family embarrassment. Will you take care of her at my sister Agatha's home in Newark until the child is born? If she goes to your office, she may encounter someone who knows her or someone in our family. I must ask that all I have told you be held in the utmost secrecy, not divulging the least bit to Frederick or to anyone."

"Of course, sir. I'd be happy to help in any way that I can."

"Thank you, Tony. You have always been a friend to the Woodsworths."

Chapter 48

OCTOBER, 1972

Luckily the evening Ed Byrne called, Mark was bowling. Victoria would not have to explain to her husband the nature of Ed's call.

"Vikky, I got some information for you. A doctor named Anthony Russo delivered a child from Helen Stanhope, but it was stillborn. Isn't he your uncle?

She didn't respond to his question.

I know that much, Victoria thought, she had discovered that herself on her trip to the Hall of Records,

When she waited too long to respond, he continued, "Agatha Woodsworth was a spinster who owned the house. She authorized Harrison Funeral Home to pick up the bodies of the mother and her child. They were buried, without a viewing, in Calvary Cemetery in Belleville. The old church that owned the cemetery burned down along with all the records. Hope this helps, Vikky."

"Do you think your friend could find out one more thing for me? I need to know how Helen Stanhope was related to the Woodsworths. "

I'll see what I can do."

"Thanks Ed. I owe you a big one."

Victoria didn't know if Helen was Agatha Woodsworth's niece who had gotten into trouble or was she the pregnant girlfriend of one of Uncle Tony's mobster friends. There were many scenarios swirling in her head. Helen could have been a pregnant widowed renter, a divorcee or even a battered wife. Then she remembered a Stanhope had married one of the Woodsworth sons. Helen had to be related to Walter Woodsworth's daughter-in-law.

The more Victoria went over the clues, the more she knew that she had to find out Helen Stanhope's blood type. She nervously tapped her fingers on the kitchen table and thought, but how am I going to find out what her blood type was? That's the key to the truth. I'll have to find a way to get into Uncle Tony's files. Maybe the answer is there.

Just then she realized that her cousin Vinnie owned the cleaning service in the building where Uncle Tony's office was located. Uncle Tony owned a piece of the building with some other doctors and had gotten Vinnie the contract. Rumor had it that Vinnie had to kick back a little to Uncle Tony.

Victoria had a plan. I'll call Aunt Teresa to find out on which nights Vinnie works there. He still lives at home and his mother knows his schedule.

"Hi. Aunt Teresa. It's been so long. I'd like to have you and Vinnie over for dinner some night. I know Vinnie cleans the professional building, but don't know what nights."

"He goes there every Monday, Wednesday and Friday from 6:00 PM and he's there until midnight. So, if you want us for dinner it will have to be on a weekend, because he cleans other buildings on Tuesday, Thursday and Saturday."

"I'll get back to you Aunt Teresa as soon as I check Mark's schedule." Victoria decided to wait until she was due for her next B-12 shot the following week.

Monday to execute her plan. She mulled over her plan of action. Sometime that night while Vinnie is working. I'll tell him that I lost my glasses when I saw Uncle Tony earlier that day. I'll ask him to let me in to see if I dropped them in the office or the examination room. This way if Vinnie should accidentally mention to Uncle Tony that I was there, he would not suspect anything because he knows I can't read without my glasses. She had to find Helen Stanhope's file if it still existed.

Chapter 49

JULY, 1940

When they had returned from their honeymoon in Bermuda sometime in April, Winifred and Frederick had taken possession of a very lovely home in the affluent community of Montclair, a short distance from the mill. Winifred did not want to live at Belle Vista and have the eyes of the Woodsworths on her every action. Harriet seemed to dote on Elizabeth, and Winifred especially did not want to go into competition with "Elizabeth, the good," as she snidely referred to her new sister-in-law to her friends.

James was having a new home built, also in Montclair, for his family. They would soon be leaving Belle Vista. The house would not be ready for at least a few months but they hoped to be moved in well before Christmas. Elizabeth, with Harriet's help, had been busy selecting furniture, drapes and the like.

James and Elizabeth lovingly poured over the house plans when they were alone in their rooms, anticipating the time when they could truly be a family. She wanted so much for it to be a haven -- light and airy, comforting and nurturing, a safe nest - unlike Belle Vista which seemed like a museum to her. The extra bedrooms would not be filled with children, Elizabeth thought with sadness. She so wanted a big family.

Winifred on the other hand was setting up her home for entertaining. She immediately signed on to all the prominent charitable and historical committees in the district. Frederick didn't know it yet. but Winifred had big plans for him. She thought she would make a wonderful senator's wife. With her upper crust background and the lavish partys he intended to throw for all the right people, she was sure she could push Frederick further than he ever expected to go.

Frederick wanted a son badly. It was all he talked about. He wanted a living reminder that he could best his brother, and when it was a reality, his brother would have to envy him because he was sure his father's attitude toward him would change. Frederick was counting on Walter to endow a grandson with a huge trust fund of Boar's Head stock. Secretly, Winifred wore a diaphragm. She was not ready for children. She told a friend, "If Fred turns out to be an idiot, I can always divorce him and live on the fat settlement I'll get. My daddy's lawyers know how to squeeze."

Harriet was at her window watching Elizabeth push Mary around in a little stroller on the veranda. She was saddened that her only grandchild would be leaving to spend her first Christmas morning in another home and that she would be totally alone with Walter. They passed like two ships in the night, barely acknowledging each other. Lately she noticed that Walter was even more distant than usual. She felt as if her life was over...both boys married and her own marriage a failure. She reflected on what life would hold for her now.

Could I ever forgive Walter? I never did give him a chance to explain. I do not want to spend my future as an embittered lonely woman, she thought. I could suggest a cruise to Walter to work things out so we both could forgive and forget.

That night she put her pride away. Dressed in her best nightgown, she stole into Walter's bed justifying her actions by reasoning Forgiveness is the cornerstone of my religion. They made love for the first time in many months. Grateful for Harriet's forgiveness, Walter agreed to the cruise.

The whole family went down to the ship that June morning to wish Harriet and Walter "Bon Voyage." They were all so happy to see their parents talking civilly to each other and hoped the cruise would rekindle their love.

When they had gone to bed that first night out, Harriet felt she had to clear the air. Without rancor, she quietly told Walter, "I gave you my youth, my love, my body, my inheritance, children and my fidelity. When this incident happened with my sister, I felt bankrupt. I had nothing left. You had all that I had to give and yet it was not enough. You took what was left -- my dignity and the love I had for my sister. Why, Walter?"

"I struck out at you and carried this thing too far because you accepted what she said as truth. I would never hurt you in that way. I have more control than that. Your sister tried to use her wiles on me to extract money. I did not seduce her, but I did give her a check. Please forgive me my pride in not telling you what happened earlier, and let me make this up to you. I promise nothing like this will ever come between us again. I will devote my life to your happiness."

Walter took her in his arms and was a most tender lover that night. It was as if he knew her again for the first time. She responded to him with a renewed passion. With her energy spent, Harriet fell into a deep sleep, but Walter lay there awake thinking.

In her quiet way, Harriet had made him feel he was in her debt and that he had repaid all the gifts she had given him with infidelity. He was ashamed, a feeling most foreign to him. He realized that when he married Harriet, she had given him all the tools he needed to become a power in the business world and king of his castle. He vowed to spend the rest of his life devoted to Harriet's happiness, but what he had done to Helen still unnerved him. He had never slipped so badly in his life. He thought, this thing with Helen could destroy everything I spent a lifetime building. I just have to get through the next few months and get Helen back to France. If anything gets out later, Helen could always make up a story about her French boyfriend marrying her just before he was killed in an auto accident. He knew Helen did not want her sister to know the truth and that gave him some comfort.

Walter now wanted to be a loving husband, father, and grandfather.

He thought, Harriet and I can travel more now that we have found each other again. Frederick and James were more than reliable on the job. I can take life a little easier now.

What he didn't know was that Frederick would use Walter's absence to give himself a raise. While papa was away on his cruise, the mouse ... no the rat, would play. Frederick wanted so much to discredit James and now he had the time and the opportunity to do so. Winifred was proving to be quite expensive. He contacted some of James' suppliers and told them he was controlling payments and that he wanted a little kickback for him and his brother on the threads and materials used to manufacture the parachutes for the military. He informed them that they should deposit the payments directly into a bank account he had set up in both names. James would never be aware of the account. Frederick was emphatic about telling the salesmen that they were never to discuss the deal with either himself or James. It was easy; James trusted Frederick. He would just initial the purchase orders expecting that Frederick ordered the usual quantity of materials. Fred later would simply adjust the office copy.

Chapter 50

SEPTEMBER, 1940

It was late in the month. As James was walking past the gatehouse, Ralph the guard stopped him. They had developed a close friendship over the months since the Woodsworth takeover. James had a lot of respect for Ralph. He knew Ralph looked out for any employee with a problem.

"Hi Jim. How's the Mrs. and your new daughter?" "Fine, doing fine Ralph. Let me show you a picture."

'Ralph put on his glasses and squinted as he viewed the photo. "She's a beauty Jim. Pity what's happened to your Mrs."

"My wife's been a little despondent lately about never being able to have another child."

"You could always adopt."

"We really haven't discussed it much since moving into our new home."

James remembered when they went through each room of their new home for the first time; how sad Elizabeth became as they viewed each bedroom. He recalled their conversation.

With her eyes downcast Elizabeth feeling so empty said, "Guess these rooms will only be occupied by guests. James, I'm so sorry I can't give you more children. I feel like such a failure as a wife."

James grabbed her by her shoulders and shook her slightly. "I married you because I love you, not for any children we might have and that hasn't changed." He kissed her long and hard making her know that to him she was all that mattered.

"Listen Jim," Ralph said. 'I know of a young woman who has gotten herself in the family way and just gave birth to a fine son, but the poor girl has no relatives to help her. She needs to find a loving family to adopt him. Do you think your Mrs. would welcome such a thing?"

"I don't know Ralph, but if it would make my wife happy, it would be fine with me."

"Well, here's the attorney's card that's handling the adoption. If your Mrs. is willing, contact this lawyer."

"Thanks, Ralph."

When James got to his office, he called Elizabeth, "Hello darling. How are my two beautiful girls today?"

"We're just fine and dandy."

"Well, how would you like to go to Mario's tonight?"

"I'd love to. We haven't been there since I told you that you were going to be a father."

James smiled to himself, ... and it's there I'll tell her she's going to be a mother again. That is, if she wants.

"I might have a surprise for you this time."

“I can't wait."

That evening as they sipped their wine at Mario's, James began, "I was talking to Ralph today. You know, the guard at the mill I've told you about. He always asks for you and Mary Harriet. He told me of a young woman he knows who has just given birth to a son. The poor girl has no family and must give him up for adoption. He asked me if we would be interested. What do you think?"

"We do have a few rooms to fill up in that big house. Oh James, God is good. He closed one door and has opened another. Of course I want another child; a brother for Mary Harriet to grow up with. Do you?"

"Yes, my darling, if it will make you happy. I didn't know Mary Harriet before she was born. I won't know an adopted child until I meet him or her. and I will love that child as much as I love Mary Harriet."

"How soon can we see him?"

"I'll contact the lawyer who's handling the adoption tomorrow. Is that soon enough?"

James could see the light come back to Elizabeth's eyes. She was ecstatic. She held his hand and kissed him, "I love you, Jim."

When they returned to their rooms at Belle Vista that evening, she locked their bedroom door. It was Elizabeth that initiated the love making that night. She wanted to make James as happy as he had made her.

"James, I'm going to take a shower." "Sure hon. I'll listen to the radio a while."

James almost fell off the chair he was sitting in when he heard, "Why don't you join me?"

She had always let him take the lead. He was continually being surprised by his beautiful bride. James stripped down and almost slipped getting to her.

He pulled back the shower curtain and stepped in to the tub. His eyes took all of her in. Her creamy white skin was soft as silk under his hands causing his manhood to rise. He lathered his hands with soap and caressed every part of her body. When a stray bit of soap landed in her eye, he dried her with a towel and carried her to their bed. He kissed her eyes, her mouth and suckled her breasts. Her back arched as his tongue entered the blonde tufted mound between her legs. Her body began to lunge back and forth climaxing in a muffled moan. Then he entered her and both were carried away in a wave of ecstasy.

Chapter 51

OCTOBER, 1940

James rose early the next morning, invigorated by the pure joy of the previous evening. He wanted to get to the mill as soon as he could to set up a meeting with the attorney. There was nothing he would deny his beautiful Elizabeth.

Taking the card from his pocket, James dialed the attorney's number.

"Mr. Farley's office. May I help you."

"This is Jim Woodsworth. How soon can I have an appointment with Mr. Farley?"

"There was a cancellation today at three thirty, but if that's too soon I..."

James didn't give her time to finish the sentence. "I'll take it."
"We'll see you then, Mr. Woodsworth."

James quickly dialed the phone again,

"Darling, we have a three-thirty appointment with the attorney this afternoon. Is that soon enough?"

"I love you, Jim. I couldn't be happier." "I'll pick you up at three o'clock"

"I'll be ready."

James called for Elizabeth at the appointed time and they drove to the law offices in Passaic. Elizabeth and James had made a pact that they would not say anything to the family until they were sure the baby would be theirs.

"Mr. and Mrs. Woodsworth to see Mr. Farley," James announced to Mr. Farley's secretary.

"Yes, you are expected. Please come with me. Mr. Farley is ready to see you." The secretary opened the door to Mr. Farley's office and announced the Woodsworths.

Farley, a man in his early forties, stretched out his hand and introduced himself.

"Robert Farley here. So nice to meet you, Mr. and Mrs. Woodsworth. Please be seated."

"Ralph, one of my employees, has told us you are handling the adoption of a child, a boy."

"Yes, Ralph told me he had given you my card. The boy is hale and hearty and ready for almost immediate adoption. The mother is of Polish stock and the father, who is unknown, is said to be of English or German background. The mother wishes to remain anonymous."

"Is it possible for us to see the child?"

"He's in St. Mary's hospital. I can take you over there if you wish." "Oh, please!" replied Elizabeth.

"Well, let's go then. My car is in the lot."

It was a short drive to the hospital. Elizabeth thought she would jump out of her skin with excitement. Laughingly she thought to herself, this child will be all joy. The hard part was done for me already.

Once in the hospital, Mr. Farley directed them to a private elevator and pushed the fourth-floor button. James held Elizabeth's hand and when he looked at her, he knew he was giving her the best gift possible. She was beaming. When they arrived at the area of the maternity ward where the babies were kept, Mr. Farley asked the nurse to bring the baby to a small consulting room. A few minutes later the nurse arrived and placed the child in Elizabeth's arms. When Elizabeth looked into his sweet face she smiled.

"Oh, he's beautiful," she sighed.

When the child put his thumb in his mouth, Elizabeth gasped, "Look James, he has a birthmark on his hand. My God, it's providence. The mark looks just like the one all the Woodsworth's carry."

James came to her side. Elizabeth took the boy's little hand and showed James the tiny triangular birthmark just above the middle finger on the back of his hand.

"Amazing. Maybe you're right. This does seem more than just coincidence."

"Oh yes, James, please let's adopt him. "

James took Mr. Farley outside the room while Elizabeth cooed over the boy.

"How soon could we complete the paperwork. Of course, I know of the mother's poverty and would like to give her a gift of say $5,000."

"I'm sure I can have all the paperwork completed by the end of the week. Once signed, you may take your new son home with you that day."

The two men walked back into the room to find Elizabeth totally enthralled with the baby.

"Well darling, Mr. Farley believes we can take him home on Friday after we sign the papers."

"I don't know if I can wait that long. He's beautiful."

James saw the sparkle in Elizabeth's eyes and he was willing to pay any price to keep it there.

Just then the nurse returned, "Time for his feeding."

She whisked the boy from Elizabeth's arms and back to the nursery. "Shall we leave so I can get those papers done as fast as I can."

"'Oh please, Mr. Farley, as fast as you can," an excited Elizabeth replied.

They drove back to the law office and thanked Mr. Farley profusely before getting into their car. Farley assured them he would be in touch as soon as everything was in place. On the ride back to Belle Vista, Elizabeth questioned, "James, how do you think your parents will respond to our adoption of the child?"

"I'm sure they will love the boy as much as they love Mary, especially when they see the birthmark. That is strange, but like you said it must be providence. God's way of telling us we're doing the right thing."

When Mr. Farley returned to his office, he called Ralph, "Woodsworth Silk Mill, Ralph here."

"Ralph, it's Farley. Looks like they went for it. The baby should be theirs by Friday. The wife spotted a birthmark on the kid's hand. I heard her telling her husband that it looked like the one on all the Woodsworth kin. I don't think they suspected a thing but coincidence. He's giving Stella $5,000. as a gift and I'll bang him for all the expenses."

"Thanks Bob. At least the kid will be with his own blood. The father of the kid, for what he did to Stella, should burn in hell. Everything he touches should rot."

"I'll have all the records sealed by the court so no one will ever learn the identity of the mother."

With his extensive contacts, Farley pushed through all the paperwork by Friday as promised. That afternoon James and Elizabeth took their new son home.

Ralph had a little kick back thing going on with Farley for each new client he brought him. Anna Kovacs had a close relationship with Ralph. He had suggested Farley to handle all the paperwork when her husband died. When she found Stella pregnant and unwilling to name the father, Ralph had arranged for Farley to handle the adoption. Ralph knew who had impregnated Stella and why she wouldn't name the father; she didn't want her mother to lose her job.

When the proud new parents arrived home, they giggled. No one knew that they had a new son.

"Well do you think, now that it's a reality, we should tell my parents?" smiled James.

"We'll invite your parents, your brother and Winifred for Sunday dinner and introduce little Walter."

Elizabeth wanted her new son to be called after her father-in-law to endear the child to him. She was afraid he would not accept the child as his grandson.

"Don't expect my brother to be happy for us." "He's mellowed some since he married Winifred."

"You think so? A leopard doesn't change its spots. He's always been jealous of me. My father had this competition thing going between us. I stopped playing that game when I was a kid. Fred is still letting dad be his puppeteer."

"Well let's not anticipate unhappiness. I don't want anything to dampen our new found joy."

"You're right. As long as we are happy, nothing else should matter."

Chapter 52

On Sunday, Elizabeth was sitting in the living room with Mary when the family arrived. Harriet ran to Mary and hugged and kissed her.

"I miss you so much, Mary Harriet," cooed the proud grandmother.

After all were seated in the living room. The maid brought in a tray of champagne.

James stood, "Family, please raise your glass. I have a surprise for you. Mother, Father, I am pleased to announce you have a grandson. Winifred, Fred you now have a new nephew. Elizabeth and I have adopted a son. His name is Walter Robert Woodsworth."

The room fell silent.

"How wonderful, another grandchild!" Harriet was the first to break the silence, her eye lashes aflutter. "Why didn't you tell us sooner, my dear, that you had planned to adopt?"

"Everything happened so quickly Mother, and we weren't sure until Friday that he would be ours."

Walter, for the first time in his life, was speechless.

"Well, where is this namesake of mine?" he finally bellowed.

Frederick and Winifred were stunned and barely stuttered "Congratulations."

James had asked that the nanny bring little Walter into the room. Walter walked toward the child and asked to hold him. As the nanny handed him over, Walter spotted the birthmark. He took the child's hand and could barely believe his eyes. Seeing the look on his father's face, James said, "Yes, father, his birthmark is very similar to that of the Woodsworth's. Elizabeth and I agreed after seeing that mark that indeed it must be providence and that he should come to us."

"How did this all happen?"

"A man at the mill said he knew of a young woman who had recently given birth to a son. Since she had no relatives to help her, she had to put him up for adoption. The man knew of our situation and gave me the attorney's card who was handling the adoption. Elizabeth and I discussed the matter and decided to take a look. We did and that was it. We had to have him. I hope you're happy for us."

"It's wonderful," Harriet smiled as she went to little Walter.

Everyone chimed in and said they were happy for Elizabeth and James.

Frederick could barely make it through dinner. His lips were pursed tight between bites of the food he barely touched. Complaining of a headache, he excused himself and Winifred before coffee was served. As soon as they got in their car, Frederick exploded into a string of profanities.

"Damn him! Damn him! How dare he give that little bastard my father's name. That privilege should have been reserved for our son. Elizabeth can't have any more kids. This was a deliberate act on my brother's part, timed before we could give my father a grandson."

"Calm down Freddy. You'll give yourself a heart attack."

"The only thing that would help me right now is if you told me you were pregnant."

"We've only been married six months. Give me a chance."

Winifred could see Frederick's knuckles were white from the angry death grip he had on the steering wheel. She hoped he would drink himself to sleep tonight. If he didn't, she knew she was in for it. When anger overtook Frederick, he was insatiable and rougher than usual.

Chapter 53

While the world was a bright and beautiful place for Elizabeth, her sister Helen, as if in a tomb, had never known such silence and confinement. She was only allowed out into the back yard of Agatha's house for one hour a day. The tall hedges that surrounded the property blocked all contact with the outside world. The only bright time was when Dr. Russo came with his nurse to examine her. She tried to get close to Agatha, but the steel in those eyes warned Helen not even to start a conversation.

Agatha had her orders and she would not betray Walter. Before dinner, in her stern voice, Agatha recited Grace. As Agatha prayed, Helen thought, it's amazing how cruel those who think themselves righteous and religious can be. She's never shown me one bit of kindness. They ate quietly barely exchanging a "good evening" in a dimly lit dining room each night.

Agatha was never able to adjust to the comfort Walter had afforded her. She rationed electricity, holding fast to her parent's credo against waste.

When Dr. Russo came to see Helen, she would talk about Paris and how she longed to go back to her art classes. He knew he shouldn't pry, but when the nurse was out of the room, he asked Helen, "Is there a chance the father of your child will marry you? "

"How could Walter Woodsworth do that?" she exclaimed.

When she saw the shock on Tony's face she sighed, "He did not tell you it was he who raped me the night of Frederick's wedding. Please, you must not tell anyone. I thought you knew, since Walter had sent you to care for me. After the child is born, I'll be going back to France permanently."

"Helen, I promise whatever you say to me will be held in the strictest confidence."

"I don't want to ruin my sister's happiness. She would never survive the truth."

Tony knew she was just an innocent kid caught between a rock and a hard place. On subsequent visits he would bring her some art books, candy, etc. to lift her spirits. He had met Agatha and knew Helen must be in a living hell.

Chapter 54

NOVEMBER, 1972

Victoria had to keep up a good front when she entered her uncle's office for her B-12 shot. Her mind was in turmoil. Her imagination was running wild with theories. Did Uncle Tony switch me at birth? Maybe he arranged for my adoption from some underworld boss' girlfriend, and that is why Uncle Tony gave me that cock-and-bull story about transfusing my blood supply when I was born. Did my parents lie to me all these years? She didn't want to ask Uncle Tony any more questions because he lied to her once and she could not count on him now to tell her the truth.

"Hi Minnie. You look busy."

"Can't keep up with all this paperwork. Your frugal uncle is going to have to get me some help. I've been with him for thirty years and he still thinks I can do everything by myself. The insurance companies demand more and more paperwork every year."

"What do you do with all the files. Guess you have to store the inactive ones some place."

"We have a record storage room back there." Minnie pointed to a door to her right. "Would you believe he has every record since 1 940 in there. It needs to be cleaned out, but I don't have the time.

OK, Vikky. Go to examining room three. He'll be with you in a few minutes. He should be finishing up with the last patient."

When Tony walked in to the examining room, he noticed Victoria wasn't her usual jovial self.

"What's wrong? You look like the weight of the world is on your shoulders. You still feeling tired?"

"No. I have to stop and see my Dad when I'm done with you. I'm worried about him. My Dad's knee is better, but he looks like he's starting to fail."

It wasn't a lie, she thought. She was worried about her dad and used it as an excuse for her demeanor.

Tony seemed to accept her explanation because he didn't question her further. As he gave her the shot, he commented, "You're a good daughter Vikky. It's never easy to see a parent weaken before your eyes. " He gave her a hug and kissed her goodbye.

She stiffened at his touch. He smiled as she left and thought to himself, I did the right thing. My sister brought her up right.

Victoria breathed a sigh of relief when she exited the building into the parking lot. She was glad she hadn't blurted out her thoughts and questions to her uncle.

As she was parking her car in front of her dad's home, Victoria noticed there were more dents in Victor's car. Her dad found it hard to remember things lately. He was failing and she would have to come to terms with that. How could this happen to my strong-as-a-bull father. How am I going to tell him I don't think he should be driving anymore? she thought.

Her shoulders slumped as she climbed the stairs to Victor's front door.

Opening the door with her key she yelled in, "Dad, it's Victoria." "I'm in the kitchen," he called out.

"How are you doing, Pop? Did you eat?"

"Yeah, I ate the lasagna you made. Pretty good. Almost as good as your mother's."

Victoria wanted to make sure he had enough food and checked the freezer and refrigerator to see if he had eaten the meals she had prepared for him.

She called Mark and told him she had to spend some time with her father and asked him to order out for himself and Diana and that she would be home as soon as she could. She hadn't told Mark what she really intended to do that night, nor did she tell him what she suspected about being switched at birth. He would have a fit if he knew what she was up to. Victoria had dinner with her dad, did the dishes and watched some television with him, but her eyes were constantly checking the clock. The later it got the more edgy she became. When she felt the time was right, she kissed her dad goodnight and left his home determined to find answers.

It was a little after eight o'clock when she rapped on the door of Uncle Tony's building. "Come on Vikky. You can pull this off," she whispered to herself. She wondered where she had gotten the nerve to do this. It certainly wasn't as dull as washing clothes, she thought. She had never been this sneaky or deceptive before. She kind of liked the rush. Looking through the entrance doors, she could see cousin Vinnie vacuuming the lobby. She waved her arms and rapped again and finally caught Vinnie's eye. He opened the door and was surprised to see her. He kissed her and asked, "Hey cuz, what are you doing here?"

"I came to see Uncle Tony today and I think I left my glasses in his office. Do you mind if I take a look?"

"Yeah, go ahead. I got to finish in here." he said busily.

Victoria quickly slipped into the elevator which led to Uncle Tony's second floor office. She flipped on the lights and made her way to the huge bank of files in the storage room. "Stanhope, Stanhope" she muttered to herself. Skimming through several cabinets she finally came across a series of old files. There it was - Helen Stanhope. She turned on the Xerox and quickly copied the few pages. She found her mother's file in the same cabinet and copied that as well. Carefully, she re-filed the folders and placed the copies in her purse. She turned off the copier and the lights and took the elevator to the lobby. Vinnie, who was still vacuuming, looked up when he saw Victoria approaching. Victoria waved her glasses at him indicating that she had found them. He turned off the machine.

"I found them. Thanks Vinnie. I'll call you soon and we'll get together for dinner."

Turning his vacuum back on, he waved at her and nodded his head. She quickly made her way to the door hoping he wouldn't see how red her face was; a telltale sign that she was rushed or doing something she shouldn't.

When she got into her car in the parking lot, she let out a sigh of relief. She put on the overhead light unable to wait to read the files. Helen's baby was born a few minutes before her own time of birth, but there was no blood type listed, just a record of each time Uncle Tony went to Agatha's house to see her. "Damn it. I thought I'd get lucky. My whole friggin life maybe a lie," she gulped.

Victoria couldn't tell anyone what she found. She still was not positive that she was Helen Stanhope's child even though the evidence was mounting. Her Uncle Tony was the only one who knew the truth. If it was as she had suspected, then her father and mother never knew. That knowledge, she felt, would surely kill her father at this stage of his life. Mark doesn't know who he may be married to. If my family finds out I'm not blood, will they treat me differently? Her mind was a dizzying whirl of ifs. The only person Victoria could talk to was Father Gennaro in confession. Even though he could never divulge what she would tell him, she decided not to confide in him either. At this point, she trusted no one.

When Victoria arrived home, she found a note saying that Mark had gone to the golf range with Diana to hit some balls. The telephone was blinking indicating she had messages. It was Ed Byrne asking her to give him a call tomorrow.

Chapter 55

NOVEMBER 22, 1940 - NEWARK, NEW JERSEY

A howling nor'easter had blown the night's snowfall into a blanket of purity covering the dust and dirt of the city and the gray house at 9 Forest Street. Inside, Helen was awakened by a gripping pain in her swollen belly. Her anguished scream muted that of the wailing wind outside. Sweat soaked her hair and face. Throwing off the blankets, she could see that her white nightgown was covered in blood. Just then another spasm seized her little body, eliciting another scream, "Agatha."

Down the hall, Agatha Woodsworth woke with a start from a sound sleep. Someone was calling her name. Forgetting her slippers, she ran from her bed towards Helen's room, her robe thrown over her shoulders. There in the eerie glow of the nightlight and amid the tangled bed sheets, she saw the blood-soaked Helen writhing in pain. Without a word of comfort or reassurance Agatha quickly left the room, putting her arms in the sleeves of her robe and tying the sash tightly around her waist. She ran down the stairs to the phone and called her brother Walter.

Walter had been working late in his study at Belle Vista when the call came from Agatha.

Her voice shaking, "We have a problem," Agatha rasped into the mouthpiece. "Helen is bleeding badly. She needs to get to a hospital."

"Calm down, Agatha, I'll have someone there to pick her up as soon as possible. Don't worry, there won't be any sirens," he whispered. Immediately, he telephoned Frederick and in a shaky and hushed tone ordered, "Get a hold of Tony fast. Helen is in a bad way. She's hemorrhaging. Have Tony pick her up and bring her to the hospital. No ambulance, Frederick, we don't want to leave a trail," he cautioned.

"OK, Dad, I'll handle it." Frederick replied.

Walter had to trust his son with this. His renewed relationship with Harriet was at stake. He didn't want any more phone calls that night.

Frederick hadn't awakened Tony by his call. He was already dressing.

His sister Angela was in labor and on her way to the hospital. "What's wrong, Fred?" answered Tony.

"Helen's time has come. Aunt Agatha called. Can you have her picked up but not by ambulance? My father doesn't want any attention called to Agatha's house."

"She's not due for at least another month. Is there something wrong?" "Aunt Agatha told my father she was hemorrhaging. Listen Tony, if the bitch and her brat don't make it, I'll see to it that your loan will disappear."

Frederick couldn't risk the scandal of what his father had done. If the truth ever got out, he was sure that Winifred would leave him and his career in politics would be over. If Tony didn't take care of things for him, he would have to have it done when Helen returned to France.

"Fred, do you know what you are saying? I have to go." Angrily, Tony slammed down the phone. He was stunned that Frederick would ask him to do such a thing. Quickly he called Imperial Limousine, a company his friend "Bobby Shoes" owned. Bobby had told his man at the limo company that anytime Tony called, they were to get him anything he asked for.

“Vito?"

"Yeah."

"This is Dr. Tony Russo. I need a car to go to 9 Forest Street, Newark and pick up a Helen Stanhope. Bring her to American Legion Hospital as fast as you can. Pull in the driveway and ring the back door bell."

"You got it, Doc," the gruff voice replied.

Tony rushed down the stairs and went out the side door to his garage. Good thing he had the chains put on the tires of his Cadillac. The snow was tire deep as he pulled out of his driveway. It was c1 long and dangerous trip lo American Legion Hospital. It took him over an hour, skidding most of the way.

* * *

Agatha waited by the back door. Within minutes, a black Cadillac pulled to the rear entrance of the stark gabled Victorian. Nervously, she unlocked the door for the two large approaching men. "Follow me," Agatha whispered as she quickly led them up the massive mahogany staircase to Helen's room, their footsteps muted by the burgundy fleur-de-lis patterned carpet runner. When they reached Helen, she was no longer crying. Her eyes were open and dazed. Crudely, the men wrapped Helen's body tightly in the bedspread and carried her down the stairs as if she was an old rug. They put her into the back seat and took her into the night, life draining from her pale small body. The falling snow covered the little drops of red left where they had dragged her into the car. It was as if the universe had conspired to obliterate her ever being there.

* * *

By the time Tony arrived at the hospital, his sister was almost ready to deliver. The nurse came in and informed him, "Helen Stanhope is in the next bed in labor and bleeding profusely. Her blood pressure is dropping."

"Type her and hang a pint of blood. Quickly," he shouted to the nurse.

With only a curtain between the two delivery tables, Tony ran back and forth, but before the nurse could come back with the blood, Helen had expired at three thirty in the morning while delivering her baby. He suctioned the child and when it cried, he wrapped the baby in a cloth and put the little girl in a bassinet next to Helen. He would tell the nurse to clean her when she returned. His heart sank. "That kid did not deserve this," his face twisted in anguish.

Just then Angela screamed, 'Tony it's coming."

Only one maternity nurse had made it in through the snow that night and he felt like a one- armed paper hanger. He ran to his sister and delivered Angela's baby. He slapped the baby's bottom several times, but no sound came out. He knew it was another stillborn. Angela started to weep, "God, no. Please not another dead baby."

"I have to suction." he told Angela.

He quickly carried the child into Helen's area, out of his sister's line of sight. Laying Angela's dead child next to Helen, he picked up Helen's live child, made it cry, and brought the little girl to his sister.

"Here's your baby, Angie. She's beautiful!"

"I knew this time it was going to be all right. I made several novenas to St. Gerard."

Tony was crying. Over the last several years, his sister had miscarried three times, and at her age it was probably her last chance.

When Tony had time to put together all that had happened that morning, he finally understood why Frederick was hated by everyone including his father. He was furious that Helen's death gave Frederick what he wanted. "That bastard should pay just for asking me to do such a thing."

He called Frederick,

"Helen and the child didn't make it."

"I can always count on you, Tony. You know my father and I are grateful. Your debt is paid."

As he put the receiver down, Tony thought, "Let him think what he wants to. My conscience is clear. I can't imagine what Fred would contemplate if he knew Helen's baby is alive. With a good mother like Angela, she'll have a chance at life and won't turn out like those murderous rich bastards.

Chapter 56

Early that afternoon Frederick arrived at Belle Vista to inform his father that Helen and the child had died. He climbed the stairs to Walter's study. The door ajar, Frederick walked in and announced, "Helen and the baby are dead. They are not a problem anymore. I had Aunt Agatha call Harrison Funeral Parlor to pick up their bodies at the hospital. She has been instructed to have them buried in an empty family plot in Calvary Cemetery in Belleville. This way nothing can be traced back to you."

Helen and Angela's dead baby would be interred next to Walter's parents. Their names would never be engraved on the family stone. Frederick chose this place so there would be no record of a newly purchased gravesite. Helen's imprint on the world had been erased.

Walter's face fell. He covered his eyes with his hands and whispered, "Oh my God."

Almost with a sense of pride, Frederick laid out before Walter what was done on his behalf and a list of demands for those services.

"With the help of my old friend, I have cleaned up your mess, Father, and I think we should be rewarded." Frederick wasn't about to let this moment pass without taking advantage of his father's vulnerability.

"Tony's loan should now be considered paid in full and I would like to be made President of the mill."

When Frederick saw Walter's scowl and his imminent argument against Frederick's demands, he headed it off with his last Ace.

"You were the father of Helen's child. Did you really think Helen would have come to you if it was someone else who had done the dirty deed. It had to be you or else she would have gone to Elizabeth. The only reason she wouldn't want Elizabeth's help is because she couldn't tell her it was her husband's father who knocked her up."

"Are you trying to blackmail me, you little bastard?" Walter raged. "What do you mean, you cleaned up my mess? What have you done?"

"Tony made it happen because I asked him to. She was half dead anyway from the hemorrhaging and the kid was well... was stillborn. We committed murder so that little bitch could never hold this family hostage. That's what was done to save your ass." bellowed Frederick.

Believing he had his father in an inescapable corner, Frederick now had the courage to dare to speak to his father in such a manner.

Stalling for time to contemplate the fix he was in, Walter lowered his voice, "How could you be so stupid to come here and risk having the servants hear? Didn't I teach you anything? Go home Frederick. We will talk later."

In his haste to please and blackmail his father into giving him what he wanted, Frederick now knew he had broken one of his father's cardinal laws.

Outside the door to the study, Harriet dropped the travel brochures she held in her hand. She had excitedly walked to Walter's study to tell him where she wished to go on their next trip. Harriet had overheard most of the conversation between her son and her husband. Her anticipation of a happy future with Walter was over. Hearing of her son's unspeakable deeds on her husband's behalf was so incomprehensible, her mind could not bear its consequences.

She staggered down the hallway; the pressure in her head building. Trying to steady her gait, she held on to the walls to get as far away from the study as she could. She felt a doorway to a parlor and pushed the buttons to turn on the light, but there was none. Everything was black. She had lost her sight. Feeling her way to the sofa, she collapsed.

A few minutes later the maid found her motionless and staring into space. The maid's screams brought Walter and Frederick to her side. Walter tried to bring her to by calling her name and patting her face.

"Get the smelling salts," he yelled to the maid, but when she returned with them, they proved ineffective.

"Frederick, stay with your mother!" Walter ordered as he ran back to the study.

There on the floor outside his study, Walter discovered the brochures Harriet had been holding. He realized then that his wife must have overheard everything. "Oh God, no!" he whispered. It was one of the few times in his life that he would appeal to deity.

Harriet hung between life and death for weeks. She was the victim of a stroke. They would not take her home from the hospital until Christmas Eve. Paralyzed and no longer able to speak, the only sound she could make was a groan. Poor Harriet's body would be in the care of around-the-clock nurses. Caught between two worlds, Walter's beautiful wife was just a shadow of her former self.

In her last lucid moments before succumbing to the stroke, she had learned that she was married to a monstrous husband who would defile a child in his care and had spawned a murderous son who would enlist his friend to dispose of Helen and her child. Her body responded to what her mind could not bear. The stroke freed her of all the mental torture she would have had to endure.

Chapter 57

JANUARY, 1941

Since his mother's stroke, Frederick had not brought up Tony's loan or becoming President of the mill to Walter. He would let his father have time to contemplate his options.

The holidays passed quietly for the Woodsworths. At dinner, one evening, Elizabeth remarked that she had not received a call or letter from her sister Helen. She was very concerned now that France had been invaded by Germany. She asked Walter, "Father is there anything you can do to get my sister Helen out of France. 1 fear for her life."

"I will do my best, Elizabeth. In fact, I will try to reach out to my friend in the State Department now. Excuse me." he replied as he left the table and walked to his study. He could not look into Elizabeth's pleading eyes any longer. Frederick glared at him when he left.

Walter knew he had to tie up this loose end. Agatha had told him of Colette corresponding regularly with Helen. She had copied Colette's name and address down for her brother, giving it to him when the letters first started to arrive at her house. Walter called

Richard Miller and they arranged to meet at The Thicket. Richard knew that there were no business deals pending and couldn't imagine what was so important to warrant a trip to Pennsylvania, particularly in January. The tone in Walter's voice bothered him.

They walked the rocky path around the lake, taking in the quiet. Richard thought it was strange that Walter had not brought his shotgun along. Walter's face was somber and he looked quite a bit older than the last time they had been together. Richard tried not to second guess the reason for his being there. It was a while before Walter opened the conversation. Walter found it difficult to begin. He was trying to find the right words to confess his crime to his most trusted ally.

He began, "I am ashamed to tell you that I have committed a grievous deed. I lost control and now find myself in a desperate situation." He told Richard all of it, including Frederick's attempt to bribe his friend Tony by canceling his loan to make sure that Helen and her baby did not survive.

Wearily accustomed to dealing with the sins of the rich men he served, Richard spoke without emotion.

"We have a discreet person at the National Bank of Paris. We can arrange for him to contact Colette. He will give her a letter of instruction in a sealed envelope informing her that Helen and her baby had died in childbirth. In the letter of instruction, she will be asked to write to Elizabeth in her own hand informing her that Helen and Jacques, a Jew, had been taken by the Germans, they were put on a train and had not been seen since. Colette will be compensated with $1,000, and will be instructed to destroy all that was sent to her. Upon receipt of the letter by Elizabeth, Colette will be contacted and a second payment of $1,000 will be delivered to her."

"Do you think of me as a monster, Richard?" "I'm not here to pass judgment on you."

Richard was the closest thing to a friend that Walter would ever have. He would never truly have Richard's friendship in the conventional way, but Walter knew his lawyer would carry out his wishes to the letter, whether he was dead or alive. Richard was the best money could buy.

Unemotionally, Walter told Richard, "I have another problem. My son Frederick is blackmailing me. He wants to become President of the mill. If I give in to Frederick's demands, I know that sadistic bastard will make James' life a living hell. I wouldn't put it past him to sabotage the mill to oust James. I hate that sneaky bastard and I don't want him to have anything.

"I would like you to set up a trust or a set of documents where I can make sure Frederick gets next to nothing when I'm gone. I want him to know that blackmailing me was the worst mistake of his life outside of marrying that snob. Winifred thinks her family is so far above us. She thinks the Woodsworth's are peasants. Frederick has taken to extorting money from the mill's suppliers to keep the bitch in mink. I didn't get this far to not know when I'm being robbed.

"I know this Tony Russo, and I know he could not have deliberately let Helen and the child die. I can't prove it but I have a hunch that Helen's child still lives," Walter said confidently.

"I want to create a trust with a caveat put into it for a term of fifteen years after my death. If anyone comes forth within that time frame with the birth date of November 22, 1940, born at American Legion Hospital in Newark and can prove that I am the father, that child shall have half my fortune. The other half will go to James upon my death."

As his eyes welled up with tears, Walter confessed, "I was a beast to Helen. I caused her death and I owe her child... if it has survived... that much...it has my blood." Just as he uttered his last word, he remembered his stumble that killed the swan, and thought about how arrogant he was. It had foreshadowed his loss of control with Helen that eventually caused her death. He would never forgive himself, but he could try to put things right with the tools he had.

"The stock I own in Winifred's father's company is all that Fred will inherit. Let him blackmail his father-in-law and see how far he gets on his own wits," Walter said with a sneer. "Oh, and my Marc Chagall of Cain and Abel; he is to get that as well. Fred let his hatred of James hold him back all these years. Maybe he'll get the message."

Richard's quick mind had found a solution and he suggested to Walter, "All of your assets should be incorporated into a trust except the stock in Winifred's father's company. That asset will go through your will. Give Frederick the Presidency with a yearly percentage of the profits to him and James and you can make Fred a gift of some mill stock. Let him believe that you have given in to his demands. If you should die, the trust will sell the stock in the mill forcing it into bankruptcy. James will be able to draw on his half of the trust. The other half shall remain until the fifteen years are up. Then, it will revert to James and his family if no claimant comes forward."

"Richard, I indeed chose well when I selected you as my attorney and friend."

Chapter 58

Victoria called Ed Byrne on her lunch hour from a pay phone on the corner. She didn't want anyone in the office to hear her conversation. Ed was supposed to see if his friend, the private investigator, could find out what the relationship was between Helen Stanhope and Agatha Woodsworth.

"Hi Ed, it's Vikky. Got something for me?"

"I have the information you wanted. Helen Stanhope was the sister-in law of James Woodsworth, Walter's eldest son."

"Thanks a million, Ed. If I ever get to the end of this story, we' II have a lot to talk about."

"You'll tell me when you're ready. Take care, Vikky."

Ed knew Vikky's birth date was the same as the child and mother who died on that date. He had his suspicions as to what was going on. His friend A.K., the private investigator, had filled him in.

Victoria now had a clearer picture. She theorized, Helen must have become pregnant and probably didn't have a husband. The Woodsworths must have shipped her off to the spinster's home in Newark to avoid a scandal and away from people who knew her.

In her mind, Victoria recapped all the information that she had managed to find through her own investigation and through Ed's friend. A female child was born at American Legion Hospital that a Helen Stanhope had given birth to. The child was the only other female born there that day other than herself. The child was born on the same morning, had the same delivering doctor, and was born a few minutes before she was. The woman with whom Helen lived was the sister of Walter Woodsworth. Helen's sister was married to Walter's son.

Victoria had determined this because, when she did her research at the Paterson Library, there were wedding announcements in the local newspaper of the marriages of Walter's two sons. Frederick, the other son, had married a Winifred Teasdale. So when Ed Byrne mentioned that Helen was James' sister-in-law, she knew it was not Frederick's wife.

Then there was the Boar's Head Company. Victoria couldn't figure out yet the relevance it had to her first dream on the veranda where the boar's head appeared next to her, looked at her, became frightened and then disappeared. She conjectured, Maybe the man who owned Boar's Head Company, Walter Woodsworth, was frightened because I'm finding out the truth; a truth that had been buried for so long.

Victoria had hidden the box containing Helen's artwork and letters that the woman on Forest Street had given her in her closet. She hadn't had the time or been alone long enough to read the letters. She would tackle that next.

She picked up a sandwich and went back to work. It was a difficult afternoon...her mind kept wandering. When the day was done, she made her way to the subway. As the car clacked along the rails she realized that she didn't have to pick up Diana at the usual time because her daughter had band practice today. Victoria would be alone when she got home for an hour or so and would have time to read the letters.

They were addressed to Helen and were from a woman in Paris, a Colette Brizzard. There were vague references in the letters that Helen's time was growing short before she could return to Paris and several mentions of a Frenchman named Jacques who had asked about Helen. Later the letters warned that the Germans had invaded France and that Helen should consider a change of plans. Perhaps Helen could go to Switzerland and Colette could meet up with her there. Another letter thought it would be safer if Helen remained in America until the war was over. "I'm sure the father can find you a safe place, maybe in another state," wrote Colette.

Victoria wondered if Helen's sister knew of her pregnancy. She must have known, Victoria thought, if her father-in-law and his sister were taking care of Helen; but maybe not. Maybe I should write to this Colette. After all these years she didn't know whether Colette still lived at the address on the envelope. Victoria had nothing to lose but the postage.

Dear Ms. Brizzard:

You do not know me, but I have come into possession of letters sent by you to a Helen Stanhope. She delivered a female child in the same hospital, on the same day, minutes apart from my own birth.

I have since found that my parents had 0-positive blood, while mine is B-Negative. Do you have any knowledge of Helen's blood type and who had fathered Helen's child. I know this must seem like an enormous imposition, but I must know who I am, and there is a real possibility that I was switched accidentally at birth.

Sincerely yours,

Victoria Valentino

Chapter 59

Weeks had passed and still there was no word from Colette. Victoria thought she was silly to expect that this woman would still be living at the same address or living at all. It had been over thirty years. Right now, Victoria had more pressing concerns.

Her Dad had recently had a mini stroke and she could see the handwriting on the wall even though he seemed to recuperate quickly. Her father was the strongest man she had ever known. He was always healthy as a horse. It saddened her deeply to see his deterioration. She knew the inevitable was not long off.

Victoria had discontinued the B-12 shots. She doubled up on her vitamins. It was too painful to see Uncle Tony and she did not know if she could contain herself in his presence. She was afraid of blurting out all that she knew. Right now, she could not bear what he might tell her whether it be lies or the awful truth. Victoria just could not handle anything more emotionally.

After four long months and several hospitalizations, Victoria's father passed away. His care had taken a toll on her. She barely had enough strength to get through the wake and funeral, family and friends. The weeks after her father's death were filled with paperwork; thank you notes, arranging for the monument to be engraved, the surrogates office to have her father's will probated and all the other necessary things to do when there's a death and you are left to handle the final wishes of a loved one. It would be a month before she could begin to clear out her dad's house and get rid of his furnishings. The house needed to be put up for sale. This wonderful old house; the site of her happy birthday parties, the house she was married from, soon would no longer be there for her to ramble through and relive the happy times. She felt orphaned.

When all was done, her past put away, she had the final dream of the mansion.

Victoria was in the attic, a place she knew she had always feared. It was filled with beautiful flowering plants. The large windows there created a greenhouse effect. All the plants were healthy and hearty. A voice told her,

"See, you were always frightened of this place, but there is nothing to fear here any longer. Look at the beauty."

When Victoria woke, her heart was not pounding, It was 3:30 AM, and she felt fine. She knew it was over. The terror was over.

Chapter 60

MARCH, 1941

The grand charade had begun when Walter summoned Frederick to his office in Manhattan. In tones only a loving and grateful father would use, Walter put his arm around Frederick's shoulder and smiled.

"Son, I've had time to consider what you have done for the family, and you deserve to be President with a salary befitting your position... and there's more. You shall receive a share of the profits at the end of each fiscal year and stock in the mill."

From his father's expression and generosity, Frederick thought, at long last he has finally come to appreciate me.

"What about Tony's loan?" he blurted.

"It is paid in full. I want to take life a little easier now that I know I can depend on you to oversee things at the mill. After all, when the chips were down, I could count on you to do whatever it took to get the job done. Your brother would have never had the stomach to do what you did." Walter knew that Frederick would perceive this as a compliment, not as a denigration as Walter truly meant it.

"Dad, I don't know what to say. You will always be able to depend on me."

Frederick thought he finally had his father where he wanted him and, over time, could influence Walter to give him more and more control.

As Walter came from behind his desk, Frederick rose from his chair and before Frederick could say anything further, Walter put his arm around him,

"Son, you can let the mill suppliers off the hook now."

Frederick's eyebrows raised and in a cowed voice replied, "Yes, father."

Frederick knew better than to push his father for more. Walter knew of his little kickback scheme. Now they had something on each other.

Walter had not lost his talent for deception. He could tell that Frederick bought his feigned capitulation and gratitude. Disgusted by the niceties he had heaped upon Frederick he washed his mouth out with scotch.

When James found out that Frederick was made President of the mill, he went straight to his office.

"Fred, I just heard. Congratulations!" James gave his brother a big bear hug. "Let me take you to lunch to celebrate."

Fred was so disturbed by James' genuine happiness for him, he wanted to throw up. He would have preferred James' envy, but there was none in him.

No matter what Frederick had done to James over the years, he could never stay mad at him for long. Frederick was his brother. He loved him. James overlooked pretty much every rotten thing Frederick had said or done to him. The only time James pounced on Frederick was when he found him beating their dog. He threatened Frederick, "If anything happens to Sparky, you'll lose that eye I just blackened." He could take anything Frederick could dish out, but he could not abide Frederick harming anything he loved.

James was still in Frederick's office when the telephone rang. It was the telephone operator looking for James.

"Jim, Bess has a call for you. Do you want to take it here?" "Fred, tell her I'll take it in my office."

While the call was being transferred, Elizabeth waited on the line quietly sobbing. She was happier than she thought she could ever be. Their house was truly a home filled with love and joy. Then the postman arrived with Colette's letter. As she read the gruesome news, her happiness disappeared. Her sister Helen had been taken by the Germans along with her love Jacques, a Jew, and had not been seen since.

The phone was ringing when James arrived at his office. He quickly picked it up, "Jim Woodsworth."

"I have your wife on the line, Jim," Bess responded. "Please put her through Bess."

"Jim, I have terrible news. Helen is missing in France. The Germans have her. Please come home. I just received a letter from her friend Colette." Her voice quivered.

"Darling, please be calm. I'll be right home, but first I'll call my father and see what he can find out."

James immediately dialed Walter at Belle Vista.

"Dad, it's James. Elizabeth just received a letter from Helen's friend Colette. The Germans have Helen. Can you do anything?"

Knowing that Helen and her baby were rotting in their grave, Walter convincingly lied, "This is a terrible turn of events. I'II put more pressure on my friends at the State Department. If anyone can find her, they can."

James went to his wife. Elizabeth lay on their bed sobbing, her body shaking with grief. He held her in his arms and told her,

"Elizabeth darling, please don't cry. My dad is doing everything he possibly can. His friends in Washington will find her."

"No James, I'll never see my sister again. I've lost her."

Chapter 61

OCTOBER, 1941 -BELLE VISTA

A heavy snow had fallen that Friday afternoon. Belle Vista was eerily quiet. Even though the fireplaces were all lit, there was a daunting chill in the air. Walter had retired early and was snug in his bed when the nurse caring for Harriet awakened him.

"Mr. Woodworth, please come. Mrs. Woodsworth has taken a turn for the worse."

Walter quickly wrapped himself in the heavy black and red brocade robe that lay at the foot of his bed and slipped into his woolen slippers. He walked as fast as he could to Harriet's room. Kneeling at the side of her bed, he softly called her, "Harriet, love. It's Walter." Lying there gray and ashen, she turned her face to his voice and for the first time, opened her blue eyes. For an instant Walter saw her as he had the first time their eyes met in her father's office so long ago. It destroyed him. A primitive sound emanated from deep within him. He plunged his face into the bed next to her body, held her hand and wept uncontrollably as she slipped away.

When he was able to leave his wife's lifeless body, Walter went to his study and poured himself a brandy. He put his head on his desk and sobbed for hours. Finally, just before 5:00, he managed enough composure to call the funeral director. After Harriet had been taken away, Walter called James,

"Son, I have some very bad news."

"Have your friends located Helen?" James asked cautiously.

His voice faltering, "No James. It's your mother. She has passed away.

Please call your brother and tell him. If you could all be here at noon..." "Yes father, of course."

When they all had assembled, Walter informed them, "I have decided that your mother's wake and funeral will be private; family only."

"Father, we have so many friends that would wish to express their condolences," stated Frederick.

Walter stared at Frederick, his black and bloodshot eyes sending a direct message to his son's core not to continue.

"OK father. If you think that's best."

Walter did not want those who knew Harriet looking at the shadow she had become, and he could not bear the company of strangers and their inane expressions of sympathy.

His hatred of Frederick deepened. He blamed his son for Harriet's stroke. If he had only used the phone. This hatred helped him to obliterate the fact that it was his rape of Helen that had brought down a curse upon his house and that it was he who had set the terrible events into motion.

Two days later Harriet's body was laid to rest. The viewing was just before Mass at the local Catholic church Harriet had attended before her stroke, followed by the entombment at the newly built mausoleum. Walter had ordered its construction months before.

Harriet's sister Vivienne attended the funeral. She had returned to the States when the war had come too close for comfort. She was living in New York City. Her beauty waning and her funds low, she had been looking to hook up with a man who could support her in the lifestyle she had been accustomed to.

Chapter 62

DECEMBER, 1941

In the weeks after her sister's death, Vivienne attempted to get close to Walter. Feigning ignorance about financial matters, she telephoned him. "Walter dear. Do you think you would have time to advise me on my investments? I really don't know about such things."

"Sure Viv. Come to Belle Vista on Sunday and I'll look over what you have."

When Vivienne arrived, the house was in turmoil. There had just been a news bulletin on the radio that Pearl Harbor had been bombed. Summoned by Walter, both James and Frederick were there when she came into the house.

Vivienne was shown into the dining room. The boys and Walter had the table filled with papers.

"What's going on?" asked Vivienne.

"Haven't you heard, Aunt Viv. The Japanese have bombed Pearl Harbor. We're at war," James said with a certain degree of anxiety in his voice.

"Oh my God."

"Viv, I'm afraid I will not have time to go over your financial records today. The boys and I have to make arrangements to increase production at the mill."

"Walter, I'll just leave the papers with you and I'll come back next Sunday if you have completed your review of them by then, or call me when you have."

She kissed them all goodbye and was driven back to Manhattan. Several Sundays had passed before Walter invited Vivienne back to Belle Vista to discuss her finances.

"Viv, you're going broke. Let me handle your investments. You can no longer afford that flat in the city and your extravagances. Come and live here and manage my household and I'll build up your assets."

Walter hated living alone. He needed someone to relieve him of his loneliness.

"Thank you, Walter. Maybe we can be of help to each other," she said with a twinkle in her eye.

It took several months for Vivienne to settle things in New York and move to Belle Vista.

James was not happy about his aunt moving in and had expressed his displeasure to Walter. His mother had slipped one day and he had asked, "Mother, why are you and Dad not getting along. There has been a coldness between you since I returned from my honeymoon. Did anything happen after my wedding reception to cause this."

"Your Aunt Vivienne is to blame. She intimated that something untoward had happened. I don't want to talk about it."

Walter convinced James that it was all in his mother's imagination.

* * *

Harriet had barely been in her grave six months when her sister decided to make a move on Walter. Wearing her sexiest black negligee. she slipped into Walter's bedroom and softly called his name.

"Walter."

His eyes shot open and saw Vivienne in the night light. Her sagging breasts were held firm and upright in the French lace nightgown. Her wrinkles were not so apparent in the dimness of the light. Walter simply pulled back the covers and invited her into his bed.

He kissed her with such hunger that Vivienne could hardly breathe. She pushed his head down towards her breasts and allowed him to feast upon them for a while. Simultaneously his hand invaded her intimate part arousing her passion. She pushed him to his back and straddled him, but Walter could not become erect. Vivienne tried everything in the book, but it was not to be.

As she slithered off him and lay facing Walter, she softly said, "Don't worry Walt, it happens," tenderly brushing his hair with her hand.

"Never before," he said with embarrassment. He had expected her derision given her history, but instead she was kind and understanding.

"You've just been working too hard with the war and everything." Vivienne held him in her arms until he fell asleep and then crept back to her bedroom.

The fact that he could not perform bothered Walter enough to see a doctor. Soon afterward Walter had to have his diseased prostate removed.

Vivienne took care of Walter while he recuperated from the surgery. No one could have had a better nurse and companion. In the evening she arranged for their supper to be served in his bedroom. After some light conversation, she would read to him until he fell asleep.

Walter quickly recovered and dove into work. He wanted to be back in control of his business ventures, but more importantly, in control of his emotions. He had spent too much time with Vivienne and was beginning to soften towards her wish to marry him. He did not want her as an heir or to have standing as a wife in his estate in case she decided to contest any provisions he had made.

Chapter 63

SEPTEMBER, 1962

Since Vivienne's passing in 1955 from cirrhosis, James and Elizabeth would have Walter over for Sunday dinner. Frederick and Winifred managed to make excuses not to attend, frequently citing political functions they had to attend. The sight of his father fawning over the children and the whole happy family scene caused Frederick no end of pain because he did not have a child of his own. To Winifred, James' and Elizabeth's children were a constant reminder of what she could not give her husband. Winifred would never have children. She was barren as a result of scar tissue from an abortion she had in her teens.

Over the years, making the right contacts, Winifred had positioned something over James. Frederick could be a senator. Walter was always invited to her parties, where she extracted as much money as she could from him to support her husband's run for the Senate.

During the campaign, Walter suddenly died of a cerebral hemorrhage. He had collapsed under his ceiling on the marble floor of the great room. The year was 1962. He was out on the veranda when the maid brought him the mail. He was about to go to his study when, while leafing through the mail, he noticed a letter in a hand that he did not recognize. It was marked personal and confidential. There was no name or return address on the envelope. Curious, he quickly opened it. The letter read,

Dear Mr. Woodsworth:

You do not know me, but in September of 1940 I gave birth to your grandson. Your son Frederick and I had an affair. I was just seventeen when it began. He had promised me marriage and I foolishly believed him. The day I told him I might be pregnant, he pushed me down a flight of stairs hoping that I would lose the child.

My mother's friend, Ralph, the guard at your mill's gate, arranged to have my baby adopted through an attorney he knew in Passaic. I never knew where my child was or who had adopted him. Recently, on his deathbed, my mother's friend summoned me and told me that it was he who sent your son James to attorney Farley to arrange for an adoption. Your son James nor his wife ever knew who the biological parents were.

It was the worst pain anyone could imagine to have my son ripped from my arms. My mother was devastated to lose a grandchild, but insisted that I sign the adoption papers. The shame of it all put her in an early grave.

I felt I must come forward now to let you know that James' adopted son is of your blood. He is truly your grandson as he carries the Woodsworth birthmark on his left hand. If you had denied him your full measure of love, know that you can give it freely now. I can only hope that he has had a good life growing up in your family. I'm sure he had been afforded much more than I could have ever given him. I have never stopped loving my son.

I have used the money your son James so generously provided through the attorney to go to college. I am a teacher, a wife and mother. Rest assured I will never divulge these circumstances. Please never tell Frederick of his son's existence. I had known nothing but cruelty from him. I am sorry to have laid such a heavy burden of truth upon you, but I felt you should know.

There was no signature on the letter. Frederick had given him the grandson he had so longed for; but if the truth were known, it would destroy James and Elizabeth. Little Walter hated his uncle and Winifred. They always treated him as if he didn't belong. Walter was rushing to the stairs to destroy the letter in his study when he felt a searing pain in his head. In seconds he had lost consciousness and collapsed on the floor; the letter clutched in his hand.

Hearing a thud, the maid ran to the great room. When she saw Walter lying on the floor, she screamed. The chauffeur came running. He put his finger on Walter's neck and then his wrist looking for a pulse and said, "He's dead Margaret."

"My God, what are we to do."

The chauffeur picked up the mail and the letter in Walter's hand. He handed them to the maid and said, "Put these in Mr. Woodsworth's desk. I'll call his son James."

Margaret ran up the stairs grateful to get away from Walter's dead body. She went into the study to the desk, opened the middle drawer and put the letter and mail into it. She was so nervous, that she slammed the drawer shut causing Stella's letter to fall from the drawer to the back of the desk.

The chauffeur dialed the number tor the mill and asked the receptionist to put him through to James telling her, "It is urgent that I speak to him immediately."

"Jim here."

"It's Henry, sir. Your father sir. He has collapsed and I believe he has passed away. I find no pulse."

“I’m on my way."

James left the building without a word to anyone and raced to Belle Vista. He ran through the back door where the maid and the chauffeur were waiting tor him saying, "Your father is in the great room." When he got to Walter's side, he could readily see that Walter had died.

"Margaret, please bring a sheet to cover my dad."

"Yes sir, right away."

"I'm sorry sir. He went quick and did not suffer," Henry offered trying to console James who had begun to weep.

"Please get me Wryles Funeral Home on the phone Henry."

"Yes sir."

"Mr. Wryles, this is James Woodsworth. My father Walter Woodsworth has passed away at Belle Vista. Would you please come."

"Of course, James. I shall come immediately. My sincerest condolences."

James dialed the mill. The receptionist answered, "Woodsworth Silk Mill"

"Bess, it's James. ls my brother Fred there?" "No sir. He's out to lunch."

"Please have him come to Belle Vista upon his return. It's urgent."

“Of course, sir."

James' next call was to Richard Miller. "Richard Miller here."

"Richard, it's Jim Woodsworth. I have some terrible news. Father is dead. He collapsed in the great room."

"James, stay calm. I'm on my way. Your father left me in charge of his final arrangements and I am the executor of his estate.

Please see to it that nothing is tampered with and please lock the door to his study."

"Sure, but why?"·

"Your father was a very private man and I don't want his papers disturbed."

James took the keys from his father's belt and locked the door to the study. When he had returned to the first floor, he went into the library.

Frederick had arrived and was somberly greeted at the door by Henry who directed him to go to the library.

"I got your message. What's so urgent?"

"Father's dead Fred. He's in the great room where he collapsed. I'm waiting for Wryles Funeral Home to get here."

Frederick walked to the great room and saw the outline of his father's body under the sheet.

Finally he's out of the way. I can do what I want at the mill, Frederick thought. I'll know what he's worth now. The old bastard kept that a secret long enough.

"I need a drink Fred. Let's go to the library."

"No, Dad had his best stuff in his study."

"Sorry. Richard Miller said I was to lock it and allow no one to enter until he can go through dad's papers."

"That's ridiculous. Give me the keys." "No. Richard is on his way."

Almost simultaneously, Wryles' car and that of Richard Miller arrived.

Richard was shown into the library where the brothers were seated.

"My deepest sympathies to you both," Richard said grimly as he shook their hands. "I have seen Mr. Wryles on the way in and I have instructed him as to your father's wishes."

"What!" Fred said indignantly.

"As I told James, I am the executor of your father's estate and he left me explicit instructions as to his final arrangements."

"Why have you locked us out of our father's study?"

"Because that's what he wanted. As executor of your father's estate I must protect all his assets. James, may I have his keys?"

"Wait just a minute. You have no right to take over here. Where are your papers?"

"I brought them with me anticipating your attitude, Frederick."

Richard produced an affidavit which stated, "At the moment of my death, Richard Miller, my attorney, will take possession of all my effects, property and holdings and he shall be the administrator of my intentions as outlined in my will."

"Are you satisfied, Frederick?"

Frederick scanned the papers and did not respond.

Once Walter's body had been removed, Richard informed the servants that there would be compensation and severance pay due them, and asked them to leave. He walked back to the library and requested. "Would you both be here at Belle Vista tomorrow morning at eight-thirty? At that time, I will discuss with you your father's final arrangements."

Chapter 64

The brothers and their wives arrived at the appointed time. Richard informed them that it was Walter's wish that the services be attended only by family members and himself.

Winifred was aghast.

"My father-in-law was a giant of industry and his friends and associates should have the opportunity to express their sympathy."

"I respect your concern Winifred, but I have my orders. You can have a memorial service at a place of your choosing and at your own expense after Walter is entombed."

Her painted-on eyebrows arched and her mouth opened as if to argue, but no sound came out. Winifred was insulted and in shock. No one had ever spoken to her as Richard dared. She had wanted to use the event to garner support for Frederick's run for the Senate.

James said very little. His father's death had hit him hard and he was glad that Richard was handling arrangements so he could deal with his loss.

* * *

It rained buckets that morning. Walter was laid to rest at Resurrection Cemetery in Paterson; his coffin placed next to Harriet's in the grand mausoleum that would eventually house them all. As they were leaving the cemetery, Frederick asked Richard, "When are you planning to read my father's will?"

"On Monday next at Belle Vista. Please be there at one o'clock". Richard entered his waiting limousine and returned to his office in Manhattan.

Frederick was already counting his inheritance. He was just short of having controlling interest in the mill. With the anticipated inheritance which he expected would be evenly divided between himself and his brother, he would have total control of the mill.

As they were leaving the cemetery, James and Elizabeth invited Fred and Winifred for brunch at their home, but Frederick quickly refused feigning a headache.

Chapter 65

Richard arrived promptly at 1:00 PM the following Monday at Belle Vista. Frederick and Winifred were waiting in the parking lot for him. As they entered, Frederick commented, "My brother and his wife are not here yet."

"They are not included in your father's will therefore their presence was not required. Please come into the library."

Frederick was ecstatic. Richard positioned himself behind the elegantly carved antique mahogany desk; Frederick and Winfred in the high boy oriental patterned red silk upholstered chairs in front of the desk.

"Walter's will is quite simple, with one bequest to you Frederick. You will inherit his entire holding ... "

Fred moved to the edge of his chair in anticipation of hearing that he was sole heir to his father's entire fortune.

"...of stock in Cheshire Foods, and his painting of Cain and Able by Chagall."

Fred, waiting anxiously for Richard to continue with the list of assets, was stunned when Richard said, "That concludes the reading of Mr. Woodsworth's will."

Frederick jumped from his chair and angrily questioned, "Where is the rest?"

Looking Frederick straight in the eye, Richard replied, "Your father has placed everything other than what was given to you in a trust of which you are not a part."

When Winifred rose and made an attempt to speak, Richard cut her off before she could begin.

"You have no standing here. Your husband is an heir, not you." She sat down in a huff.

Trying to keep his voice from cracking, Frederick inquired, "Who is the beneficiary of that trust?"

"That is none of your business," Richard replied curtly,

Infuriated at Richard's remark, Frederick moved toward him in a threatening manner, calling Richard a long string of profanities.

Richard would not be intimidated. He stood solidly to warn Frederick that a move toward him would be a mistake.

"Your father hated you. He did not want you to have anything. Take what is being given to you. If you contest your father's will, you will lose the stock as well. If you don't like it, call a lawyer."

Richard avenged in Walter's stead. Walter's money was well spent. As Frederick grabbed Winifred's arm to leave, he warned Richard, "You will hear from my lawyer. That's a promise."

In a rage, Frederick pushed Winifred along to their car and drove erratically to their home in Montclair, Winifred was so angered by the events at Belle Vista, she smashed all of her china.

“You fool. I told you being President of that stupid mill was nothing. You should have demanded stock in Boar's Head. How much do we own in daddy's company?" she screamed.

"I don't know yet!"

"I have no intention of living like a pauper. You had better find out."

That evening after Frederick had drunk himself to sleep, Winifred called her father.

"Daddy, Walter left Fred practically nothing except for some shares in your company and a painting. I don't know how many shares. Can you find out how much? It may be a while before Frederick finds out. Walter's lawyer was horrible to me and Fred."

Larry knew how devious Walter could be.

"I don't think Walter owned that much or I would have known. The largest investor in my company is an investment firm whose corporate offices are in Switzerland. I'll check it out and get back to you."

Larry knew that Walter would not just dabble in his company's stock. He was worried now. It would be just like Walter to secretly hold a large interest in Cheshire to use it against me or my daughter, he thought.

Chapter 66

At 3:30 PM James and Elizabeth arrived at Belle Vista. Richard was there to greet them and asked that they come into the library.

"Why isn't my brother here?"

"He is not part of the trust. Your brother will receive his inheritance through your father's will."

Richard seated himself behind the desk and James and Elizabeth took the chairs his brother and sister-in-law had shortly before vacated.

"James, you will receive half of the trust's worth when several transactions ordered by your father are completed. The other half of the trust that your father has set up will be conservatively invested for a term of fifteen years. This half would be for another beneficiary. If that beneficiary cannot be found by the end of the fifteen year period as stipulated in the trust, the remainder will be paid to you or to your heirs."

James was mystified. "Who can it be. Who is the other beneficiary?" he asked.

"I'm sorry, James, I cannot divulge that per your father's instructions. I must also caution you that you must not reveal the terms of this trust; not even to your brother. It was your father's wish. I know all this is very difficult to understand, but trust me, your father had valid reasons for handling his final affairs as he has."

"Richard, it is hard for me to fathom, but my father trusted you more than anyone and so will I. What about my father's personal effects and the furniture?"

"I will arrange a convenient time for you and your brother to meet me here to select the items you wish to have. The rest will be sold and the proceeds will go into the trust as directed by your father."

When they met the following week, Frederick immediately informed the attorney that he wanted his father's desk from Walter's study. Somehow, he equated power with that desk and he meant to have it. James took the desk that his mother had so lovingly picked out for the room she had decorated for them upon their return from their honeymoon.

Walter's desk was shipped to Frederick and Winifred's home the following week. The delivery men placed it in Frederick's office. Immediately Winifred summoned the maid.

"I want every inch of this desk scrubbed and polished. My father-in law smoked cigars and I want the smell of him removed from this desk.

"Yes ma'am," the maid replied, and without haste set out to gather the cleaning supplies necessary to accomplish her task.

When the maid pulled out the middle drawer a piece of paper fell out and she quickly brought it to Winifred. She dismissed the girl and went to her purse to retrieve her reading glasses. Her eyes widened as she read Stella's letter to Walter. It was dated two days before her father-in-law's death. She read the letter three times, not believing what she was reading.

The scandal would certainly ruin Frederick's future in politics, she thought. She wasn't ready for that to happen yet. Before anyone came in, she had to hide the letter and decided to take it to her bank and place it in her safety deposit box. She didn't know when, but someday she thought It might come in handy.

On her way home. Winifred wondered about how Frederick would feel about having a son -- a child she could never give him. He had treated little Walter like an uninvited guest since Elizabeth and James had adopted him over twenty-two years ago.

When Frederick arrived home that evening, he was beyond approach. "What's wrong, Freddy?"

"That son-of-a-bitch Miller, my father's attorney. He sold the shares my father had in the mill and it has made mine almost worthless. This will certainly drive the mill towards bankruptcy."

Winifred handed him a glass of scotch and tried to calm her husband down so she could learn how badly this would affect them. He went back to the bottle several times. He was very drunk when he started talking, "My father hated me. I tried to please him. I did things for him that could have sent me to jail."

"Jail. What do you mean, Freddy?"

"Elizabeth's sister Helen didn't disappear in France. That old bastard..."

"What did he do?

Just then the glass fell from Frederick's hand and he passed out on the sofa.

Chapter 67

After his lawyer had done an intensive investigation, Larry found that Walter owned a substantial amount of stock in his company. Worried that Frederick would do something stupid, he called his daughter.

"Princess, you are going to have to do daddy a favor. You must get Frederick to add your name on the stock he inherited. I found out that Walter used a dummy corporation to buy quite a bit of stock in my company and Frederick could use it to destroy our family. By doing what I ask, you would receive at least half in a divorce settlement if that became necessary."

"But I want to be a senator's wife, daddy." she moaned.

"Let's see how he makes out in the race first. The important thing now is that you get your name on that stock."

Frederick soon realized that his only ally was Winifred. She still believed in him and worked really hard trying to get him elected. It was her birthday and when Frederick asked her what she wanted, she promptly told him, "Fred, I know things have not gone well with your father's estate and I don't really need anything expensive now; just add my name as co-owner of the stock in daddy's company and that will be enough. You can make it up to me when you are elected senator." She kissed him passionately as she walked him upstairs to their bedroom.

When the news circulated that the mill was closing and that Frederick was practically penniless, his support from those that had nominated him began to decline. James had donated a sizeable sum to Frederick's campaign upon Winifred's urging, but no amount of money could get a perceived loser elected. The insiders had already given orders to the ward bosses. Frederick lost the election.

Their prominent friends now refused Winifred's invitations. She decided there was nothing left in New Jersey for her. While Frederick was away in Florida golfing to get over his loss, Winifred called her father, "Daddy, it's time. I want to come home."

"I'II arrange everything princess. "

Before Winifred entered the limousine, her father had sent for her, she left a note for Frederick which simply read, "I want a divorce."

Chapter 68

MARCH, 1973

The long- awaited letter from Provence, France, arrived. It was from Colette. Victoria nervously tore open the letter by her mailbox. She was too excited. She could not believe what she was reading. Helen indeed had B Negative blood. Colette was able to get the information from Dr. Fermi in Paris. She gave Victoria his name and address as well and a copy of the letter of instruction she had received from a lawyer named Richard Miller all those many years ago.

Armed with this final bit of information, Victoria called her Uncle Tony, "I have to talk to you privately."

Tony had an inkling of what she wanted to discuss with him. The private investigator that Ed Byrne used to get the information for Victoria worked at times for Tony's underworld friend, Bobby "Shoes". Bobby told Tony of his niece's inquiry.

"Are you ill?"

"No, It's something else. Can we meet at your office tonight after hours?"

“Why?” I overheard.

“Is seven-thirty OK?"

“That’s fine."

Tony was waiting for her at the building's entrance. He could see that Victoria had a briefcase with her as she walked from the parking lot to the door. The presence of the briefcase unnerved Tony. It contained all the evidence she had amassed. They walked silently into Tony's office. When Tony had seated himself behind his desk, Victoria in the chair in front of it, he asked, "What's all this cloak and dagger about?" his face questioning, his mouth wearing a sardonic smile.

"Helen Stanhope is what it's about." Victoria's face was stern as she placed Colette's letter before him. "....and no lies Uncle Tony. I know."

Dissolving into tears, he cried, "Yes, I switched you at birth. Your mother had several miscarriages. She was desperate to have a child. Your parents never knew. I didn't want you to go to an orphanage. It was the only way to keep you safe and my sister from having a breakdown. Helen, your birth mother, did have B-Negative blood. She was too far gone when they brought her in that hellish night. There was nothing I could have done to save her. She was a beautiful and innocent woman and an aspiring artist that Walter Woodsworth raped. She was like a lovely little white swan. She had sworn me to secrecy because she didn't want to destroy her sister Elizabeth's life with the truth. Elizabeth, your aunt, had lived in Montclair at the time, but I haven't spoken to the Woodsworths since. I don't know if she still lives there."

Tony was sobbing more than he thought he could. He didn't mention James. It would only make clear that he was her half-brother and her uncle. Tony could not bring himself to tell her what Frederick had asked him to do that night; that Frederick had wanted her dead. He thought she had enough to digest.

Victoria kissed him and said, "It's OK Uncle Tony, it's OK. Just keep this between you and me. No one knows about this. I don't even know what I'm going to do. First, I have to tell my husband. I'll keep in touch."

He hugged her. "You're still my niece and you always will be."

Victoria picked up Colette's letter and placed it back in her briefcase, walked to the exit and out to the parking lot. On the drive home, she tried to rehearse how she would begin to tell Mark about her start in life. Mark was watching a ball game when she came into the living room. She walked over to the TV and pushed the off button.

"What the hell!" he bellowed as she ended his game.

"I have something to tell you," she said ominously.

Mark could see from the expression on her face that it was serious. As she related her story to him, he could not fathom its enormity.

"I don't know how to begin, but the long and short of it is that my mother and father were not my biological parents. My mother's name was Helen Stanhope and my father was Walter Woodsworth."

Mark was alert now and quickly asked, "Were you adopted?"

"No, I was the product of a rape. Walter raped his daughter-in-law's sister, Helen. She died giving birth to me. Uncle Tony switched me with the stillborn my mother had."

Mark held Victoria in his arms. "Oh God, how did you find out all of this?"

"You really don't want to know. It was a combination of things." She showed him Colette's letter and told him of her investigation and that of Ed Byrne's friend, the PI. "I can't tell Diana. She's too young to deal with the truth. Helen had a sister Elizabeth, my aunt, and she lived in Montclair at the time this all happened. She doesn't know about me."

"Are you going to try to contact her?"

"My mother, Helen... gee, it sounds strange to say that…never wanted her to know about the rape. I don't know what I'm going to do."

"Why don't you contact the lawyer named in the letter Colette sent you? He probably can tell you more about your family." It seemed weird to Mark when he said the words "your family." He always thought he knew them and now he knew nothing.

Chapter 69

The next morning Victoria called Miller and Weiss and asked to speak to Richard Miller. When the secretary asked who was calling, she replied "Helen Stanhope's daughter, Victoria." Immediately upon hearing the name from his secretary, Richard picked up the phone,

"Richard Miller here."

"I'm Mrs. Victoria Valentino. I believe I am Helen Stanhope's daughter."

"Before we go any further young lady, what is your birth date and the name of the hospital in which you were born?"

"I was born in American Legion Hospital in Newark on the twenty second of November, 1 940."

"If you blood matches that of Mr. Woodsworth's, we will have much to discuss."

"What do you mean?" she replied.

"Walter Woodsworth had a feeling that Helen's child did not die; that somehow you were still alive. He passed away leaving a sizable trust set up for anyone who could prove they were his child.

We will need a sample of your blood. Mr. Woodsworth, before his death, had a vial of blood cryogenically preserved so that any claimant could be tested. I would like to set up a meeting at my office in New York to discuss the details with you."

"I knew nothing of a trust. I did not call for that reason. I know I have an aunt. Please do not tell her of my existence yet." My God!. The realization hit her, "I have brothers as well. They are not to know either."

"I will keep your confidence Mrs. Valentino, but let's not get ahead of ourselves. First, the blood test."

Victoria was seated at her kitchen table and was unable to believe what Richard Miller had told her. I have to call Mark, she thought, but hesitated. It's too much to tell him over the phone, she reasoned.

Victoria decided instead to take a ride to clear her head and somehow found her way to Calvary Cemetery. It was a small cemetery. Maybe she could find the Woodsworth monument. She needed to make a connection to Helen and that was where she was resting. She drove from Nutley to Belleville in somewhat of a dream state. It was as if her mind and body were in neutral. Pulling into the cemetery, she parked near Aunt Mim's grave. She would visit there first. An elderly couple approached her. The man asked, "Are you her daughter?"

"No. She was my aunt through marriage. She was married to my mother's brother Nick."

"We're the caretakers here," the woman said., "Oh we remember him. Such a sad case. We always felt so sorry for the man. He would sit by her grave and cry for hours. We've seen him here many times over the years."

"He passed away."

"We figured that when we didn't see him anymore." "By the way, is there a Woodsworth monument here?"

"There sure is. It's on the other side. Follow me and I'll show you where it is," the man answered.

As they approached the large stone, Victoria's eyes began to well up with tears.

"Are the Woodsworths part of your family?"

Victoria nodded, "Distant relatives."

"All four graves are full now. Strange, they never had the fourth name engraved on the stone," the caretaker remarked.

The couple left her and continued with their chores.

Looking at the stone that marked her biological mother's grave, Victoria thought, who are these people? Seeing the engraved names of Arthur and Mary, she thought, these are my grandparents. Then there was Agatha's name, her aunt who Uncle Tony had described as a pinch-faced spinster; stern and unfeeling except to Walter.

Somewhere in there, anonymous, lay a mother she had never known. She was buried amongst strangers; Walter's parents, and near Agatha, who had treated her horribly the last days of her life according to Uncle Tony. The thought that this young and innocent woman was so cruelly treated caused a gasp to escape from the depths of Victoria's body followed by a flood of tears. Her whole body shuddered. Her strength gone, she fell to her knees, finally able to let go of all her emotions. In a small voice she told Helen, "You have found me, mother, and I have found you."

Seeing Victoria on her knees from a distance, the caretakers looked at one another.

"I guess the relationship wasn't so distant." the man said.

They averted their eyes and went back to their work. When she had composed herself, Victoria stood up and brushed some grass clippings from her slacks. On her way out of the cemetery she neared the kindly couple. She could barely raise her voice to say

"Thank you" and weakly waved goodbye. By the time she reached her car, she felt totally depleted. She drove home slowly, her mind not thinking or feeling but simply caught in a kind of nether world, her body heavy with sadness.

When Mark walked into the house that night, he found Victoria sitting alone in the living room. The TV was not on That's strange, Mark thought. It was a Friday night and Diana was at a sleep over at a classmate's house.

"I called Richard Miller today. He wants a meeting with me on Monday at ten-thirty to discuss the details of a trust Walter Woodsworth set up in case I ever came forth. I have to have a blood test. If all goes as expected, we'll be very wealthy."

Mark was in shock. He stood there agape for a few seconds. He could see Victoria had been crying. He hated it when she cried. He knew if he said something ridiculous and off subject, it would snap her back. "Well, if you are going to be that rich, do you think we can order some supper in? I don't smell anything cooking."

Victoria smiled, "I haven't got the money yet."

Mark had a real wry sense of humor. He knew a serious conversation was coming and had to break the tension.

"I'll front you the money. If you don't get it, I can always take it out in trade."

"What are we going to tell Diana? I never want her to know that I was a child of rape and that my whole life has been a lie."

Mark sat next to his wife on the sofa. She was in tears. That calm type of weeping, the type that scares men to death. He put his arms around her and said, "Your life was never a lie, Victoria. Your Mom and Dad may have been poor, but they loved you more than life itself, and that's no lie. They never knew you were not their flesh and blood child. Your biological mother must have loved you just as much. It must have been her who bugged you with all those dreams so you would know that she existed and that you should have your inheritance. Now you won't have to work so hard. We can drive into

Manhattan on Monday for the meeting with Mr. Miller. If you want me to be there with you, I'll take the day off. If not, I'll go to work and meet you for lunch. Whatever will make you more comfortable."

"Come with me. I'm too emotional. I won't remember a thing he says to me."

Chapter 70

Mark worked on Fifth Avenue, a half block away from the Miller and Weiss offices. He worked for American Chemical Co. as their Director of Traffic.

On Monday, one of the company trucks delivering hazardous material had been involved in an accident early that morning. There had been a terrible spill on the turnpike in Edison, New Jersey, and there was no way he could attend the meeting with Victoria. She had to go alone. They had called him at 5:30 AM and Mark had to leave the house as soon as possible to be at the office managing the cleanup and dealing with the EPA.

Victoria was such a nervous wreck she couldn't drive, so she boarded a bus to Port Authority. When it arrived in Manhattan, she grabbed a cab to Fifth Avenue. As she entered the building, a tall thin man who had just exited an elevator was raving at another man walking with him. The man doing the raving was so engrossed berating his companion that he bumped into Victoria almost knocking her down. He stared at Victoria for a few seconds as if she had some nerve to be in his way. His eyes were filled with fire. He didn't even excuse himself, but went back to screaming,

"What kind of lawyer are you? I want to know everything about that trust."

The man with him replied, "Frederick, I've done everything possible." Then they disappeared through the large glass doors of the entrance.

Straightening herself and calling him a few choice words under her breath, Victoria took the elevator to the top floor.

Very impressive, she thought when she got her first glimpse of one of the most prestigious offices she had ever seen. It was fitted in rich mahogany paneling and rugs so thick you could sink into them.

"Victoria Valentino to see Mr. Richard Miller." she announced to the receptionist, who then buzzed Richard's secretary. A few minutes passed and then a tall, gray haired, distinguished looking man in his late sixties or early seventies approached Victoria offering his hand.

"Mrs. Valentino, I'm Richard Miller. Please come to my office."

She followed him and after they had seated themselves comfortably. Richard Miller told Victoria, "You know a blood test is necessary to support your claim. I have taken the liberty of having my own personal physician come in today to take a blood sample from you. If you agree, we can begin the process."

"I have a lot of questions about my family. I know nothing about them."

"When the results come back, we can discuss the family and the details of the trust. Until then I cannot give you any information."

Nervously, she asked, " No one in the Woodsworth family knows about this?"

"No one. We'll have the results in a couple of days. I'll call you when they come in. May I show Dr. Grant in?"

"OK," Victoria replied shaking just a little. She hated needles.

Richard left the room and Dr. Grant entered. He walked over to her and took her hand. "I'm happy to meet you. I'll be taking a sample of your blood today. Please be at ease. You won't feel a thing."

His eyes mesmerized her. Victoria stared at him awe struck. He was gorgeous and had a charm about him that just exuded money and style. He was the epitome of tall, dark and handsome. Victoria thought to herself, Blood. I wouldn't care if he took a kidney.

"Fine, I'm ready," she said still gazing at him.

As she extended her arm, his deft hands wrapped a rubber band on her upper arm. Victoria, almost in a rapture, never felt the needle go in. When he finished and had put all his paraphernalia back into his black bag, he took her hand again and wished her a good day. Victoria nodded, unable to speak.

A few seconds later Richard came back into the room and Victoria snapped back to reality.

"I hope that was not too uncomfortable for you."

"No, not at all. Dr. Grant was very gentle."

Richard rose and offered his hand, "Mrs. Valentino. I will call you in a few days."

"Thank you, Mr. Miller. Is there a phone I could use before I leave?"

"Of course. Please come with me."

Richard led her into an unoccupied office and left the room. Victoria dialed her husband,

"Mark it's Victoria."

"How did it go."

"Mr. Miller had a doctor here and he took a sample of my blood. He'll call in a few days with the results. I'm leaving now to go home. How's it going there?"

"It's a big mess. I don't know what time I'll be in. See you when I see you."

Chapter 71

Richard Miller called Wednesday evening, "Victoria, it's Richard Miller."

"Yes, Mr. Miller. I have been waiting for your call," she replied nervously. "I have some very good news for you. You are indeed Walter Woodsworth's daughter and I am pleased to tell you that you are the beneficiary of a rather substantial trust."

Victoria gasped.

"Victoria?"

"Yes, I'm here, but quite bowled over at the moment."

"I would like to send a limousine to pick you up on Friday morning to discuss the family and the trust."

"I'd rather you didn't," Victoria answered. "I don't need my neighbors questioning me. They will think someone died. That's the only time a limo is seen in my neighborhood. My daughter knows nothing of this and I am not ready to tell her yet."

"As you wish, Mrs. Valentino. Can you be at my office by eleven o'clock."

"Yes, I'll be there at eleven."

Upon her arrival on Friday, Victoria was shown into Richard's office. He extended his hand to her, as was his custom and got right to it.

"Victoria, the trust that has been set up for you totaled four million dollars at the time of Mr. Woodsworth's death. With our prudent investments, your inheritance has appreciated considerably nearing ten million. It is available to you immediately. I also have this letter for you from Walter." When he looked up from his paperwork, Richard saw Victoria's mouth agape and her eyes fixed. "Mrs. Valentino?"

"Did you say ten million?" Victoria muttered.

"Yes, I did. You are now a very wealthy woman. Don't suppose you will be wanting to take the bus home," he laughed. "Do you want to meet your mother's sister and James, your half-brother and uncle? They have a daughter, your niece Mary Harriet. There is also your half-brother Frederick."

"The last time I was here a man almost knocked me down. He was yelling at a man I assumed was his lawyer, the attorney referred to him as Frederick. Was Frederick Woodsworth here that day?"

"I'm not sure, but yes, Frederick has been after the details of his father's trust for years. It's been close to seven years and he keeps hiring new lawyers, but I have made sure that he will never know. You have nothing to worry about in that regard. I'm sure I can arrange for you just to meet your aunt if that is your wish."

Victoria, with a sad and haunting look replied, "No. My mother didn't want to cause Elizabeth the heartache of knowing that her husband's father had raped her. She has accepted her sister's death. I would not want to resurrect the past and cause her any more pain."

Richard asked her if she would reconsider. "You are Elizabeth's only living relative outside of her daughter and an adopted son."

"Maybe someday, not now."

She offered her hand to Mr. Miller and asked if his offer of a limousine was still open. She was too excited to walk to the bus and wasn't the least bit worried about her neighbors.

"Of course, Mrs. Valentino, I'll have my secretary make our car available to you when you leave. I have compiled a listing of all your assets and have enclosed Walter's letter to you in this briefcase. Please review all the materials and let me know if you wish to retain our firm to look after your affairs. I'm sure you are overwhelmed by all that has transpired. Please take as much time as you need to get back to me."

"Thank you, Mr. Miller. I have a lot to think about."

Richard assessed the complicated woman who had just left his office. He. liked her. She was real, not phony. She had integrity. He had had some of his people investigate her as soon as he knew she was a claimant. It was easy for him to put two and two together when he found out that Dr. Tony Russo was her uncle. He remembered his conversation with Walter at The Thicket the day he confessed to him. Walter believed that Tony was not the kind of man who could have killed a baby. Tony had given the child to his sister. I'm sure he switched the babies to protect Victoria from Frederick, he reasoned. Richard knew Frederick would know no boundary to get his hands on Walter's fortune. He did not envy the internal turmoil Victoria had been through nor the adjustment she would have to make becoming a rich woman so suddenly. Instant wealth can destroy the recipients and their families, he mused.

He never knew the contents of the letter he had given to Victoria from Walter. His old client had shared his deepest, darkest secrets with him, but in this once instance, he had not. Richard was curious. Then there was the matter of a whole new family waiting in the shadows for Victoria if she so chose. He wondered if she would ever change her mind about meeting Elizabeth.

Victoria smiled as she left the building. The sun was shining, a cool and refreshing breeze was blowing, a limo was waiting for her in front of the building, Could life be any better? she thought. Victoria was finally free from the terror that had stalked her and now was wealthy enough to realize all her good dreams.

On the ride home from Manhattan, her mind was trying to take in all that had been discussed with Richard and its implications for her family. She didn't call Mark before leaving Richard Miller's office. I can't tell him over the phone, she thought, there is just too much to say and I don't want him blurting out "Ten million dollars" over the phone where someone in the office could hear him. Then there's the matter of Frederick; that horrible stick figure of a man. The thought of him made her entire body cringe.

Chapter 72

Frederick had been living in an apartment in Manhattan after his divorce from Winifred. With half of Aunt Vivienne's estate, the proceeds from the sale of his home in Montclair and the sale of his Cheshire Foods stock, he opened an accounting firm located on Park Avenue in New York City. Though seven years had passed since Walter's death, Frederick could not let go. He had to find out the details of the trust. Every chance he got he would· try to browbeat James into revealing what he had received from the trust and if there was anyone else that might be a beneficiary. Frederick was so incensed that his latest attorney had not been able to force Miller and Weiss to reveal the terms of the trust, that when he met James for golf one afternoon, he started hammering him about it.

James replied, "I'm sorry Fred. It would be a breach of the affidavit I signed and you know my word is my bond."

"Damn you and your ethics and damn that ole bastard. "

"Don't refer to our father that way, Fred."

"You think you knew him so well. Well you didn't. You'd be surprised at what I know about our dear departed father."

Frederick almost blurted out the whole sordid truth when he caught himself. Not yet, he thought, Not yet. Someday I might need Jim and I'm sure he would pay royally for information about Helen.

It was on his way home from golf that an idea struck Frederick. Can't get any info from my brother nor from any of the attorneys I hired maybe a private investigator can do it. Got to find a way into that bastard Miller's office files. He remembered using a sleazebag private investigator from Newark for one of his clients who was going through a divorce. Frederick called A. K. Smith as soon as he returned home.

"A. K., it's Fred Woodsworth. I have a little something I want you to find out for me. Can we meet somewhere private?"

"Sure thing. How about Reiter's Rathskeller in Newark, say tomorrow afternoon at two. The lunch crowd will be gone by then. They'll be just a few drunks left."

"See you then."

Reiter's place had seen better days. It was a beat up old German bar and restaurant that was hanging on after the race riots drove a lot of businesses and people out of Newark.

A. K. was waiting at the bar for Frederick when he walked in. "C'mon, I got a table in the back. Want a drink before we sit?" "No thanks, but I'll buy one for you," answered Frederick.

"Irish again Mac, neat."

When A. K. got his drink, the pair made their way past the tables to a booth in the back. "Welcome to my office Mr. Woodsworth. What can I do for you?"

"I need you to find out the contents of a trust my father set up. I know my brother Jim has access to it, but he won't give me any details nor will my father's damn lawyer. He said I wasn't a party to the trust. I'll give you $5,000 up front money and $10,000 If you get the goods. I need you to get into my father's attorney's files. I've written down all the information you need to get started."

"I'm not much at breaking and entering, but there's other ways."

A. K. looked over the paper and asked, "This lawyer Miller. Who's he got working for him?"

"Some old broad that's been with him for twenty years." "I need you to point her out to me."

"How about you dress up in a delivery man's uniform and I give you a letter for Miller. Then you can take a look for yourself?"

"Sounds like a plan."

"I'll have a messenger deliver the letter to you here tomorrow at noon."

In his early fifties, A. K. was still a pretty good-looking guy. He had charmed his way into many a panty in his heyday. With two failed marriages under his belt, he didn't want a relationship with anyone. He only turned on the charm when it was for business or for a quick "slam, bam, thank you mam."

The following afternoon at three-thirty, A. K. showed up at the offices of Miller and Weiss. He advised the receptionist that he had a personal and confidential letter for Richard Miller with instructions to deliver only to Mr. Miller's private secretary.

Mary Keenan came out to the front office and signed for the letter.

A. K. had on dark glasses and a mustache. His disguise was almost unimportant. She barely looked at him. Just signed his receipt and walked back to her office.

Not much to look at, he thought. Probably wouldn't be so bad if she didn't look so clerical in that black suit and white blouse. A pair of sling backs might at least show off those nice legs instead of those nun's shoes. He looked down at the receipt she had signed; Mary Keenan for R. Miller.

That night he was on stakeout across the street from her building. When he saw her· come out, he followed her. She took the bus to Pennsylvania Station then the Path train to Jersey City. He tailed her right to her house a few blocks away. She lived in a small white house. An old woman was sitting on the porch. He saw her kiss the old woman and help her inside.

A. K. tailed Mary all week, but on Friday she didn't take the train at Pennsylvania Station. She walked a few blocks from her building to the Old Sod Bar and Grill. She slipped onto a stool at the far end of the old mahogany bar.

When A. K. entered a few minutes later, "Danny Boy" was playing in the background. The place looked like it hadn't changed in fifty years. Everything was well worn, including the bartender.

A. K. sat two seats away from Mary and ordered a Guinness. He looked at Mary a few times trying to catch her eye. Finally, when she looked up at him, he raised his glass and said, "Here's to your health," in his deepest Irish brough.

"Thank you," she replied and lowered her eyes.

"My dear mother has just passed. Can't drink to her health anymore." "Oh, I'm so sorry."

"It was a blessing. She suffered so," he sighed. "Is your mother still living."

"Yes, but she's quite old and frail now."

"Bet you take care of her. Us Irish always take care of our Mums." "And how do you know that I'm Irish?" she glared.

"It's in those beautiful blue Irish eyes. I can always tell." "Go on with your blarney now." She shyly smiled.

"Do you come here often?"

"Usually on a Friday night. Just a little vacation I call it." "My name is A. K. and yours is... "

“Mary Keenan."

His beer finished, A. K. tipped his hat and bowed a bit. Smiling at her he said, "Well Mary, it was nice to make the acquaintance of a lovely Irish lady, and I hope to be seeing you again sometime."

"Nice to meet you as well, A. K."

He didn't want to push his luck too far on their first meeting. He would be back the following Friday and several Fridays after that. Each time they met he gained a little more of her confidence.

* * *

Mary Keenan walked with a bit of a spring in her step this evening. It was Friday again and she was particularly happy at the prospect of seeing A. K. again at the Old Sod. They had struck up quite a friendship over the past weeks and their conversations brightened her. A. K. had told her he was a private investigator and without revealing names, related some of the stories involved in his cases. She hung on his every word.

When she arrived, A. K. was already seated at the end of the bar and motioned to her that he had the seat next to him saved for her.

"Hi Mary love. Did you have a good day?"

"Busy as usual. Glad to get a little time to relax. And how about you?" "Been a little slow lately. Guess you'll have to be the story teller tonight. Does your firm have any good cases?"

"Not exactly cases, but something unusual did occur recently. My boss had this old trust set up for a very influential man who had died a while ago. Of course, I can't tell you his name but he had interests in New York and New Jersey. In the trust, the client stipulated that if there was anyone who could prove to be his child, born in a certain hospital in Newark on November 22nd, then that person would inherit an enormous amount. My birthday is November 22nd, that's why I remember the date. A young woman showed up out of the blue and proved she was the man's daughter by submitting to a blood test performed by my boss' personal physician."

" How old was the woman?" "Probably in her early thirties."

"Amazing. Boy, I'd love to know the whole story on that."

"Only my boss knows and he's like a steel trap. After all the years I've been with him, he only tells me what I absolutely need to know."

"Well my dear Mary, you certainly topped my stories with that one."

Mary smiled and blushed a little. It had been a long time since anyone had found her interesting.

A. K. excused himself to go to the bathroom. He knew there was a pay telephone in the niche by the men's room. He dialed Frederick's number.

"Frederick Woodsworth here."

"It's A. K. I found out that a trust drawn up by Richard Miller was recently claimed by a woman who was able to prove she was the daughter of the man who created the trust; a man with interests in both New Jersey and New York. Oh yeah, my informant also told me the woman was born on November 22nd, in a Newark hospital."

There was dead silence on the other end of the phone. "Mr. Woodsworth, are you there?"

"Yes. I'll call you in a few days," the stony voiced rasped.

"I'll kill that son of a bitch," Fred shouted as he slammed the phone down.

Fred remembered that date all too well.

A. K. went back to his seat at the end of the bar. Mary was finishing her beer.

"I've got to go A. K. Mom's waiting. I'll see you next Friday."

"Sure thing, Mary. You take care of yourself now."

A. K. hung his head a bit. When he saw Mary leave the bar, he ordered an Irish whiskey neat. He hated this part of the business... taking advantage of the trusting, vulnerable people. He probably wouldn't be seeing Mary again. He knew she was too ethical a person to be pushed into revealing much more. He threw the golden brew down his throat in one gulp and ordered, "Barkeep another."

Chapter 73

Victoria arrived home in style. The chauffeur opened the door for her just as her neighbor Pam opened her door to walk her dog. When the limo pulled away she said, "Hey Vikky, did you just hit the Irish Sweepstakes or something."

Victoria flustered, "I wish. I had to deliver some important sketches to a client in New York for some big advertising campaign. The company sent me in a limo to make sure they were delivered on time."

Not wanting to continue the conversation with Pam, Victoria ended it, "Sorry I can't talk. I have to call the office and confirm the sketches were delivered. I'll talk to you later."

Victoria quickly ascended her back stairs hoping that Pam didn't suspect her lie because she could feel the heat building in her face, a sure giveaway. Wealth was something she never thought she would have to deal with in her lifetime and it scared the hell out of her. She wondered what effect all that money would have on her marriage, her family and on her. She decided to call Uncle Tony. Although he had worked for his, he knew how to deal with wealth.

"Uncle Tony, it's Victoria."

Excited and overwhelmed, disjointed sentences emanated from Victoria,

"I just came from seeing Richard Miller, the Woodsworth's attorney. I had a blood test that proved I was Walter's daughter. He set up a trust in case someone came forward to claim that they were his child. I'm a very wealthy woman and I just don't know how to deal with everything. He wants me to meet Elizabeth. I told him not now. Then there's James and Frederick."

"You don't want to meet Frederick," Tony said sharply. "That son of a bitch wanted me to kill you."

He hadn't meant to blurt that out, but the cat was now out of the bag. He told her of the phone call and the offer Frederick had made him that night so long ago; his loan to be forgiven for getting rid of Helen and her bastard.

"I think I may have run into Frederick when I first went to see Mr. Miller. He ran smack into me while he was distracted and screaming at someone who I suspected was his attorney in the lobby of Mr. Miller's building. He was upset that his attorney could not find out something about a trust."

"Vikky, be careful. If he knows who you are, your life could still be in danger. The man has no soul. He would stop at nothing to get at that money."

"Mr. Miller assured me that no one in the family knows of my existence or that anyone has come forward as a claimant to the trust. I just will never identify myself to Elizabeth so no one will ever know. More importantly how will my new found wealth effect my family. Uncle Tony, I'm scared."

"Calm down. Forget about it for now. Pretend you never got it. Give it some time and the answers will come. I'll always be here for you, Vikky. We'll figure a way for you to suddenly become rich so that you won't have to tell the family the real story."

Tony would receive another phone call that night. It was two o'clock in the morning when his phone rang. With his eyes still closed, he picked up the receiver, "Dr. Russo. "

"You rotten bastard. You cheated me."

“Who is this?”

"Fred. You let Helen's baby live. I guess you switched her with a dead one or sold it. Tell me who she is. You owe me that after I had my father forgive your loan."

Tony got up from his bed not wanting to wake his wife. Quietly, he made his way down to his home office on the first floor.

"Listen you, murderous animal. I owe you nothing and I will never tell you who she is. You think I'm like you; that money could buy my soul... and don't think you can threaten me. You may have more money than I do, but I have friends you don't want to meet and who can get to you real easy, Coppice?"

"Don't threaten me you Guinea bastard."

In a slow and ominous tone, Tony let the words slide from his mouth, "It's not a threat, it's a promise if you continue with this."

His hand still on the cradled receiver, Tony's body shook with fury. He had never threatened to use the favors owed to him by Bobby Shoes, his gangster friend; his friend, who over the years, had risen up in the infamous Jersey mob. He had to keep Victoria and her family safe. His sister Angela would come back from the grave if anything happened to her. He had already warned Vikky, but he didn't know how far Frederick would go to find her.

Frederick was still steaming when he hung up from Tony. He quickly dialed again.

A. K.’s phone woke him from a sound sleep. He grappled with the receiver until he had it firmly in his hand and answered, "A. K. here."

"It's Fred Woodsworth. You have to find out the name of every female born in American Legion Hospital the night of November 22, 1940. Then we'll know where to begin."

"Sure Mr. Woodsworth. That's easy to do. I'll have the information to you in a day or two."

Chapter 74

A. K. did what he was told and secured the information. The clerk had told him the same thing she had told Victoria many months before. There were only two females born that night; a Victoria Grasso and a stillborn child to a Helen Stanhope.

The information set off a bell in A. K.'s head. "Holy shit. I got this information months ago for Ed Byrne, the cop. When I told Bobby Shoes about it. He seemed real interested. Maybe I can make a few extra bucks." He spotted a pay phone in front of the Hall of Records and called Bobby Shoes,

Bobby picked up his phone and said,

"Speak."

"It's A. K. I think I have something that might interest you that I picked up on a case I'm working."

"I'll be in Newark at Dante's coffee shop on Bloomfield Ave. about four this afternoon. Be there and I'll see if it's worth anything."

"You got it, Bobby. I'll be there."

Bobby walked into Dante's at 3:45 PM. with his two bodyguards and seated himself at a table in the back. The two men who were built like a pair of Sherman tanks sat a few tables in front of him.

The girl behind the counter quickly brought out a demitasse of espresso and placed a bottle of Sambucca on the table. The bottle was only brought out for special customers. Dante's did not have a liquor license.

"The Cannoli's are fresh, Mr. Savino. Can I get you one?" the girl asked. "No, I'm in the mood for a Svoidelle today."

"I'll bring the pastry right away, Mr. Savino."

A. K. walked in and Bobby motioned for him to sit. "So, what have you got?"

"Remember me telling you about Tony's niece asking that cop Ed Byrne to find out who lived at 9 Forest Street some months back?"

“Yeah.”

"Well, I had this job. A guy named Fred Woodsworth. He wants me to find out what females were born at American Legion Hospital on November 22, 1940. Guess what? Tony's niece was born there that day and a stillborn from a Helen Stanhope. Helen Stanhope lived at 9 Forest Street. Somehow Tony's niece is connected to a big trust Fred Woodsworth had me looking into."

"Did you report this to that Woodsworth guy?" "Not yet, but I told him I'd call him tonight."

"Hold off on telling him about Tony's niece till I get back to you." "Sure Bobby."

Bobby slid a couple of crisp new $100 bills across the table under his hand. A. K. palmed the cash into his pant pocket and got up to leave.

Bobby went to the back of the coffee shop and used the pay-phone to call Tony.

“Dr. Russo.”

"Tony, it's Bobby. I think you and I have to meet ASAP. I have some information you need to know about your niece. Meet me on Park Avenue in Newark by Tony's D's hot dog truck at six o'clock. We'll take a little walk in the park."

A stone-faced Tony whispered "OK" and hung up the phone.

Tony finished with the last two patients in his office and then set out for Park Avenue. As he drove towards Tony D's, he scowled at how bad his old neighborhood had become. He and Bobby had attended Barringer High School across the street from the park. Now it looked like someone had bombed the place with garbage.

When he saw Tony's Cadillac pull up, Bobby ordered up some dogs with Tony D's special hot onions. After Tony exited the car, one of Bobby's men leaned on the side of it. Tony walked to the truck and Bobby handed him a dog.

"Don't worry about your car, Mikey will take care of it. Come on let's take a walk in the park. Remember all the lunch hours we spent doing this when we were across the street in Barringer High School...only then we were making out with the girls and not walking or eating too much. Tony, I got some information today. It seems someone is nosing around about your niece. They had a friend of mine checking her birth records. Want to tell me what somebody wants with Victoria?"

"This guy who's nosing around, could he be a Fred Woodsworth?"

"Could be."

Tony spilled his guts. He told Bobby the whole sordid story.

"I'm scared for her, Bobby. You don't know this guy. He'll do anything to get even, not only with me, but he'll find Victoria and make her life a hell until he gets his hands on the money his father left her."

"Don't worry about it. I can take care of the bastard."

"I don't want any blood on my hands. There's got to be another way."

"We'll just feed him some phony information. He'll just hit a lot of dead ends. I promise you he won't lose a drop of blood."

"Thanks Bobby."

Putting his arm around Tony, they walked back out of the park towards the hot dog truck.

"I'm glad I can do this for you ... pay you back for once. You never took anything from me when I needed you. I promise this will all go away, and Victoria will be safe. Want to bring some dogs home for the family... on me."

"No thanks. If my wife knows I'm eating hot dogs, she'll take a fit...says I got to lose some weight."

The old friends embraced before Tony got in his car and sped off. Bobby called A. K. from the payphone on the comer.

"Listen up. You tell that Woodsworth guy he's to meet you tomorrow night on the beach in Asbury Park on the left side of the pier that has the rides. You tell him you found out who claimed his father's trust and that you will be expecting the rest of the money he promised you."

"What's the deal Bobby?"

"Never mind. You just get him there say around eleven. Collect your money and leave first. Tell him to wait until you are out of sight and then he's to leave."

Chapter 75

That night A. K. met Frederick under the pier. The only light was the moon shimmering on the water. When A. K. handed the envelope containing Victoria's birth record over to Frederick, he looked inside and recognized the name. It was Tony's niece. Before he handed the $10,000 to A. K., he asked him if he knew a hit man. He had a client who needed something done.

"Sure, I can get one for you. How much is in it for me?" "Another grand when you arrange a meeting with him." Fred handed him the money.

"You wait until I'm off the beach and then leave. This way there are no witnesses. I didn't see you and you didn't see me."

Fred nodded.

When A. K. was out of sight. Two men in wet suits and diving gear grabbed Frederick from behind and knocked him to the ground face first. One held his face to the sand so he couldn't scream while the other tied his hands. That done, they quickly turned him over and slapped duct tape across his mouth. The larger man took the envelope that A. K. had given Frederick and slipped it into the pants of his wet suit. Fred's eyes bulged as they walked him into the ocean. Before they left him, they took the duct tape off his mouth and the rope from his hands. An early morning beachcomber found his body the next day.

Chapter 76

With a smirk on her face, Winifred dialed Elizabeth's number to set a date and time for lunch. Ever since her divorce from Frederick, she arranged these get-togethers once or twice a year. They had grown up together in Westchester and still had many friends in common. It was an opportunity for Winifred to tell Elizabeth the latest gossip about their old friends. Twice a year was about all Elizabeth could take of Winifred. Elizabeth and James had attended Winifred's wedding to Gary Huffington several years after she had divorced Frederick. Today's visit would be different.

Winifred's driver had picked up Elizabeth and drove them to a small French Restaurant in Montclair. They were seated at a table in front of a banquette of windows overlooking the Well-manicured garden on the grounds of the restaurant. Winifred would wait for the right moment to leap upon Elizabeth. She made small talk throughout their luncheon and after the coffee was served asked Elizabeth, "Have you ever told little Walter that he was adopted?"

Elizabeth was taken aback by Winifred's out-of-the-blue question.

Startled, she blurted, "Why would you ask that?"

"It might be very traumatic for him if he wasn't told and then suddenly found out about it... and who his real father was."

Elizabeth's blue eyes turned to steel.

"What are you getting at Winifred. If you have something to say, say it. I'm in no mood for games when it concerns my children."

Winifred almost relished soiling the tidy little life Elizabeth had so enjoyed. She was still in love with her husband after all these years. Her daughter, Mary Harriet, had married a New York attorney and there was a baby on the way. Little Walter had just opened a law practice and was engaged to a local doctor's daughter. Life had worked out well for Elizabeth and in a way, Winifred envied her.

"Well my dear, I'm in need of some funds. I'm going to be divorcing Gary. That idiot ran daddy's company into the ground. His taste for other women and fast cars has cost me plenty. I don't know how much my attorneys can salvage."

"And what has this got to do with me."

"After our father-in-law died, Frederick took possession of Walter's desk. It seems that when I was having it cleaned, a letter fell out of it. It was from a woman that dear Freddy had a fling with. She was a mill employee's daughter who gave birth to a son....and guess who were the adoptive parents?"

"My God, no! The birthmark on his hand. I should have known. I don't know how James will take this. His heart is not strong these days. Fred has always treated little Walter like a second-class citizen. My son despises him. It would kill him to know Frederick is his father."

"Oh, and by the way, when Freddy was drunk one night, he intimated that our dearly departed father-in-law may have caused your sister's disappearance. I'll throw that bit in for nothing. Did your sister ever say the old man came on to her?"

"No, but after your wedding to Frederick, she left Belle Vista in a hurry. She was supposed to stay a few days longer than she did.

I never knew what the reason was for her early departure, but something must have happened." "I hate to do this to you, being an old friend and all, but I will give you

the original letter that was found in Walter's desk from your son's mother in exchange for $200,000. I know Walter managed your inheritance and I'm sure you got a pretty penny."

"You must give me some time to think about how I can get the money without my husband noticing."

Elizabeth wasn't sure what her next move would be. She wanted to kill Winifred and only agreed to pay at some future date just to end their meeting.

They barely spoke on the drive back to Elizabeth's home. When Winfred's driver opened the door for Elizabeth to get out, Winifred said, "You'll call me soon I'm sure." Elizabeth did not respond.

She was beside herself with anger and worry. Her whole world could come crashing down around her. She rarely if ever had to make big decisions without the counsel of her beloved husband. How could she tell him she needed $200,000 without telling him what it was for. She couldn't tell him that Frederick had fathered their son, and how could she even broach the subject to him that his father had caused her sister Helen's disappearance. She reasoned, If James knew, I would have seen it on his face all those nights when I cried myself to sleep in his arms wondering what had happened to Helen. It was then a thought hit her, Richard Miller! If anyone would know, it would be him. She knew how much her father-in-law trusted his attorney.

Elizabeth checked her watch it was almost four-thirty. She quickly made a call.

"Miller and Weiss."

"This is Elizabeth Woodsworth. I would like to speak with Richard Miller."

"One moment. I'll connect you."

"Elizabeth, what can I do for you?"

Her voice shook, "I desperately need to see you Richard. A rather delicate situation has presented itself and I need your advice. It's rather urgent. Can you see me tomorrow some time.

"Of course, Elizabeth. Is two o'clock convenient for you?" "Fine. Thank you, Richard."

She had barely cradled the receiver when James walked in. "How was your lunch?" he smiled as he kissed her.

Pretending to look at the stack of letters on the hall table and deliberately avoiding his eyes, Elizabeth responded, "The usual with Winifred... gossip, gossip and more gossip. She's divorcing Gary. I've got a bit of a headache. Do you mind if I have a lie down before dinner?"

"Go ahead, but are you sure you're OK darling?" "I'm fine. Just a little too much Winifred."

The phone rang as Elizabeth was ascending the stairs. She paused. "Jim Woodsworth here."

"Mr. Woodsworth, this is the Asbury Park Police."

Elizabeth saw James' eyebrows raise and heard him repeat, "The Asbury Park Police?"

"Do you know a Frederick Woodsworth?"

"Yes, I do. He's my brother. What is this about?"

"I'm sorry but I have some very bad news. We believe we have found your brother's body on our beach late this morning. There was a wallet with his driver's license and your card in his pant 's pocket. It appears he has drowned. Do you think you can come down to identify the body?"

James dropped the phone. Elizabeth rushed to it,

"What's wrong? This is Mrs. Woodsworth."

"Will James be coming to identify his brother's body?" "What happened?"

"It appears he has drowned."

"My husband...he has a heart condition...1'll call you back."

James was seated in the hall chair. His face was pale and he was sweating.

"Darling, darling, please speak to me." "Better call the doctor Elizabeth."

Henry, the butler, appeared in the doorway. "Miss Elizabeth what's wrong?"

"Please Henry, call an ambulance and Dr. Parker. Have him meet us at Mountainside Hospital. Then please call my son Walter and have him meet us there as well. If Mary should call, please don't tell her. Just say we have gone out to dinner. I don't want her upset in her condition."

Elizabeth did not want the news to bring her daughter into an early labor.

The ambulance arrived in minutes and sped off into the night carrying James and Elizabeth to the emergency room. While James was being examined, Elizabeth paced alone in the waiting room. A few minutes later Walter arrived.

"Mom, what happened?"

Elizabeth began to cry and leaned upon her son's chest. "Your father received a call from the Asbury Park Police informing him that your Uncle Frederick was found drowned. They wanted him to come down to identify the body. He dropped the phone. The shock of it all. He was rubbing his chest. Oh Walter, he has to be alright."

Dr. Parker, James' cardiologist, came out to speak to Elizabeth and Walter.

"Elizabeth, please don't worry. James did not have a heart attack, but he has suffered a shock. He told me the awful news about Frederick. We'll keep him here and run some more tests just to be on the safe side. You can go in to see him now. I've given him a shot and he'll be asleep soon."

"Thank you, Doctor Parker. Are you sure he's not in any danger?" "He's holding his own. Go say goodnight before he drops off." Before Walter could follow his mother, Dr. Parker grabbed his arm.

"A word with you Walter, please."

"Is there something you haven't told my mother?"

"I really don't want your father to deal with all the details of your uncle's death. Is there an attorney or someone else to handle it? Your father's heart is not very strong."

"I'll handle the identification and the arrangements." "Good. The strain would be too much for him."

Walter walked to his father's bedside and stood next to his mother. He held his father's hand and said, "Dad, I'm here. Just get well. I'll take care of mother and Uncle Frederick."

James nodded and closed his eyes.

Walter drove his mother home and stayed with her until she was asleep. Dr. Parker had given him a sedative for Elizabeth before he left them.

Chapter 77

It was almost midnight when Walter sped to the Parkway from Montclair. He had called the Asbury Park Police before leaving the house and told them he was coming to identify his uncle's body.

The long ride to the shore gave Walter some time to question the night's events. How did Uncle Frederick drown? What was he doing in Asbury Park" He certainly wouldn't be swimming there. He was much too hate-filled to commit suicide. This whole thing doesn't make sense, he thought.

It took Walter almost an hour to arrive at the police station. The town was deserted and the wind had started to kick up. He identified himself to the sergeant at the desk and his purpose for being there. Detective Manzini was paged and came out to the front desk.

"Sorry about your uncle. How's your dad?"

"He's doing OK, but the shock has put him in the hospital for a few days."

"I'm sorry about that. My condolences. Let me take you to the morgue. I'm going to need a positive ID before we go any further. Then, if it is your uncle, I'll have to ask you some questions. OK."

"Yeah. Let's get this over with."

Walter steeled himself and got into the detective's car. The morgue was at the Bay Shore Hospital. It took just seven minutes to get there. When they reached the lobby of the hospital, Detective Manzini showed his badge to the guard and they proceeded to the elevator down to the basement. After flashing his badge, Detective Manzini stated to the attendant, "We're here to identify the body brought in this morning from the beach."

"Drawer number three, Detective."

The attendant pulled out the stainless-steel drawer and uncovered the face.

Walter could only gasp, "Yes, it's my uncle Frederick," and turned away.

Frederick had always treated Walter as if he did not deserve the air he was breathing, but for his father's sake, he ignored his uncle's disdain. He didn't think the sight of Frederick's dead body would bother him, but in a strange way it did... more than he thought it would.

On the way back to the station house, Manzini asked Walter if Frederick was depressed recently.

"No, my uncle could make you depressed, but he certainly was not." "You know there has to be an autopsy?"

"I can't believe my uncle would drown himself. Do you think this could have been murder?"

"Won't know 'til the autopsy's in and that might not be definitive. Did your uncle have any enemies?"

"Probably everyone he's ever had contact with. How soon can the autopsy be done?"

"Tomorrow probably. It might take a few days to release the body and a few weeks before the toxicology reports are back."

"I'd like to get everything over with before my dad gets out of the hospital. His doctor said the stress might be too much for his heart."

"You just have to sign some papers. I'll need your address and telephone number, then you can get back home."

Manzini swung into the parking lot and asked Walter to follow him to his desk. Walter handed him his business card after signing the paperwork.

"A lawyer?"

"Mostly corporate law."

"I'll be in touch, Mr. Woodsworth."

Walter was on the Parkway returning from Asbury Park just as the sun was coming up. It had been a long night and he needed a shower. He pulled off the road to get a cup of coffee and called his mother's house from a phone at the rest stop. Henry, the butler answered.

"The Woodsworth residence."

"Henry, It's Walter. Please tell my mother when she wakes that I have gone to my apartment to shower and change and to make the arrangements for my Uncle Frederick. She can reach me there."

Henry delivered the message to Elizabeth, who was grateful that she had time alone to call Richard Miller. She would not be able to make her two o'clock appointment with him to discuss Winifred's blackmail scheme. Due to Frederick's untimely demise and her husband's illness, she would have to give him the details over the phone. The last thing she needed was to have Winifred pressing her now.

Elizabeth placed the call and told Richard of the previous evening's events which prevented her from meeting with him.

"I'll come to you, Elizabeth, and we can discuss the delicate matter you spoke of."

"No Richard. The matter is not something I can speak of freely in the presence of my husband or children. I will have to tell you of it now over the phone, as I don't know when I will be free to discuss it what with the funeral and my husband's illness. Richard, I am being blackmailed by Winifred, my former sister-in-law. It seems a letter fell out of Walter's old desk when it was delivered to their home. The letter was from my son Walter's biological mother stating that Frederick was the father and that James and I were the adoptive parents. Winifred never showed the letter to Frederick, but kept it and is now using it to blackmail me for $200,000. She also stated that when Frederick had too much to drink one evening, he intimated to Winifred that his father was responsible for my sister Helen's disappearance. Do you know anything about that Richard?"

"Elizabeth, don't worry yourself right now about all of this. Let me handle this situation. You just take care of James. May I have Winifred's phone number please. I will tell her that you authorized me to handle payment. When James is better and things have calmed down, we will have our meeting."

"Richard, you have always been this family's rock. There are no words· adequate to thank you for your loyalty."

Chapter 78

Tony could not believe his eyes when he read the Star Ledger.

"Man found drowned in Asbury Park. A suspected suicide, the body was identified as Frederick Woodsworth of New York City, former President of Woodsworth Silk Mills in Paterson and former candidate for New Jersey Senator."

"What has Bobby done? He told me he wouldn't spill a drop of Frederick's blood."

Tony quickly placed a call to his old friend. "Bobby, it's Tony. What…"

"Before you start. I saw the paper. I swear I had nothing to do with it. Even I don't work that fast."

"Thank God. I'd never rest if I felt I was the cause."

"I know that. I promised you, didn't I? Sometimes fate takes care of things. Now your niece will never have to be afraid again and you can live with a clear conscience. I guess there is a God."

"Thanks Bobby. I'll see you soon."

Bobby put down the phone and smiled to himself, "Yeah, and maybe sometimes God needs a little help."

There was nothing he wouldn't do for Tony. He remembered, what he did for Mama and Pop.... Dealing with their cancer as if they were his own parents...never sending me a bill. How do you pay that back? Tony is family and family takes care of family.

Tony had barely hung up with Bobby when he decided to call Victoria.

"Vikky, it's Uncle Tony. Have you seen the paper?" "No. I haven't had time to read it yet."

"Frederick Woodsworth was found drowned in Asbury Park." "My God. What happened?"

"They think it was suicide. You won't have to worry about him giving you any trouble now."

"It's strange Uncle Tony; just too strange, but then again, nothing is normal anymore."

"How did you enjoy your trip to Las Vegas?"

"It was good...saw a few shows, did a little gambling. It was a great idea of yours to explain to the family our sudden wealth. I'll tell them we hit the super jackpot at Baily's."

"Yeah, what happens in Vegas, stays in Vegas. Do you have any plans yet?"

"We're thinking of having a house built in Bernardsville. I want to get out of Essex County. The schools there are so much better for Diana. So many possibilities now, my head is spinning. Mark still wants to work for a while until our new status has time to set in. I haven't told Diana anything yet about our sudden good fortune, but when I do, it will probably be the Vegas story."

"Go slow Vikky. Money can hurt as well as cure." "Thanks Uncle Tony. I love you."

"See you soon kid. Stay well."

The news of Frederick's death bothered her. She never was quite sure if Frederick was the man who bumped into her in the lobby of Mr. Miller's office building. Victoria's wheels were turning. His wake, if there is to be one, would be a perfect opportunity for me to be certain if it was him and to see my mother's sister Elizabeth, my half-brother James and their children. I bet I could go to the wake without being noticed. If I'm questioned on how I knew Frederick, I could always say I was one of his campaign volunteers.

Victoria looked at the obituary page, but there was no mention as yet of Frederick's final arrangements, "Damn it's not here. It'll probably be in tomorrow's paper." Then a thought hit her. Richard Miller would probably attend the wake and would have the time and date. She dialed Richard's office and asked to speak to him. His secretary put her call through to him.

"Mr. Miller, it's Victoria Valentino. Do you have the date and times of Frederick's wake?"

"Yes, Victoria. Are you planning to be there?"

"I'm curious. I think it was he who bumped into me in the lobby of your office building. Will you be there?"

"Yes, for James and Elizabeth's sake. Are you ready to meet your aunt?"

"I'm not ready to reveal the truth yet, but I do want to see Frederick. Please, Mr. Miller, if we should meet at the wake, do not acknowledge me. If I am questioned as to how I knew Frederick, I will say I was a volunteer in his campaign for the Senate." "As you wish, Victoria."

Chapter 79

Winifred did not have the good sense to be absent from Frederick's wake, but she was smart enough to sit in the back of the room after she expressed her condolences to the family. She stayed just long enough for Richard Miller to pull her aside and ask, "Can you be at my office at one-thirty the day after the funeral? Due to the James' delicate health, I would like to settle this matter as quickly and quietly as possible."

"Yes, I can be there at one-thirty."

Winifred smiled to herself. Finally, that son of a bitch will deal with me. I'll have standing this time. She never forgot Richard's dismissal of her, "You have no standing here. You are not an heir." when he was reading the contents of Walter's will and she tried to interject.

It was just after his conversation with Winifred, that he spotted Victoria making her way to the casket. She knelt and said a prayer he assumed. Then she was greeted by James who introduced her to his two children and then to Elizabeth. While staring into the deep brown eyes of the woman before her and as she held her hand, she asked Victoria, "How did you know my brother- in-law?"

"I worked on his campaign for the Senate," she uttered stiffly. "How very kind of you to come today. Thank you."

Victoria was the first to let go of their hand clasp. She was beginning to shake and the tell-tale reddening was warming her face. A hasty exit is in order, she thought. She had come to see if it was Frederick, and now she knew that he indeed was the man who bumped into her that day in the lobby. Her knees were beginning to buckle. Before she could make her escape, someone had asked her to sign the guest register before she left. Quickly, she scribbled her name and left for the parking lot.

Richard Miller was standing outside having a cigarette.

Looking around to see if anyone else was in earshot, Victoria blurted, "I had to see them. They look like a wonderful family." Tears were falling from her eyes. She held Richard's hand and whispered, "I have to leave."

He watched her as her car pulled slowly out of the driveway and into the street. She was dabbing her eyes with a tissue. Helen protected Elizabeth from the truth. Now her daughter was doing the same thing, Richard lamented to himself.

Richard returned to the wake and went to James and Elizabeth to say goodbye. He had to get back to the office. When James got up to welcome another visitor. Elizabeth asked Richard to sit next to her for a moment and quietly said, "There was a woman here before...a redhead about thirty something. She said she worked on Frederick's campaign, but somehow, I think that isn't the truth. There was something about her that seems so familiar. When I was holding her hand, I felt a connection. Isn't that strange?"

Richard's eyes glazed over. "It is strange. I must leave. Don't worry Elizabeth, everything will be fine. Don't hesitate to call me for anything."

Chapter 80

Winifred was seated in one of the leather chairs in front of Richard Miller's desk when he came into the room. He was holding an envelope in his hand. He seated himself in his well-worn chair and without any pleasantries calmly asked, "Do you have the original letter?"

Winifred reached into her bag and waved it at him. "Do you have my money?

He waved his envelope at her and said, "May I inspect the letter?" "Sure, it's real. See the date on it."

As he examined the letter, he asked "Are there any copies?" "Of course not. Elizabeth is my friend."

"Friends don't blackmail friends," he answered and glared at her over his glasses."

"It's not blackmail, it's a business transaction. I need the money."

Richard took out his old Zippo lighter and set the letter on fire. "What the hell are you doing?" she yelled, her eyes blazing.

With disgust in his eyes, Richard looked at Winifred and said, "Don't make a sound and further incriminate yourself. This conversation has been recorded."

"You, old bastard. How dare you?"

"I think our business has been concluded. As an attorney I would advise you to leave and betray no more or your pompous little ass will go to jail."

After Winifred stormed out, Richard placed a call to Elizabeth.

Elizabeth was doing thank you cards for the family and going through the guest register when she saw the unfamiliar name Victoria Valentino and realized that she must have been the red-haired woman who said she worked on Frederick's campaign. Her eyes lingered over the name. Why do I feel there is something more here? she asked herself.

It was then that Richard Miller called to tell her, "The Winifred situation has been handled gratis all around. The letter has been destroyed. I believe you won't be hearing from her again."

"Richard, I can't thank you enough. Tell me, is the name Victoria Valentino familiar to you? I believe that's the name of the red-haired woman who came to Frederick's wake...the woman I told you about."

“Elizabeth, I can’t answer that question. It’s client confidentiality."

"You do know her! Please Richard ask her if she will have lunch with me...anytime…any place. There's something. I just know it."

"I'll be in touch. No promises." Richard made the call to Victoria.

"Victoria, Richard Miller here. It seems you started something with Elizabeth by attending the wake. She wants to have lunch with you. Do you think you can handle it?"

"Maybe it's time or she would not have asked to meet me. Tell her Thursday at one o'clock at Mario's in Clifton. No one knows me there."

Elizabeth was overjoyed upon hearing of Victoria's choice of Mario's Restaurant for their meeting. She hadn't been there in quite a while. It was where she announced to James, he was to be a father and it was where James had given her the news of the baby boy they would adopt.

Elizabeth arrived first and was nervously toying with her napkin hoping that she would not be stood up, when Victoria walked to the table.

"I was so glad you chose Mario's. Most of the good in my life was announced here."

"My husband took me here on our first date," Victoria smiled. "We have a lot in common already it seems."

"More than you know," Victoria smiled. "What caused you to seek me out?"

"There was something about you, especially when I held your hand. I knew there had to be more. I could see it in your eyes."

"When Mr. Miller called me with your invitation to lunch, I knew you would be as tenacious as I have been to uncover what has been buried for years. I guess it runs in the family. Eventually, I am sure, you would have found out, so I might as well tell you."

Elizabeth's face showed total bewilderment. Family? What could she mean?

"The story I am about to tell you is tragic and I must have your promise that it should remain our secret. Too many lives will be affected."

"Please, go on," Elizabeth said with quiet reserve.

"Your father-in-law, Walter, raped your sister Helen the night of Frederick's wedding reception. She found she was pregnant a few months later in Paris. She came back to the States and confronted Walter. They arranged for her to live in his sister Agatha's home in Newark until I was born. After which, she was supposed to go back to France. Your sister died from a hemorrhage giving birth to me. Frederick wanted us both dead and had asked my uncle, Doctor Tony Russo, his friend from college, to make sure we did not survive. My uncle couldn't do it. To protect me from Frederick, he switched me with the stillborn which his sister had delivered within minutes of my own birth. Angela, my mother, never knew I was not her biological child.

"It was shortly before my mother's death that I began having dreams of a brownstone mansion. One day, quite by chance, I came upon Lambert Castle and knew I was connected to that place. A lot of investigating on my part uncovered my true parentage. I am your niece and Walter's daughter. did not come forward sooner because my mother, your sister Helen, did not want you to be burdened with this awful truth. My daughter and my extended family know nothing of this and I prefer to keep it that way. Only my husband and my Uncle Tony know...and of course Richard Miller."

By the time Victoria had finished, tears were streaming from the eyes of Elizabeth's still beautiful face. Holding Victoria's hand, she whimpered, "Everyone has always protected me, my husband, my sister, you. I needed to know. I can finally mourn Helen. My dear husband has a bad heart. I will never tell him what his father did. This story must remain between us. My children must never know. They loved their grandfather. What good would it do to destroy their memories of him?"

Victoria held Elizabeth's hand and said, "I brought something for you to look at. It was left in the attic at Agatha's house. The woman who purchased the home from Agatha's estate gave these to me. I have a story to tell about that too, but not now. It's the drawings Helen did while she was living with Agatha." Victoria handed them to Elizabeth.

Her hands shook as she slowly flipped through Helen's drawings. When she came upon the last page the one of the mother and child, a gasp came from deep within Elizabeth. Helen had loved the baby she was carrying. She could see it in the eyes of this self-portrait.

"I've brought something else with me. A letter from Walter that Mr. Miller gave me after the blood test proved that I was his daughter. I just couldn't open it. Maybe it's fitting that we open it together...you hearing it for Helen."

Victoria used the place-setting knife on the table to open the yellowed envelope. Her hands trembling, she read,

Dear Child,

You are reading this because you have lived and have proven to my attorney that you are indeed my child.

I have much to atone for. I have sinned against both you and Helen, your mother. I have deprived you of the love of a wonderful girl; for that was what she was when I committed a most deplorable act upon her resulting in your birth and her death. I am sure my maker will not deal kindly with me for my sins. I only hope that you were loved and provided for by those who raised you.

All I have to give to you is wealth. I have spent my life focusing on its accumulation. Please do not let it lead you to arrogance as it did me, and don't let the power that will come from it corrupt what is truly important in life...family.

I was not held to account for what I did, but know that ever since, I have condemned myself. I have not put any conditions on your receiving the benefits of the Trust, therefore if it is your wish to inform my family of your existence, I leave that to your discretion. I would prefer to be remembered by my children and grandchildren with love and respect, but I leave it to you to take either pity or revenge upon me.

Your repentant father, Walter Woodsworth

When Victoria had finished reading the letter, Elizabeth asked, "What will you do?"

"I guess we've already decided. It will not be revenge nor pity. It will be silence. We both have family to protect."

"Victoria, now that we have found each other, you can't just disappear out of my life. Can we continue to meet so we may get to know one another better? You can tell me all about how you got hold of these drawings and bring me pictures of my grandniece and your husband. We can unravel the mystery of each other's lives."

"I'd like that Elizabeth. There are so many questions I have about Helen and Walter and of a family I have never known."

"It will be our little secret."

AFTERWARD

I had been having dreams of a brownstone mansion for eight years when, by chance, I happened upon Lambert Castle Museum in Paterson, New Jersey and realized that the veranda there was the scene of my first dream. From my research at the Paterson Library, I learned that in 1892 Lambert Castle was built by Catholina Lambert, a nineteenth century silk magnate, who named it Belle Vista. Mr. Lambert died in 1923. Subsequently, his son sold Belle Vista to the City of Paterson, who eventually sold the property to the County of Passaic.

The dreams continued for a total of twenty-two years. I was never able to uncover the reason why the dreams came to me, why I was so frightened upon waking each time at three-thirty in the morning from seemingly innocuous dreams, and why this place called Belle Vista had reached out to me in so many ways.

It was the not knowing why that left me with a great deal of unrest. Although the dreams of Belle Vista had finally stopped, they were always just below the surface of my consciousness. I had to find a way to resolve my unease even if closure was dealt with only by fiction.

Victoria Valentino's dreams in The Undoing happened, only they happened to me. Her character is the vehicle I used to express, in a condensed version, what I experienced during those twenty-two years.

Most of "The Undoing of Walter Woodsworth" is a work of fiction and is a product of the author's imagination.

Made in the USA
Middletown, DE
05 May 2021